The Little Boy Inside and Other Stories

Published by Concord ePress
152 Commonwealth Ave.
Concord, Massachusetts 01742
www.concordepress.com

Designed by Alphabetica
www.alphabeticadesign.com

This is a work of fiction. All of the characters, organizations, and events portrayed in this novel are either products of the author's imagination or are used fictitiously. All song lyrics or other quotations used are the property of their respective copyright holders.

ISBN: 978-0-9847078-7-4

The Little Boy Inside and Other Stories

By Glenn Gray

Illustrated by Stephen Fredette

CONCORD
ePRESS

For my girls:
Kris, Monica, Melanie, and Kayla

Table of Contents

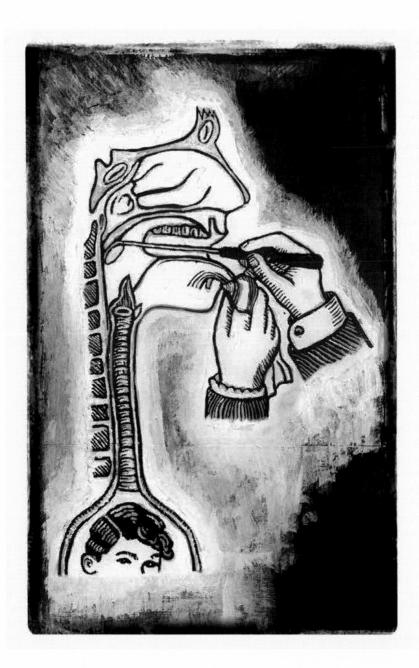

The Little Boy Inside

GREG THOUGHT HE MIGHT BE CHOKING AT FIRST. After all, he did have acid reflux and maybe his esophagus was inflamed and irritated. He lost his breath for a moment and then it felt as if he would vomit, gagged a little, and coughed up the little boy right on his desk.

The boy was naked and he was tiny, no bigger than a pen cap.

The boy was alive, somewhat lethargic, but alive and covered in mucous.

Greg was shocked and thought that maybe the couple of beers he had downed might be the culprit. *Am I that buzzed?* Greg jolted up from his desk, scared and appalled, not knowing quite what to do.

His first impulse was to get some tissues and clean the boy up but he didn't want to leave him alone. What if the little guy disappeared or woke and ran away? He didn't want that.

Greg scanned his study, grabbed one of his medical journals from the stack on the floor, the firm glossy blue one, the *American Journal of Neuroradiology*, and carefully slid the little boy onto the cover.

Greg tip-toed to the bathroom, one hand holding the journal, the other cupping the edge so the boy didn't slip and fall off. He rested the journal on the counter and studied the boy closely in the brighter light, noticing the sandy hair with the bowl cut, matted down from the phlegm.

The boy lay on his side now, in the fetal position, looking cozy and comfortable.

Greg ripped some toilet paper from the roll on the wall and patted the boy gently, drying him off, and the boy seemed to enjoy it, bending his knees closer and hugging himself tighter.

Greg draped the tiny body with a few sheets of dry tissue and the boy fell asleep.

Greg rummaged around in his garage until he finally found it, the cardboard box that his new computer came in. He hadn't thrown it away yet, just in case something went wrong.

But now it would serve a different purpose.

He tore off the top portion and flattened out the bottom.

Greg got one of his t-shirts and a couple of old socks and arranged them along the bottom of the box.

He gently slid the sleeping boy onto the fuzzy sock, covered him with some pieces of another soft shirt he had ripped up.

The boy rustled but didn't wake.

The boy looked relaxed and snug.

Greg crumpled up a chocolate chip cookie and let the crumbs fall next to the boy. From his kitchen garbage, he fished a cap from a two-liter bottle of diet soda, rinsed it and filled it with milk, plopped it in the box.

Greg stared down at the boy in his new box-home, fascinated, and thought that, without a doubt, he must be losing his mind.

Greg didn't know what to do.

He brought the box to his study and placed it on his desk next to the computer. He poured himself a Jameson's and sat there staring down into the box.

The boy slept soundly.

Greg got up and paced around the house, then sat back down.

He thought about going to the ER, but then reconsidered. What would he do? Walk in with the box, open it, and say, *Look, I just threw this up?*

Besides he couldn't see going to the hospital where he worked. He could just hear the staff now: "Dr. Baxter in Radiology has lost his mind. Walked in with a mini-boy in a box, said he threw it up. Guess he's had too much radiation exposure."

No way.

And out here in the sticks there wasn't another ER for a hundred miles.

Greg thought maybe he should get a CT scan in the morning. What if there were other boys living in his abdomen. A whole swim team? A fraternity? But Greg felt fine now—he didn't even have the slightest hint of bloating or epigastric pain he usually experienced every day for the past several months.

He felt totally normal.

Greg admitted to himself that he would need some help, someone to talk to. And he knew who he had to call—Cindy.

Greg had just met Cindy. He thought he was falling in love with her. No, he definitely had fallen in love with her.

But he didn't want her to think he was a freak.

Could he really call her now and tell her he just threw up a mini-boy and could she please come over? Could he? They had been dating for only two months.

And he had just broken up with her last weekend.

Screw it.

Greg grabbed the phone, held his finger above the number pad for a long moment, then punched her number.

"Cindy?"

"Greg?"

"I know it's late, but I need to talk to you."

"You're kidding, right?"

"No. No I'm not. I need to see you."

"Hellloo? Greg? You said you didn't want to see me anymore. Getting too serious, remember?"

"I'm sorry, Cindy. Really, I am. It's just, well, something's happened."

"Yeah, so?"

"I'd like to talk."

"I wanted to talk, you didn't. Now you want to talk."

"I know. I need to talk now."

"I was trying to get close. You ran."

"Not really."

"Now you call, late Friday night, and say you want to talk."

"Well, I need to show you something."

"You tore my heart out, Greg."

"I didn't mean to."

"And I'm not doing it again."

"But I have this thing..."

Click.

Greg stood for a moment in his study with the phone to his ear.

The old clock on the wall ticked and ticked.

A few seconds later, he clicked the phone off and placed it on his desk, next to the box.

He looked into the box.

Greg startled.

The little boy was lying on his back, eyes wide open, a swath of material pulled to his chin like a blanket.

Greg reflexively backed off, as if he were not supposed to be looking, caught peeping. Then he slowly peeked over the edge.

The boy met his gaze and tilted his head.

Greg stared. He leaned closer. He could hear his own breath whistling through his nostrils.

The clock.

"Who," Greg finally said, coming out like a whisper. "...who are you?"

The little boy looked puzzled, scrunched up his face.

The boy's voice was a distant soft squeak. "I don't know."

The little boy's eyes shut and he nodded off to sleep.

Greg watched the sleeping boy for an hour. He downed another Jameson's and a beer. Then he brought the box into his bedroom and placed it on the floor next to his bed.

Greg changed into flannel pajamas and climbed into bed.

He woke up every hour to check on the boy.

In the middle of the night Greg heard a strange noise. He flicked on the lamp, leaned over to look in the box. The little boy was hunched over on his stomach, sobbing.

"Hey, little boy," Greg said, leaning on an elbow. "You okay?"

The boy turned to his side, looked up at Greg. He took a few breaths and wiped his face. "I feel scared."

"What's that? You're scared?" Greg lowered his body, angled his head so he could hear better while reaching into the box. "It's okay, little guy. It's gonna be okay. Here."

Greg splayed his fingers, creating a welcoming flat surface. The boy hesitated, then crawled onto Greg's fleshy palm.

"There you go." Greg lifted him out of the box, brought him close to his face. "Everything's gonna be just fine, little boy."

The boy twisted, pushed, and stood, a scrap of cloth twisted about his waist. He smoothed his face with both hands. "Thank you."

Greg lay back in bed against two pillows, turned his wrist and let the boy roll onto his chest. "You're safe here."

The boy curled into a flannel fold of Greg's pajamas.

A moment later, they both fell asleep, Greg's chest rising and falling like rolling waves, his heart thudding beneath the boy.

Greg woke at dawn, still on his back, the little boy curled up on his chest. He cupped the boy in his hand and gently maneuvered his little body onto the bed next to him, in a fluffy roll of covers. Greg watched him sleep.

Greg thought about going over to the hospital. It was Saturday and Radiology would be quiet. He thought again about getting a CT scan, just to check. He knew Mike was the tech working today so there wouldn't be many questions.

He also thought that maybe he would bring the little boy, put him on the table next to him. Secretly, of course. And then he thought about the radiation dose and if it would be okay, given the boy was so small. He figured they often scanned little preemie babies when necessary and if it's just once that should be harmless.

He had to see what this boy was made of.

Greg showered, got dressed and had breakfast. He kept checking on the boy, still sleeping comfortably in the bed.

He figured he'd phone Cindy again, see if things were different now, given it was morning and she had time to think.

There was no answer, just the machine. He hung up.

He remembered Cindy sometimes worked Saturdays. She was a physical therapist at the hospital and often spent Saturday mornings working with difficult patients, giving them extra time and attention.

When Greg entered the bedroom, he abruptly stopped in the doorway. The little boy was running and jumping on the bed. Sliding down some of the bunched up covers, rolling around.

Greg went to the bed and kneeled at its side.

The boy stopped and smiled at Greg. The boy was breathing heavily.

Greg said, "Hi."

"I'm jumping."

"I see."

"I feel better now."

"You want to go on a trip?"

"With you?"

"Of course."

"Where?"

"To where I work."

"Okay."

Greg put on his navy blazer and slipped the boy into the breast pocket. "Ready?"

The boy pulled up on the edge of the pocket, peeked his head out. "Yes," he said. "This is fun."

"I'm having some abdominal pain," Greg told Mike the tech. "I just want to get a quick non-contrast abdomen and pelvis. Check things out."

Mike smiled, made a goofy face. "You're the doctor, Doc."

Mike helped Greg onto the CT gantry and position him. Greg didn't say anything, but he had the little boy in his hand and he was going to place him on the table at the right time.

"Okay, Doc." Mike said. "I'll do a scout view and you know the drill."

"Right."

Mike went into the CT control room, watched from behind the glass as the CT whirred into action. Greg's right hand was hidden from Mike. He let the boy out on the table. On the way over, he had instructed the boy about what to do. The boy lay on his back alongside Greg's abdomen.

After the scan, Greg cupped the boy in his hand, met Mike in the control room.

Mike was looking at the images on the screen. "That good, Doc?"

"Yes, yes. Fine," Greg said. "Just save it to CD and then delete the case from the system. This is off the record, okay?"

"You're the doc, Doc." Mike grinned.

Greg changed back to his shirt and blazer, got the CD from Mike.

He went to the reading room and punched in the extension to physical therapy.

"Cindy?"

"Greg?"

"I'm here in the hospital. Just did a CT."

"You okay?"

"Fine. Had some abdominal pain," Greg lied. "Can we talk?"

"I have a lot of patients."

"I really need to talk to you. Seriously."

"I thought we had something, Greg. This isn't easy for me."

"I know, I know." Greg said. There was a long silence. "Cindy?"

"Yeah."

"I love you."

An even longer silence.

"*Now* you love me?" Cindy said.

"I always did."

"Christ, Greg," Cindy said. "You're like a child."

"What'd you say?"

"You're like a child. A typical man."

Greg's head was spinning, thoughts rifling through his mind. He looked into his pocket. The little boy was looking upward, smiling.

"Greg? You still there?" Cindy said.

"Oh. Yes. Yes, yes."

"You were telling me you wanted to show me something."

"No...I wanted to talk to you."

"Last night. You said you wanted to show me something."

"I did." Greg wasn't ready to tell her about the boy. Not yet. He thought quickly. "Well, I wanted to show you...my love."

"You've lost your mind."

"I'm lost without you."

Greg could hear Cindy inhale and breathe out heavily. "So you wanna swing by PT?"

Greg stood at the door to the physical therapy department, watching Cindy work with a stroke patient on a mat. The gaunt, skeleton of a man was hemiparetic, his right arm and leg paralyzed, spasm twisting his limbs inward. Cindy was gently stretching his arm, doing various range-of-motion exercises.

Greg realized then how much he loved Cindy. She was loving and caring. She understood things. It was the first time in his life he could remember feeling this way. A sense of calm overcame him. A soothing warmth infiltrated his mind.

Greg decided that he wanted to marry her. Cindy looked over and smiled at Greg. She gave the man an elastic band, had him start an exercise on his own. Then turned to walk over.

She stopped in front of Greg, held his gaze.

Greg said, "Hi."

"Hi."

Greg moved in close and hugged Cindy, pulling her toward him. Cindy was stiff at first but softened.

"You know," Greg said. "There *is* something I want to show you."

Cindy made a face. "Oh?"

"Really. But you have to come over. Now is not the time or the place."

"Is this a joke?"

"No. We need to talk anyway. I've been doing a lot of thinking. I made a big mistake."

"Really."

"Yeah, really."

"How so."

"I don't want to lose you. You, you make me whole. I love you, Cindy."

"Hmm." Cindy narrowed her eyes, smiled. "I guess we can talk."

As Greg exited the hospital through the sliding glass doors he realized that probably for the first time in his life he felt happy. Not just a pleasant transient happiness but the deep kind of solid genuine happiness that is filled with hope and great possibilities.

The air outside was crisp and he cherished the feel of it across his face. The sunlight glinted off a mountain in the distance and he felt as if he could climb that mountain, dash up the green slope and reach its peak, breathless.

He hurried to his Lexus and climbed in, careful not to squish the little boy in his pocket.

As he pulled off the lot onto the road, he thumbed open the pocket of his coat, "You okay, old chap?"

"Yes," the boy said. "I feel happy too."

"Well, good thing," Greg said and slapped the steering wheel, sounding silly. "Cause we're going on a special mission, my boy."

Two hours later Greg pulled into his garage, twisted the key from the ignition and exhaled. He was giddy. "Can't believe I just did that," Greg said in a sing-song voice.

The boy was in the cup holder on the center console. "I'm glad you did."

Greg reached in his coat pocket, pulled out a small box, flipped it open.

"So am I," Greg said. He pulled the two-carat flawless princess-cut diamond ring from the velvet and held it up. A kaleidoscope of light shimmered before their eyes. "It's a beaut."

"It makes me happy," the boy said.

Greg couldn't contain himself. He was so excited.

He called Cindy and arranged to meet. She would come over in a few hours. He thought about waiting, maybe going on a special trip like Paris or something and pop the question there. But he decided he couldn't wait, that he would do it tonight and then show her the boy.

Things were good.

He and the boy had lunch. A sandwich and apple for Greg and a tiny chunk of apple for the boy, followed by a tiny pinch of turkey breast and more chocolate chip cookie crumbs.

Greg and the boy played a bit on the living room rug and then Greg ran warm water in a bowl for the boy to bathe.

After, the boy settled down for a nap.

Greg cleaned the house and then remembered the CD.

He went to his study, slid the CD into the computer and waited for it to load.

The phone buzzed.

"Greg?"

"Yes?"

"Hi Greg, it's Frank."

"Frank. Everything okay?" His boss never called on weekends.

"Everything's fine with me, Greg. It's *you* I'm concerned about."

"How so?"

"I heard you were in the hospital today."

"Well...yes. Had some abdominal pain. Just wanted to get a CT."

"Turn out okay?"

"Yes, fine. Probably gastritis."

"Good. I came in to do some paperwork. One of the transporters said he saw you. I spoke with Mike and he was real reluctant to talk. Don't blame him. I pressured him."

"There's nothing to hide, Frank."

"Well. Some of the other docs, even some techs, they say you're not yourself."

"I'm fine. Just the gastritis."

"Even Mike. Said you were acting weird. Fidgety."

"I have a lot going on. A little stressed."

"That's what I'm saying, Greg. As chairman of your department, but also as a friend, I think you should take a week or two off. Relax a bit. We'll be fine. I've got coverage, no problem."

A long silence.

"Greg?"

"Um. Okay. Sure. I'll take the week. Thanks, Frank."

"Good. I'll give you a call."

Greg set the phone in its cradle.

He went to the bedroom, saw the boy sleeping soundly on the bed.

He went to the kitchen and poured a Jameson's and noticed the clock.

Cindy was due to arrive in twenty minutes.

Greg couldn't get the conversation with his boss off his mind. He took a quick shower and shaved. He put on fresh clothes.

Who was talking about him? Frank made it sound as if everyone thought Greg was acting strangely. A subtle paranoia started to take hold and Greg pushed it aside. Told himself that he would relax, forget about that and just focus on Cindy.

Just a few hours ago he was on top of the world. He tried to transport himself back into that zone. He thought about Cindy, watching her at work, and the warmth rose up in him again. The happiness was breaking through.

He went to the bedroom and saw the boy, awake now, sitting on the bed. Greg explained what had happened.

The boy said, "You'll be fine."

"You're right. I'm just dandy. And I'm gonna ask Cindy to marry me. Tonight. I'll just put you in your little box-mansion here and later, I'll introduce you."

"I love you," the boy said.

"What?" Greg was taken aback. He picked the boy up and brought him close to his face. "Well, I love you too."

Greg placed him in the box.

There was a knock on the door.

Greg padded across the living room floor, nervously fiddling with the buttons on his shirt. He could make out Cindy's silhouette through the stained glass. The ring in his pant pocket pinched his thigh. He pulled the heavy wood door open and there she was.

The warmth rose up in Greg, flooding his muscles.

Cindy tilted her head and smiled, pushing right into his arms in the foyer.

Greg shuffled back, intertwining his body with Cindy's. They said nothing. He pulled Cindy close, a bear hug, his nose at the nape of her neck, inhaling deeply, feeling like some kind of addict, her scent the drug.

After a long moment, they backed away, eyes still connecting.

"It's so good to be here, Greg." Cindy seemed as if she might cry.

"I really missed you," Greg said. "Really really missed you."

"We've gotten real close, real fast."

"I know."

"Does that scare you?"

"Not anymore."

"We can do this."

"I know." Greg took her by the hand into the kitchen.

"You want a drink?"

"What did you want to show me?"

"Not yet," Greg said. "Well, two things now. Wine?"

"Two things? A little white would be nice. Anything bad?"

"*No no no.*" Greg reached into the fridge, pulled the cork from a half-filled bottle of pinot, poured. He cracked a beer for himself. "Come out to the porch."

He led her out onto a wood deck behind the house, which had a wonderful view of the mountains. They sat on a cushioned loveseat, sipping their drinks, cuddling.

The strong scent of evergreen wafted from the line of trees bordering his property. The sun was low, the sky reddish brown.

Greg couldn't take it anymore. He felt as if he would explode.

In one motion, he reached in his pocket and dropped to his knees in front of Cindy.

She looked surprised. Greg brought up the box, clicked the top open, held it up.

He waited a beat for Cindy to comprehend. He met her eyes.

"Cindy?" Greg inhaled, cleared his throat. "Will you marry me?"

Cindy's face stretched, eyebrows arched, eyelids lifted, teeth. She was holding her breath, then let it out.

"Oh my God, yes. Yes yes." Cindy gushed, and then a shriek. "YES!"

They embraced and kissed and Cindy stood up, hopped around a bit, and they hugged some more.

When they settled down, Greg finally said, "Now for the second thing."

"It's in here." Greg had Cindy's hand, guiding her into the bedroom. The box was on the bed.

"It's in that box?"

"Yup. Come here."

Greg and Cindy peered into the box simultaneously.

Cindy gasped.

Greg's mood flipped from jocular confidence to one of utter seriousness. "Hold on."

Cindy pressed her hand to her mouth. She stepped back.

Greg reached in and picked up the boy.

The boy had somehow solidified. He looked like a little sculpture, perfectly chiseled as if from a master artisan. He was a dull gray, but perfectly formed.

"Greg?" Cindy said. "What is that?"

Greg had to think quickly. The woman he just asked to marry him was clearly terrified. He had to think of something.

"Ah. Just a joke is all." Greg floundered. "Yeah. You said I was like a child. Just a joke. Thought it would be funny."

It was half-hearted. Cindy backed up a few more steps. Greg placed the boy back in the box, took Cindy by the hand back to the porch.

"Are you okay, Greg?"

"I'm fine. Sorry about that. Thought it would be funny."

Cindy was uneasy, and started to turn the ring on her finger.

"What are you doing?"

"I need a day to think, Greg." She set the ring on the glass-topped wicker table with a clink, next to her wineglass.

"Cindy, please."

"I'm sorry, Greg. It's all been so fast. Something tells me to sleep on it. I don't know what's happening here. With that little statue. Why did you have that thing in a box? Like you made a home for it? It's weird."

"I was just kidding. Please. Believe me."

"You know." Cindy seemed to loosen a bit. "I do love you, Greg. I really do."

"I love you too, so much."

"I think I better go." Cindy looked around, her hands fidgeting. "Why don't we talk more tomorrow?"

Greg figured maybe it was the best thing. He was thrown off and she was uncomfortable. He needed to play it cool.

"Yeah, okay," Greg said. "I'll call you in the morning."

After Cindy left, Greg went back to the box. The boy was still there, immovable.

He remembered the CD in the computer. The CT scan.

He scrambled to the study and clicked the mouse. The scan was on the screen as he had left it, when Frank called. He scrolled through the images and there he was.

The little boy.

He was right along side his abdomen on the CT table, right where he put him. He zoomed the images. If the boy was made out of stone or clay or whatever he would have appeared as a dense block, similar to calcification. Like bone.

But the lungs were aerated. The soft tissues were the same density as his own. The flesh was real. The bones were dense and the organs were proper organ density. Liver, spleen, pancreas and gallbladder. Stool in the colon. Fluid density in the bladder.

Greg rushed back to the box and saw that the boy hadn't moved.

Greg spoke to him. Called him.

Nothing.

Greg cried.

He poured a Jameson's over ice and sat with the boy on the desk in front of him for two hours.

Greg waited for something to happen.

Nothing happened.

He spoke to the boy until he was talked out.

Finally, Greg took the boy to the bathroom. He thought maybe some water might somehow bring him back. Rehydration? Yeah, that's it. He opened the faucet and ran warm water.

With the boy in the palm of his hand, he tested the boy's foot first. He let the water trickle, then course over the foot and lower leg.

The foot started to dissolve.

It began washing away like a sugar cube dissolving in a hot cup of tea.

Greg jerked his hand back.

He pinched some of the granules with his other hand, rolled them around between his fingertips, and then they were gone.

Greg started to sob softly, tears falling into the sink. He ran more water over the boy's thighs after the feet were gone, and then the abdomen, all dissolving into nothingness. Then the chest and finally he was left with the little boy's head wobbling on his palm.

The boy's eyes were closed and he was smiling. He appeared content.

Greg sighed, said, "See ya, little guy," and let the warm water course over his face, running in rivulets around the curves of his cheeks, nose, eyes.

After a minute, Greg's hand was empty and the water flowed through the creases in his palm, trickled between his fingers and around his wrist.

Greg stood and examined his own face in the mirror. He thought he looked different, older.

He shut off the faucet.

Greg gave a weak grin and dried his hands on a small cotton towel. His movements were slow, robot-like.

He shuffled back to the study, pushed the button on the front of the computer and retrieved the CD. He turned it over in his hand as if looking for some hidden code or message. It was just any old CD. Finally, he folded it and folded it until it cracked and then cracked again. He dropped it in the trash and sighed.

Greg lumbered to his bedroom, drained. He set the box on the floor. He undressed and lay flat on his back. He stared at the ceiling, the shadow from the lamp casting a wide, undulating arc.

Greg wondered where the little boy had gone. He hoped he was okay—wherever he was. He thought about Cindy and smiled, the warmth seeping in, beginning to caress his body.

Bigorexia

A WEEK BEFORE THE CONTEST, while perched on the toilet, Erich noticed the faint spray of oil spitting up from a tiny hole in his skin when he flexed his arm. Like a miniature oil well. Probably residual needle hole, he concluded. He swung his arm, elbow bent, fist clenched, biceps peaking out at twenty-nine inches now, and saw the micro-geyser moistening the skin. He spread the oil around, muscle glistening like polished bronze. He flexed the other arm— same thing, only the oil shot up a little off center from the biceps.

He got off the toilet, stood at the mirror. Hit another pose, arms in front, fists balled as if hugging a tree. Held it hard and long. There it was again. Little jets of oil sprayed from around his nipples. He laughed and shook his head, the whole thing absurd. He had to make it one more week. Just get through the contest, hopefully win the thing and then he could give it a break for a while.

He figured the few bottles of synthol he had left would be plenty.

Erich flicked the last bit of hair off his left pectoral muscle with the disposable razor, arched his back under hot water and let the clumped hair and soap wash clean, running off the angled curves and valleys, damming up at the drain. He examined the shaved forearms, thought they were smooth enough, watched cords of muscle undulate and dance as he wiggled his fingers. He neatly placed the razor back in its spot, blade down, handle out.

He slid palm over pecs, satisfied. They were smooth without evidence of stray stubble. Ran both hands over studded abs, stopped abruptly, sensing a thin layer of subcutaneous fat. He pinched skin and decided he had to get his body fat index checked again.

"You about done in there?" Debra said through the locked door.

Erich let the water cascade over his forehead and cheeks. Smoothed his hair, shut off the faucet. He waited until the last droplet swelled at the showerhead, then released. Stepped out of the stall, stood before the floor-to-ceiling mirror. Hit a few quick poses, shook his head in disgust, grabbed a towel and wrapped it around his waist, tucking the right corner downward, the line of the towel edge perfectly straight, right down the middle.

"One minute."

"I'm running late for work," Debra said. "And so are you."

"A minute." Erich smirked as he massaged a palmful of aloe vera gel over his shoulder. He admired his slick expression in the mirror, wondered how he was going to tell her he had no job, fired just the other day.

Synthol. Pump N' Pose. Posing oil. 85% medium-chain triglyceride oils, 7.5% lidocaine, 7.5% benzyl alcohol. Yeah, whatever. Erich liked the more official, scientific sounding name—Site Enhancement Oil. SEO. Sure. *I'll be administering the Site Enhancement Oil now, thank you. Just some fine tuning, enhancement of the site, thanks.*

It was just two months prior that Erich retrieved the wonderful cardboard box UPS had dropped on his porch—the case of synthol he had ordered online, twelve glass bottles stacked in neat and tidy rows.

That first day, while Deb was out, Erich sat in his study, filling ten disposable syringes with synthol, putting them in even rows of two, and propping up the instructions he had printed out from his favorite online bodybuilding forum.

Erich studied the amber oil in the syringes. He had reached the plateau, that's all. It's a well-known phenomenon. He paid his dues, did his time. Juicing it up for two years now. He had swallowed enough d-bol and anavar to choke a pig. Rammed so many syringes full of test and deca into his ass that parts of the skin were numb.

It was definitely time for some enhancement.

He laughed out loud at the thought of guys who claimed using SEO was cheating. Right. Juice monsters shooting and eating every drug in the book, destroying their livers, sprouting acne from hell, bloating, water retention and those annoying painful and swollen nipples—the notorious bitch tits. Gimme a break. Gear is okay? Oil is cheating? Sure.

Needle punctured skin. He started with several cc's into each delt, visualizing the oil infiltrating, creeping along and insinuating its molecules between muscle fibers like living amoeba. The muscle belly puffing like a striated blowfish.

Man, he really needed some posterior delts. *Puncture. Push.* Those things were hard to build up, despite hammering away at reverse cable crossovers for endless hours.

He slammed 2 cc's into each bicep right at the top to give it a nice peak. He thought of Arnold on the cover of *Education of a Bodybuilder*, with that sick bicep peak, as if an extra scoop of ice cream had been plopped on an already tall cone. Guns were the key to life. Gotta have guns. He was gonna spend some extra time on those bad boys. He did the same for the pecs, filling them out, looking like a warrior's armor plates.

And the tri's. He wanted that nice horseshoe sweep. The true sign of a polished arm. Artwork. And add a little roundness to the quad, the *vastus medialis* down front, give it that awesome teardrop look.

He knew he'd have to take it slow, several cc's at a time, a few times a week. Gradually build it up. This wasn't an overnight thing.

When Erich was satisfied, he hustled over to the gym, just like the instructions said. Get a good pump, spread the oil around, get the blood flowing, work it between the muscle fibers so you don't get any weird bumps or lumps.

So it looks nice and natural. Like you were born that way.

Erich swung the bathroom door and there was Debra, hands on hips in a flowered sundress, grinning.

"I thought you were late," Erich said.

"Not really," Debra said, slithering closer. "I exaggerated a little."

"How come?"

"Well." Debra flitted lashes. "You know. Figured, you know, we could, ah...do it. Been a while, huh?"

Erich inhaled, didn't want to answer too quickly, seem eager. "Well...I gotta workout."

"Sooooo?"

"So, sex uses energy. Extra energy. I told you I'm in that contest next week."

"You kidding?" She hiked the dress, spun a little pirouette, displaying a pink thong buried between two smooth, perfectly molded gluteus muscles. "You gonna turn this down?"

Erich squinted. He had to get out of there, get to the gym and do legs. Today was squat day and it was gonna be brutal. "Told you. I got the contest."

Debra let the dress fall. Her expression changed instantly like someone pulled a plug. "You look like a freak already. What the heck are you doing anyway? You're not using that crap again are you?"

"Nope."

"Why do you look so greasy?"

Erich glanced down, saw some oily streaks flowing along his arms. Had to think fast. "Aloe."

"Everyone's saying how freaky big you are. That you don't even look real. I overheard someone say you look like a cartoon character. I hardly recognize you."

"They're full of crap."

"No," Debra pointed. "You're full of crap."

"That's not very nice, Debra."

"Not nice? And don't call me Debra. You live at that gym. Your mom calls last weekend, you tell me to say we couldn't have dinner because you were sick? You really wanted to workout. Nice." Her face changed again, as if she had a sudden thought. "Since when don't you want some of this? Huh?"

"Just wanna be ready for the show."

"That's all I hear. The gym. A show. We're supposed to start a family too. Hello? Kids? How we gonna do that when you won't come near me? Huh?"

"After the show."

"Always after the show. Work, gym, work, gym. That's all it is."

"Well," Erich said, taking a breath. "It won't be quite like that anymore. At least not for a while."

"Whadaya mean?"

"Well," Erich said, letting a beat pass. He looked around, scraped an oily armpit. "I got fired."

"Well, Erich," Doctor Reed said. "Your blood work is fine. Liver enzymes a tiny bit elevated but not surprising given the amount of anabolics you've used."

"See, Doc?" Erich sat on the edge of the examining table in his underwear, crunching paper, the table creaking under his weight. "Who says juice is a bad thing?"

Reed leaned against the counter in his white coat. "You seem to be using them responsibly."

"I cycle, Doc. On time, off time. Give the body a break."

"Still, Erich," Reed said. "This synthol you're telling me about. Seems all wrong. Downright strange."

"Everyone's doing it, Doc. Just gives you that edge before a show."

"But your body is looking quite unnatural, Erich. I'm sorry to say. The muscles don't seem to follow natural contours."

"Freaky, right?"

"Not in a good way, Erich. And I think you've overdone it. This oil you're showing me. I think there's just too much in there."

"The contest is in a week. I'm gonna cool out after that."

"I'm tempted to send you for an MRI. See what the muscle looks like. There may be excessive pressure buildup. Don't want to risk some kind of fasciitis, or hinder the blood flow."

"No worries, Doc." Erich jiggled his pecs. "Not happening here."

"Not yet. Never know, though."

"I'm a machine, Doc. Feels just perfecto."

"Erich."

"Doesn't feel tight. I feel like an animal. Just a little more fullness around the delts, give 'em that cannonball look. A nice sweep to the tri. I'll be good."

"Erich."

"Yeah?"

"After the show."

"Yeah."

"After the show," Reed said. "I'd like you to see a therapist."

"Therapist? Doc, I'm not injured. I'm fine. I'll work through all this."

"No, no, no," Reed said. "A psychotherapist."

"What?" Erich sat up straight. "The heck for? I'm fine."

Reed rubbed his chin, a serious expression clouding his face.

"Erich," Reed said. "I think you have bigorexia."

"Ha!" Erich arched back. "You're kidding right?"

"No."

Erich shook his head, spread his arms, glanced at his limbs, as if checking to see that they were still there. "Sure, I like to be big. So what?"

"It's a real medical term, Erich."

"Come on. We throw that word 'round the gym. A joke."

"Well it's a real term. Falls under body dysmorphic disorder. Like reverse anorexia."

"Gotta love it."

"You fulfill all the criteria," Reed said. "And your life's a mess."

"Damn right. But it's not a bad mess. It's just falling into place. You wanna be big? Live in the kingdom of huge? Then you gotta make some changes. It's a commitment. A lifelong process. Not for the weak. You wanna play? You gotta pay. Simple."

"You told me you just lost your job."

"The hell with them. Doc, I've been an electrical engineer for ten years. Working in a cubicle's a death sentence. Sitting in a box. Circuit boards. They wanted to promote me to a more sedentary position. Screw it."

"Erich. You have to earn money."

"I *am* earning money. Decent money too. Got a job at the airport. Gym buddy hooked me up. Baggage handler. Evening hours. Can get to the gym in the morning. Lifting stuff all the time, keeps the blood pumping."

"Forgive me, Erich. But that job doesn't sound right for someone who graduated from RIT."

"Hard to get those jobs, believe me. Damn good benefits too. And I'm staying in shape. Thinking about the next workout."

"All I'm saying is bigorexia is treatable. No drugs. Just cognitive therapy. It can balance your life."

"You're serious, huh?"

"I've known you and Debbie a long time. Hate to see things fall apart."

"Nah."

"Will you consider it? I know a good therapist locally. Specializing in body issues."

"Body issues? That's hilarious. Somebody specializing in that. What a joke. I could give a seminar on body issues. How most people are fat-asses."

"Here's his name."

"Everyone has body issues. Me? I'm trying to perfect my body. Sculpt it, like Rodin. What's wrong with that?"

"Nothing. If balanced."

"I'm balanced. Two hundred forty pounds of symmetrical crafted stone."

"That's massive, Erich."

"Could use ten more pounds of muscle."

"Two fifty?"

"Be absolute perfection."

"Much too much."

"Nah."

"For your height, Erich."

"Nah."

"But Erich," Reed said. "You're only five-six."

After the doctor, Erich went to the gym. He needed a workout. Needed to pound some iron. Think about all that crap Reed told him. Bigorexia. Therapy. Balance.

Typical. Somebody trying to succeed, do something laudable. *Boom.* Take 'em down.

No way was he going to any therapist. He knew what he had to do. Train.

"Wait," Tony said, pointing. "What the hell is that?"

Erich and Tony were in the locker room at Iron Plate Gym. Erich stood in front of a huge wall mirror in white cotton briefs, his sweats in a heap at his feet. He was holding a side chest pose. Tony stood behind Erich, a little off to the side.

"What?"

"Wait. Hit the calf again. There."

Erich crunched his toes to the floor, raised the heel. His calf shortened and expanded, as if a kitten were under his skin, curling up for a nap. A jet of oil sprung out.

"Didn't see anything," Erich said.

"Right there. I saw a little spritz." Tony leaned over and jabbed a finger. "Right there, man. That ain't right."

"Didn't see anything."

"Fine. You're scary looking," Tony said, shaking his head. "Hate to say it. But you're a synthol freak, bro."

"Let's train, okay?"

Erich got home just after Debra. She was in the kitchen making a salad. Erich entered the room, tossed his gym bag on the chair.

She regarded him carefully.

"So I saw Doctor Reed today," Erich said. "Like you suggested."

"And?"

"He says I'm fine."

"Really?"

"Yeah."

"That's not what he told me."

"What?"

"I spoke with him."

"My visit is confidential. He can't talk to you."

"I'm your wife, Erich. Remember? Besides he didn't go into detail."

"Good."

"He said he recommended therapy. For bigorexia."

"Damn Reed!"

"No. Damn you, Erich. This is out of control."

"Everything's fine. I just have a contest in a few days."

"Been like this a long time."

"So?"

"You know what today is?"

"Wednesday."

"Right. Our first wedding anniversary."

"Yeah."

"I made reservations for that Italian place. For tomorrow."

"You know I can't eat that crap. I'm on a strict pre-contest diet. Tuna. Chicken breast. Water."

"Surprise surprise." Debra turned back to the counter, started chopping a tomato with loud deliberate clunks. "So you gonna go to therapy?"

"No way. It's a bunch of garbage."

"Erich!" Debra spun round.

"People just don't want me being big."

"Erich!"

"They're jealous."

"Ha!"

"So are you!"

"This is nuts. The gym's like a mistress. But even worse. You're having an affair with yourself!"

"Fine," Erich said, looking around. The sink, the cutting board, the window. "After the show, I'll cut down on the gym to six times a week."

"What?"

"Okay, maybe five."

"This is not gonna work, Erich." Debra hastily swiped the lettuce and chopped veggies into the sink. Some scattered to the floor. "You don't want kids, you don't care about me."

"What're you sayin?"

"I married an engineer. Now you're a baggage handler."

"It's honest work!"

"It's not you!"

"Maybe you just don't know me."

"Maybe not."

"You're getting me all worked up. Come on. It's not good to stress out before a show. I gotta eat."

"Erich?"

"What?"

A long pause. An intense stare. Daggers. "I'm leaving you."

Erich locked Debra's gaze. She looked dead serious and he didn't know what to do. Was this a good thing? No way. He loved Debbie. Right? All he could come out with was, "Good."

"Good?" Debra's mouth smiled, but her eyes didn't.

Erich stared, feeling awkward.

Debra narrowed her eyes, honing in on Erich's mid-chest. "What's that stuff dripping down your shirt?"

Erich looked down, felt the oil running from his nipples, bubbling down his shirt to his abs, staining the front like streaks of blood. Soaking and spreading.

"Nothing." Erich brought his hands up for cover. "Sweat."

Erich sunk into the low leather couch in his den, the wood coffee table at his knees. On the table, spread out in a neat row, were ten synthol-filled disposable syringes.

One more day.

Debra bolted to her mother's in Jersey for the weekend. Said maybe they'd try to work through things after the show. He knew that was crap. Because if she couldn't support him at contest time, hell, she'd never support him in anything. He smiled thinking that the whole thing made sense now, a test.

He had to find himself a muscle chick. A chick who trained, who understood—a babe who lived in the world of muscle.

He also had to replace the synthol he was losing. And fast. It was coming out steadily now, a real slow trickle. Around the nipples and bi's. Yesterday it had started along the quads, oozing out around the kneecaps. This morning some dribbled at the junction of the long triceps head as it tucked under the lateral head of the delt.

As long as he didn't flex too hard for too long, he'd be okay. Just a subtle baseline ooze.

He needed to maintain it for the contest.

He began the injections in his pecs, using the first syringe in line. He took his time. Swipe with alcohol, puncture, push. Puncture, push. When all the syringes were empty, he felt euphoric. The muscles tight. Engorged and swollen. Mountainous cascading lines and deep cavernous valleys.

He was *gigundohumongous.*

Hell, more like *syntholfreakenormous.*

Erich stood. Did several deep knee bends, mimicking a loaded bar draping his back like a heavy squat. Flowing through a crude version of his posing routine, Erich achieved the slow hot burn of a pump. His skin tightened. It leaked a tiny bit and he smeared it around.

He lumbered to the bathroom and faced the floor-to-ceiling mirror, evaluating the chiseled mass in the glass. The bright overhead light created shadows that accentuated every hill and gash. His body looked like the closest thing to perfection he had ever seen.

Adonis himself would be proud, and would have to relinquish his crown in defeat.

Erich woke at 5:00 a.m. Contest day. He had tossed and turned all night, a bit wired. His metabolism was kicking into hyperdrive due to the loads of thyroid hormone he'd been taking over the last two weeks. He lay on his back, staring at the ceiling, wide-eyed. He sensed wetness. The sheets were matted. He was in a shallow pool of thick oil.

He jumped and wiped himself with the covers. Dripping, he gathered all the sheets into a ball and tossed them in the wash. He went to the den, loaded several syringes with synthol, and proceeded to replenish. *Puncture push. Puncture push.*

He showered and took 50 milligrams of Lasix to get rid of any excess water.

He was ready for battle.

Erich made sure he got to the auditorium early, wearing the baggiest sweatsuit he owned. He checked in and made his way to the back holding area.

He found a quiet corner and faced the wall, removed the sweat suit, revealing skimpy fluorescent gold posing trunks. He applied several coats of quick tan lotion.

A short time later he was on stage for the pre-judging portion of the contest. Erich looked around, studied his competitors and laughed. Were these guys kidding?

He could tell the way everyone was staring that he had something special. There was whispering and head swiveling and nobody made eye contact. Perfect. They were scared. Didn't want to acknowledge the obvious god-like specimen in their presence. A literal gorilla in the room, Erich thought, a weird little grin ripping across his tanned face.

He spotted one guy he had seen before at the gym, Joey. This character might give him a run for his money but the a-wipe had spindles for legs and his calves looked like they belonged to a ten year-old girl. A ten year-old ballet-dancing girl.

Guess he never heard of synthol. Idiot. And there was a big old Jesus tat across his chest. Like he just got out of prison. Judges hated that.

Erich was satisfied. He could tell he was a lock-in the way the judges gawked at him, all subtle pointing and low talking, coming back to him several times, asking him to hit a most muscular pose three times. All of them staring, big-eyed like a little group of owls.

After the pre-judging he donned his sweat suit in a hurry and scurried to his corner. He meditated and did some deep breathing.

It wasn't long before he noticed. The entire sweatsuit was saturated with oil.

Erich heard his name echo through the hall. He stepped from the shadows into bright light, waddling to the posing platform. Hot, blinding lights. If he squinted he could make out hundreds of people in the crowd.

Time for a show.

Time to witness true perfection.

The music erupted. A mix of hip-hop and classical arranged by a DJ friend.

He hit the first pose and heard the low rumble of the crowd. Some clapping. A big crescendo beat and he swung his arms in wide arcs.

He stepped and turned. Twisted on his feet, feeling the slickness of oil between his toes.

His muscles pulled tighter and tighter, veins swelling, a result of the king-sized chocolate bar he had devoured an hour ago, creating a massive sugar rush and surging pump.

He locked the final pose. Finished. Stood there, a little contorted. Felt pain. Not the good pain of the pump but a weird pain. Racking his body.

Oil streaks oozed across both biceps and down into the crook of his elbow. He squinted and saw a subtle rip around the periphery of his left nipple. There was a droplet of blood.

He heard someone yell his name. The head judge chopped his hand, motioning for him to get the hell off stage and the lights were sizzling and the crowd was whooping and he couldn't tell if they were cheering or laughing or both. It sounded like glorious cheers of adulation to Erich.

His body ached. He turned and plodded offstage, almost toppling over, slipping on scattered pools of oil.

Fifteen minutes later Erich was back on stage, this time with the rest of the competitors. All twenty of them. The pose down. Decision time.

Erich struggled to get toward center stage, bumping elbows, trying to take the dominant position. Display his hard-earned sculpted temple. Let the judges cherish his molded girth alongside these wimpy sucked-out losers.

The men stood like gladiators, fighting without weapons, stepping, contracting arm, leg, trap. Squeezing, huffing, wiggling thighs and calves. Anything to stand out. Brutal and raw. The crowd roared.

Erich flexed with passionate rage. No holding back. Going for gold. Striking each pose with his entire soul. If Deb could see him now. Veins distended along the surface of his delts and chest, rising and crawling like swollen man-eating worms.

His breath caught. The pain was setting in, intense pain.

Jets of oil sprayed wildly from around his nipples with each contraction.

He could see the crowd, chanting, waving, pointing. At him?

Erich groaned and pumped. Slightly dizzy. Endorphins flooding.

He could make out the skyline of trophies off to the side, standing at attention like soldiers. He wanted the towering shiny majestic one in the middle, taller than he was. That was his. First prize. He thought he could hear his name exploding in the darkness.

Erich heaved and swung arms down front, knocking fists, traps lifting like fleshy mini hams and coming alive, the fibers between his pecs quivering with spasm.

And that's when the first fissure tore apart.

A crater split the length of his bicep, like a street during a massive earthquake, and despite claps and cheers, he thought he heard a sound like shredding paper.

Other rips immediately followed. Skin separated. His left nipple detached from his body, dangling by a thin strand of tissue. Fluid spewed forth and splattered wood planks, as if his pec had vomited.

His right bicep split sideways and both quads opened up lengthwise.

Viscous fluid gushed from the defects. Yellowish and streaked with rust, all of it exiting, giving a long-awaited sigh, a full body orgasm.

A collective gasp burst from the audience.

Erich couldn't understand how this could be happening. Maybe it wasn't? He had done everything right. He thought about Deb, far away, in New Jersey, glad she wasn't there now.

Erich folded at the waist, his legs unable to support weight. As his face rushed toward the hardwood floor, a sudden and complete silence echoed before he heard the bellowing voice of the head judge like a cannon blast.

"DIIIIISQUALIFIIIIED!"

Disintegration

DR. DOUGLAS BRENNER'S RIGHT INDEX FINGER TURNED BLACK. Then fell off.

Whooosh.

Doug had a hard time comprehending what had just happened. He sat at the splintered kitchen table in his hunting cabin. Upstate New York. Left hand clutched right wrist. Drew the hand close to his face.

Gone.

It didn't just "fall off" in the usual sense of the word. It *disintegrated.* The finger had been tingly for an hour, pins and needles. Went totally numb and then there was no feeling at all.

Like a rubber finger.

His concern spiked when the finger started to change color. Black from the nail down. He knew black meant ischemia, cut off blood flow. He worried about some kind of infarct. An embolus? From where? There was no pain at all. Certainly, if he flipped a clot there'd be sudden, intense pain.

Didn't make sense. Every finger was supplied by two arteries. Total finger ischemic events just didn't happen like this. Spasm then? Like a weird Raynaud's Disease? Vasculitis? No. Not just one finger. So clean.

The blackness had started at the tip, slowly worked its way down to the base, took a few minutes, like the mercury in a thermometer dropping.

And for those few minutes he sat rooted to the wobbly wood chair, watched, dumbfounded, as if enjoying a strange but nonetheless intriguing movie. When the blackness reached the base, it stopped. He tried to wiggle the finger. No go. Nothing happening there.

So he whipped his hand. A sudden jerk. The finger fell apart into a soft powdery mound of black dust, like a charred twig pulled from a fire, looking whole at first, but one touch reveals it's constructed of ash.

Whooosh.

Doug angled his torso at the kitchen sink, cold water splashing his hand as he examined the raised stump where his finger had been less than an hour ago. A slight convexity over the metacarpal head. No open wound, no bleeding. Just a patchy red film of tissue. He rubbed the tip of his left index finger over the site. Felt normal.

He inspected his other fingers. Looked good.

Doug dried his hands with a couple sheets of stale paper towel, went over to the kitchen table, looked at the little clump of dust. He creaked open an overhead cabinet, removed a chipped plate. Doug palmed the dust pile onto the plate, thinking he should keep it. Maybe get it to a lab, test it. For what? Who knows, but it sounded like a good plan.

Another idea popped. He rummaged through a warped drawer next to the sink, found a crunched box of plastic sandwich bags, pulled one out, and tapped the dust from the plate into the bag. Sealed it. Put it on the counter next to the rusted toaster with the broken handle.

What the hell could be happening? Maybe he should bolt, get back to Manhattan, visit one of his doctor buddies. Maybe Barry the cardiologist, or Pradeep in infectious disease. Crap. He wanted to Google this in the worst way, but there was no internet access. No cell signal either.

Country living.

With Amy arriving in the morning, maybe he was better off staying put. He laughed. This was supposed to be a relaxing time for him and Amy. The whole idea of this trip. Try to work things out. She was in the middle of her medicine residency and was extremely busy—fifteen hour days, frequent overnight call, studying for her boards. She thought they were drifting apart. Implied he wasn't trying hard enough.

He worshiped Amy. They were supposed to have a week to spend together. Quietly. Middle of nowhere. Work things out.

And he had no finger.

Doug dropped another log into the fireplace, wracking his brain. The fire crackled. A puff of curly smoke drifted into the living room. Maybe he should go to the local ER, but *local* around here meant miles. What would they do for him anyway? At the very least he could make a call. Yeah. Maybe some blood work. An x-ray?

He figured if he was going to do it he should leave now. It was 4:30, getting dark and a light snow, flurries really, had been falling since he got to the cabin that morning. He ambled a few steps to the kitchen.

He yanked a drawer stuffed with crinkly papers and a dated phone book. He flipped pages and there it was, Saint Margaret Hospital. There was a little map. He was right, about fifteen miles.

He grabbed his keys.

The Jeep was a few steps beyond the porch. A thin coat of snow dusted metal. He swiped the door handle, hopped in. The temperature had dropped. He flicked the ignition. The satellite radio kicked in. Set for the 80's station. The Cure blasted. He had to laugh.

The cabin was nestled into the side of a small mountain called Dingle Hill, about a mile down to the main road. Dirt and gravel. About five miles on that till he got to the main drag.

At the bottom of the mountain there was a sign that read, "Dingle Haven." As he swung onto the road he almost squashed two mangy looking dogs. The Jeep fishtailed on an ice patch. He quickly pulled straight, switched over to four-wheel drive. Cranked the volume.

The ball of the stick felt wrong. All wrong in his hand without the index finger. Had to recruit the pinky to help out. Promote the little guy. So the stick didn't slip away.

The Jeep dug in and spit up dirt.

Doug finally saw hospital signs, the blue one with the white "H". Getting close. The flurries morphed to a mixture of sleet and snow and he was thankful for the four-wheel drive. Never know.

There it was. He swung into the lot and almost ran over a lanky mutt as it darted across the gravel lot into the neighboring woods. This was a hospital? Single story square structure, decrepit, paint peeling. Looked like a vacant strip joint. He parked and headed to the door, a sign above, "Ring Bell For Emergency".

A doorbell? Doug buzzed.

With his thumb.

A moment later an older woman cracked the door. "Yeeeeuuus?"

"Evenin'." Doug took in the sight. Gray hair in a bun. Creepy smile. Navy blue scrub shirt stretched over a sizable bosom. And gut. "I need to see someone."

"What's the problem there, sir?"

"Um." Doug figured he'd just get to business. Shock value. "My finger fell off."

She raked Doug up and down. Down and up. Crunched her brow.

"Listen. I'm a physician. From New York. Had a weird thing happen. I know it sounds crazy. But I really need to talk to the doctor here."

"Wella'." She arced the door a bit more. "I'm the nurse here at Saint Margaret's. We need a doctor, we gotta' page 'im."

"Okay, then. Fine. Maybe you can get me started. Take some blood. Got an x-ray tech on site?"

"You're looking at er."

"Great." Doug slid inside, scanned the place. A small room with one patient bed. Several monitors, glass cabinets, trays. A room off to the side with an x-ray unit.

"I'm Clara." The nurse motioned for him to sit on a metal chair next to the bed. Doug spewed the whole story. The numbness, the blackness. Finger disintegration.

Clara stared at him then walked to the phone. An old dial-up model, faded yellow, with a long squiggly cord. Said she was paging Doctor Whicker. He'd be here shortly.

Clara drew some blood. Doug asked about internet access and Clara looked at him funny and said, "Nope."

Doug asked to use the phone. He dialed Amy's cell but she didn't answer. That didn't surprise him. She was out with her two sisters. He left a message, telling her he had a medical issue and can she come up to the cabin as soon as possible.

He looked back at Clara and she was staring his way.

Doug threw her a smile. "Can you shoot a film?"

"Don't see why not." Clara motioned him to the x-ray room.

Doug sat in a chair, rested his fingerless hand on an adjacent table. Clara swung the x-ray equipment into position.

"Clara?" Doug said, "what's with all these mutts round here?"

"Mutts?"

"Stray dogs. I saw a couple by my cabin. Another in your lot."

"Thems probly' ain't dogs." Clara slid a square cassette under Doug's hand. Pushed on his hand so it was flat. "Thems c'yotes."

"Coyotes?"

"Yup." Clara angled the cross-hairs over his hand. "Seein' 'em more and more."

Clara disappeared behind a half wall, said, "Don't move," and the machine made a sharp high-pitched sound. She shot two more views. Clara ran the cassettes through the processor.

Doug grabbed the films as they fell into the bin and swung them onto the view box. Clara glared at him.

"Oh." Doug gave Clara his charm the nurse smile. "I'm a Radiologist."

It seemed to work. Her face softened. "Convenient, huh?"

"Guess." Doug studied the films. The bones were intact. No erosion. No lytic or blastic lesions. Hmm. His second metacarpal looked fine. Right where the finger fell off. The second proximal, middle and distal phalanges were gone. As expected. Okay. At least the other bones were normal looking.

"Looks fine." Doug swiped the films off the view box, handed them to Clara. Attempted another smile. This one was weaker and they both knew it.

After a few minutes, a bell rattled and the door opened. Doctor Whicker.

An ancient-looking character. Stooped over, gnarled cane in hand. Long gray hair swept back off his forehead. Greased. He resembled an old-time movie star. Bow tie.

Doug loved that. The old internists seemed to all wear bow ties. Doug made a mental note to buy one, try it out, see what it did for him. He was pushing forty now. Maybe it was time.

"So what do we have here?" Whicker motioned for Doug to come into the main room, swung his hand at the bed. "Sit down."

"I'm a physician too, sir. Good to meet you." Doug shook Whicker's hand. Was deferential. Then held up his right hand, twisted up his face. "This is what we have."

Whicker's eyes narrowed.

"I lost my finger, Doc." Doug waved his hand. Wiggled the remaining fingers. "Turned black then just fell off. Turned to dust."

Whicker glanced over at Clara. She said, "Got the bloods. An x-ray. Vitals are fine. No medical history."

"I looked at the film." Doug said. "Nothing significant."

Whicker spun back to Doug. Something woke in Whicker's eyes. His demeanor changed.

"You okay, Doc?"

Whicker clutched Doug's wrist. Hard. Leaned in. "When this happen?"

"About an hour ago."

Whicker inhaled. Released Doug's wrist. "Where you from?"

"New York City. Got a cabin on Dingle Hill."

Whicker's wrinkly eyelids burst apart. "Dingle Hill?"

"Yup. Know it? Was my uncle's. Years ago. Use it once in a while. Not in a long time though."

Whicker's face reflected something dark. He seemed adrift for a few moments, then was back. "Seen any bugs there?"

"Bugs?"

"Yeah. Insects and such."

"Not really. Just the regular stuff."

Whicker palmed his gray skull. Rubbed his eyes. "My dad was the doc in this town 'fore me. I was a boy. My dad told a story of Old Man Bidwell. From Dingle Hill. Came to this very hospital. Only it was smaller then of course. Bidwell's big toe had fallen off while he slept. Came here an' lost a few more toes. Said some bug had bit him the night before."

Toes fell off? Doug felt sick. He got up and strode a few steps. "Bidwell is my mother's side of the family."

"Intrestin'," Whicker said. "You bit by any bug?"

Doug shook his head. Did a quick recall. "Nope."

"Be real sure, son."

Doug went over the morning in his head. Looked off beyond the ceiling. Then it hit him.

"Well," Doug said. "I was stacking some firewood at the cabin. This morning. In the living room. Felt a pinch. Thought it was the wood, like a little splinter. Saw a little bug scurry away but I thought nothing of it."

"Where was the pinch?"

Doug's palm came up. Didn't want to look. His gut tightened.

"Finger that fell off?"

Doug stared at his hand. "Ah...yes."

"Think you better get on back to New York City. Just in case. Get to one of those big university hospitals."

"Um...okay." The room turned hot. His senses sharpened. Doug felt numbness creeping along his right hand. Was he imagining it? "This some kind of infection? Like accelerated leprosy?"

"Don't know."

Doug went over all the bizarre infections in his head. "Doc?"

"Yeah?"

"What happened to Old Man Bidwell?"

Whicker looked at Clara. Then back at Doug. "Well. Never heard. Some said he disappeared."

"Disappeared?"

"Seems no one heard from him. Sheriff went on over to his place and he just wasn't there, is all."

Images of family faces and gatherings flashed through Doug's head like a film clip. He couldn't remember any story about a great uncle or relative going missing. Still, he felt as if he would vomit.

Doug was five miles into the ride to the cabin when he knew for sure that his right hand was numb. No, he was not imagining it. The snow was falling at a good clip and there was some rain too. The wipers were on high speed. *Flip flop flip flop.*

Insects? What? Like some weird infection? Accelerated leprosy? Or just total small vessel occlusion? No way.

After a while he couldn't feel the stick shift and he glanced down. It looked like he was wearing a dark glove.

He swerved roadside, the wipers smashing along. He fumbled, found the overhead light. Flicked it. Lifted his hand to his face. Nope. No glove. Black.

No sensation.

Dead.

Crap.

Doug shook his arm, elbow bent. One vigorous back and forth. The hand fell away in a flurry of powder.

Whoosh.

A handless fleshy stump.

Barreling along. Sleet and rain tapping. Doug had realized he couldn't just sit on the side of the road in the middle of nowhere in this storm. He would end up freezing to death. It took him a few minutes to yank his eyes away from the smooth pink stump of his wrist.

The Jeep's over-sized tires spewed an arc of gray slush. He was speeding.

He pushed down on the stick shift with his stump. Was hard to shift so he just put it in third, then fourth with his left hand, almost losing control. Tried cruising along at a constant speed.

When he came to the beginning of the mountain he had to reach across with his left hand and downshift to first to start the ascent.

Then he realized his whole right arm was numb.

The Jeep jerked and lurched up the mountain.

Doug swung the vehicle in front of the cabin. Hopped out. Went to the door. He tried to grab the doorknob with his right arm. He realized he couldn't. It felt like he could though. He thought his right hand was there but he knew this was just the "phantom limb" phenomenon he had read about and discussed numerous times. Now his own hand was the phantom.

The stump of his right arm hit the door knob.

The sleeve deflated.

The coat sleeve fell to his side and dangled. Like a muffler backfire, a puff of smoky dust shot to the ground.

He put the keys in his mouth. Opened the door with his left hand. Stumbled inside.

Doug twisted off his coat. Angled. Pulled.

He spit the keys out onto the kitchen table. Tore off his shirt.

He went to the bathroom and stood in front of the mirror.

What?

He stood there. Right arm gone. Gone? There was a smooth rounded bulge where his shoulder used to be. Man, that looked all wrong. He massaged his left palm along the bulge. Thought he would feel smooth skin. He felt nothing.

Because his left hand was numb.

Doug bolted to the living room.

To the fireplace.

He knelt down in front of the pile of firewood stacked against the wall. About ten logs. What were these bugs? He had to know. With caution, he lifted the top piece, tossed it into the smoldering fire. He grabbed another log, left-handed, tossed that one.

And another.

He threw the rest of the logs across the floor, skittering into the kitchen. Had to look around.

On the hardwood, he saw a few bugs scurrying about. Disappearing between the wide planks. Tiny little things. A knobby thorax, jointed legs. Hairs. Surely they couldn't be responsible? But then again, all it took was one microbe to kill.

He inhaled. One of the planks was not flush with the floor. A hole where a knot had been. He slowly inserted his left index finger through the hole, not knowing what the hell might be in there. Bent the tip, hooked it in. Lifted.

The plank thunked up.

Christ. No way. Hundreds of tiny reddish creatures scrambled about, darted here and there, disappeared into the exposed dirt.

Doug lurched back. Stood.

Noticed his left hand.

Black.

Doug dashed to the kitchen, yanked open cabinets. Looked under the sink. *There.* He fisted a cruddy can of bug spray. He couldn't feel it in his hand. He scrambled to the fireplace. *Got to kill those fuckers.* Weakly held the can above the exposed dirt. His chest heaved as if he had just sprinted a mile.

He went to push the nozzle but the can fell to the floor with a clank.

His left hand was gone.

Then the arm.

Dust.

Doug realized what he had to do. Burn the infestation to the ground. But he had no hands.

He kicked flaming logs in the fireplace with his right foot. He kept kicking until a log rolled in front of the fireplace, on the rug over the hardwood floor.

He tapped it with his foot so it was over the open spot in the floor. The spot with the plank pulled up. With the evil.

He could see the bugs buzzing around. He was able to hook his foot under an adjacent plank. He kept kicking and pulling until the plank popped. He gave it one good kick and it sailed through the air. Clanked behind him. Hundreds of tiny bugs swarmed.

He twisted his foot back into the fire and hooked out another log. Swung this one over towards the couch.

His right foot was numb.

Crap.

Doug limped to the couch.

He prodded the log so that it wedged under the couch. The fabric exploded in orange flames. Mild at first. Then the whole thing went up, heat and light dancing slashes across his face.

Whoosh.

Doug was halfway to the kitchen table when his right foot disintegrated. He fell to the floor like a heavy punching bag detached from its chain. *Thump.*

The couch was now a raging inferno. Succumbing to the heat. The rug in the living room burned black, crept and stretched around the couch.

Doug pushed to his knees. Got onto his left foot and right ankle stump. He hobbled to the kitchen table. With dried lips, he leaned and gnawed at the Jeep keys. He got them in his mouth, turned.

His knee gave. Twisted. The right leg crumbled as if his bones were made of balsa wood. The right leg of his jeans wrinkled and folded under his weight.

Black dust puffed from the hem of his pants and he smashed the floor.

Doug had one leg, the left. No arms. The living room was ablaze in a brilliant yellow and red.

A shifting carpet of red undulated over the floor. Millions of tiny insects scrambled from the heat.

This can't be happening. He felt as if he were trapped in some nightmare. Doug shimmied across the floor to the kitchen wall. Teeth crunching keys. He pushed his head against the sheetrock and tried to get up. No way.

Gotta' push. Gotta' get up. Bugs. Lots of 'em.

He went flat on his back. Crunched his abs to get into a sitting position. He forced his head against the recliner. The one that bordered the kitchen and living room. With a swinging motion and great effort he managed to get on his knee. Damn that hurt. Felt like his neck would crack. He dug his head into the arm of the chair, turned, pushed himself into a standing position.

His breath caught. Smoke filled the room. Black.

He hopped to the front door, one legged. *Hop bam balance. Hop bam balance.*

Doug had to use his hip and ass to turn the knob, get the door open. He met a wall of cold. Wind swirling with snow and sleet.

His left leg turned numb.

Doug hopped into the cold like a human pogo-stick.

The ground was slick.

Snow and sleet whipped his face.

He got next to the Jeep and had to bend, using his jaw and chin to open the door. All the while trying not to drop the keys from his mouth.

He leaned. Got his head in the Jeep, smelled the familiar Jeep smell. A lurch. All he had. He thrust himself across the seat, his forehead rapping the stick shift, shoulder slamming console.

He twisted his neck, tongued the keys. Turned the metal over in his mouth. Got the ignition key to stick out. He poked and poked, looking like a chicken, until it slipped into the ignition.

It hit him. How the hell was he going to turn it? Shift? Steer?

Doug yelled. A hysterical maniacal laugh. Twisted on the seat, so he was on his side. He was exhausted, breathing heavily, giving in.

He realized he couldn't feel his left leg.

Gone.

He could see the material of his pant legs, both of them, flailing loosely.

Doug lay there, giggling. A silly, sad giggle. Whimpering maybe. What would Amy think if she pulled up right now? A pathetic limbless torso.

Snow flakes sailed in, floated about, landed. They prickled his face, stabbed him, left droplets of moisture in their wake. The cold wind felt good. Soothing.

Doug looked at the cabin. Reflected orange light cut and bounced across his face. Smoke and flames shot from the cabin door, reached out. The fire crackled, then the house gave out a crash as the roof fell in.

He was just a torso. Armless. Legless. Pathetic. So this was it? Maybe just his limbs would be affected? If he could survive the cold till morning, when Amy got there, at least he had a shot. The cabin was engulfed, succumbed to the flames.

The warmth felt good.

Could get him through the night.

He took a deep breath and tried to wriggle around, so that he might be able to sit upright, get the door closed somehow.

The panting was difficult to hear at first over the crackling fire.

He turned his head, his stomach sinking at what he knew he would see.

A pack of coyotes milled around the Jeep. Probably a family. Hunting for food during this hard, scarce season, winter.

The largest one already had his muzzle jutting in the Jeep, sniffing, eyes black and empty, a string of saliva dangling. A guttural growl as his eyes met Doug's. They held each others gaze for a long moment, man and beast. The gums lifted like curtains, displaying rows of glistening, jagged teeth.

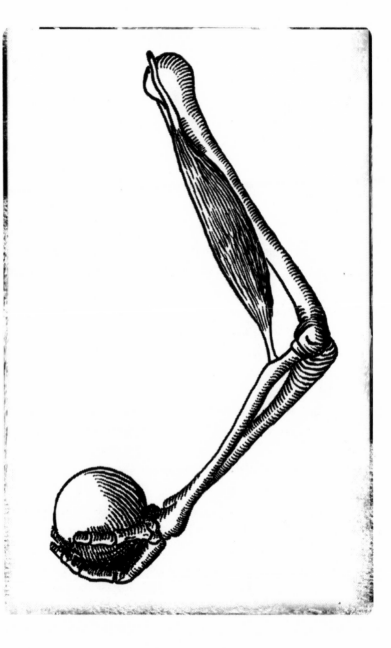

Mr. Universe

IF IT WEREN'T FOR THE HUMONGOUS JUICE DOSAGES I woulda
been Mr. Universe. I mean, if not Mr. U then something pretty close,
like maybe Mr. A. I had it all, the genetics, the proportion—and I
could pose like a professional dancer. Not like some fairy but I mean
I could flow through the moves like honey in slow motion pouring
from a bottle. I was on my way.

Then friggin' 'roid rage.

Just because I killed my best friend with my bare hands don't
make me all that bad a guy either. It was the shit. Christ, I loved the
guy like a brother.

We're in the locker room at Iron Plate Gym, me and my best
friend Stevie, all revved up cause we just got our first juice delivery
from Big Bobby. Crazy Bobby and his white '79 Corvette. Never knew
how that guy with twenty-two inch guns fit in that thing.

Big Bob handed me a crumpled paper bag with a few boxes of
Deca and a bottle of D-bol tabs and said, "You're on your own," and
went to workout. He threw in a few darts so we'd be ready to start
right away. What a guy.

We're staring at all this gear in the bag and I'm thinking that this
was it—I'm gonna be in the big time now. That's right. I was primed
to get huge like the other freaky gym monsters. Only bigger.

Stevie fishes out a syringe and I pull out a box of Deca. I howl and
say, "Look," as I chomp off the top of the cardboard box and dump the

vial into my hand, spitting the wet flap onto the floor. We're carrying on like two goofy kids.

I pinch the glass up to the light and say, "Breakfast of champions," and we both bust out and do a high five. Joey Napoli walks in and looks at us so we cool out. We go into the small bathroom, barely big enough for two guys on their way to the kingdom of huge.

I grab the dart from Stevie, peel open the wrapper and pop off the needle cap. I snatch a bottle of rubbing alcohol from my gym bag and splash some on toilet paper and wipe the rubber top of the vial. I stick the needle in, turn it upside down and suck out the full 2 cc's of oily stuff.

I say, "Me first."

Stevie says, "Fine," and then says, "Dude, I ain't shootin your ass."

I call him a pussy and say, "I'll do it myself." I face the sink and undo my sweat pants. I let them drop to expose my glutes.

I wipe my skin with alcohol, lean on the porcelain with one hand and say, "Bombs away," then plunge the spike, push down hard, forcing the Deca into my ass muscle. It stings a little and I could swear the juice started to work right then and there—but I know it ain't so.

My life changed somehow at that moment, like I was in some new exclusive club now. I guess I was. At the time I thought the change was for the better, but little did I know.

One time me and Stevie meet this older guy at the gym, his name is Richard and he tells us if we want to really be cool we should get into Manhattan and forget about all this Long Island suburban crap. They're all losers out there, he says.

I think, *whatever*, but I have a feeling this guy is weird but may be right. So one night we go into the city, a place downtown in the West Village. I forget the name. It don't matter and all I remember is people screwing around all over in these dark concrete chambers.

It was some club and you had to be a member and this guy Rich just showed a card at the door and the bouncer said, "Go 'head boys." Guess Rich had been there before.

When I figured out it was a sex club I was like, *hell, yeah.* There was this Amazon chick in shiny leather pulling a guy around on a leash and he's licking her black spiked boots and she's kicking him and he just keeps apologizing. Man, what a pussy the guy was.

Me and Stevie look at each other and almost at the same time we say, "What the fuck," and then we just start cracking up. Richard glares at us like we should chill out or something. Like we're breakin' the rules or some shit.

Another naked lady has her hands tied to a wood beam above her head and this guy in a mask is whipping her. He's got the littlest pecker around, like a turtle head poking out from his fat sack. Not that I was lookin' or anything. This lady moans in the dark and then he rams her with the handle of the whip. She lifts her legs off the ground like she's riding a jet ski and screams so loud it hurts my ears.

After a couple beers I gotta go to the can so I weave my way through the stone chambers and smoky haze, like I'm exploring some ancient tomb or something. In slashes of light, I see this skinny guy wearing only cowboy boots lounging inside one of those long urinals like he's at the beach, one leg draped over the side. And he's loving it.

I stood in the shadows, eyes burning with the smell of urine and smoke, thinking, *What the...?* I watched two guys finish spraying the cowboy with piss like they're putting out a fire. He rubbed it in like lotion and groaned and said, "Next."

He's lookin' at me and smiling—and I really had to go, so I ended up taking a whiz on his boots.

After a few months of juicing like an animal, I'm getting huge and Stevie slows down on his shit and tells me, "Maybe you should cool it for a while."

I tell him, "No way," cause I'm getting jacked and I want to enter a show. Probably the Mr. Long Island to start things off.

Stevie says, "What about college?"

I say, "Screw that." I keep training and training and getting bigger and bigger.

Stevie is getting ready to go to college, Mr. Frat boy. I got my eye on the Mr. Teenage USA contest the August after graduation in Venice Beach, California.

Somebody tells me that Venice is the Mecca of all bodybuilding and that fires me up even more.

California here I come.

Another time a group of us cut school on a freaky warm April day. We hop in Stevie's Chevelle and cruise over to Jones Beach.

We packed a cooler full of Bud quickies we picked up at Seven-Eleven. Sherrie and Michele were in the car with us, Michele with her blonde hair falling over her shoulders, smelling like goddamn spring flowers or something. I knew that Stevie liked Michele cause she was much hotter, but Michele liked me and it was obvious. She kept saying things to me like, "Wow you're getting so big," and, "I love your muscles," as she scraped her spike-like fingernails across my forearm hair.

I could see Stevie out the corner of my eye with that stupid look on his face.

I don't like to say it, but Stevie just didn't have what I had, you know, even though he was my best friend and all, he just didn't have good genetics I guess. You need the genetics to win shows. That's what I read in *Iron Man*.

And even though he juiced for a while it didn't seem to do anything. Me, I just got bigger and people told me I could probably win a big show some day. I already knew that.

When we get to the beach we spread out a towel and blast some Van Halen and kick back. That was when I told Stevie I was gonna go to California after graduation.

He says, "That's stupid, dude."

I say, "Really?" Right then I wanted to punch him, hard. He was leaning back on the towel, hands behind his head, like he had everything under control, like some wise old man.

He started telling me about all the college crap and says, "What're you gonna do? Be a muscle man?" And how was I gonna make money and all that.

Like all of a sudden he's got some attitude like he's better or something, like he's gonna be some doctor or lawyer. Guy's clueless.

So it was great cause right then Michele comes jogging up to the towel with her tits bouncing in her tube-top, nipples hard, and says to me, all flirty like, she says, "Come down to the water, hot stuff." In my head I was laughing like crazy.

She has her hand out, so I take it and she pulls me up.

As we saunter away hand in hand, I turn back to Stevie and he's got that stupid smirk on his face again.

I'm smiling, feeling like a pig in shit.

Things were going pretty much as planned with the California trip and all except me and Michele were getting kinda tight and she was getting a bit latchy. I could never understand these chicks.

The whole thing was starting to get on my nerves 'cause I had big plans, you know? To be Mr. Universe. I didn't need some whiny chick getting in my face.

She says things like, "You know you're taking this muscle stuff a little too serious," and, "You still taking that shit 'cause your balls are shrinking like little grapes."

When she said that last thing I let the back of my hand sort of slide across her face, not really like a hard slap, but she took it that way, her face getting all red and splotchy. And all the crying. Man, it was crazy. I'm lookin' around rolling my eyes.

I said I didn't mean it. It just happened, like a little switch in my skull clicked or something. I knew the juice was fucking with my head.

She just cried.

And then she really pissed me off 'cause she said, "Why can't you be more like Stevie."

I lost it.

Lucky I didn't hit her because my fist smashed right through the basement wall.

The next time I go to the city with Richard it's just me and him cause Stevie says he has to study and we end up back in Greenwich Village. I was like, whatever.

We're in this smoky bar and two guys are making out and I say to Richard, "The heck is that?" These guys were like hairy and shit and had some muscle and it just didn't look right.

He says, "The city, just the way it is."

We leave that place 'cause he says I got all quiet, and I was. I was trying to make sense of the shit I was seeing.

So he takes me to another place that's more of a disco club and there are some chicks, but they're making out too. Hot chicks no less.

Rich just smiles, shrugs.

I say, "I'm outta here."

After a while Stevie stops training all together 'cause he says he's got some other stuff to focus on and why don't I chill too. Take a break. Like I'm thinking, yeah right.

I'm bigger than ever and my neck feels like it's gonna explode out of every shirt I wear. My thighs rub together on the inside 'cause they're like two tree trunks, and I got cuts and veins running all over my body like lightening bolts.

I up the juice dosages cause I figure it's three months to the show in California and I wanna peak out right on time.

I start cutting some classes at school but it doesn't matter 'cause it's the end of the year and I got better things planned anyway. Like I'm ever gonna need the crap I'm learning.

I'm gonna be Mr. Universe someday.

I'm right on target for huge success, but nobody sees it like I do. I feel like I'm living in my own little world. Everyone else is just putzing along.

It's going great until Michele calls me and she tells me she's pregnant.

One time near the end of all this I'm at Richard's house and we smoke a joint and suck down some beers and we're cranking some Zep.

He takes out a sandwich baggie and it's got a lot of different colored pills in it. He pulls out a red one and says, "Take this, it'll really relax you."

I ask what it is and he says, "A downer."

I shrug and take it and not long after I'm feeling really groggy and weird but it's kinda cool.

Richard falls back on his bed, looking at the ceiling and says, "Man, I know a way a stud like you can make a lot of money."

I say, "Really."

He starts telling me about how muscle dudes can go into the city and pose for guys and get paid tons of cash.

I say that sounds kinda fucked and he says, "No, it's cool."

I'm really starting to feel funny and he says, "Try it, take off your clothes. I'll show you."

I stand up, thinking I gotta get out of there and he says, "Where you going?"

I step back. He hops up and walks toward me, smiling. I see this big happy mug headed my way, a weird look on his face, just like I thought all along.

The last thing I remember is his hand cupping my nuts before the switch clicked.

When I can see straight again, he's crumpled on the floor with a bloody face staring up at me and he's breathing funny and trying to talk.

I just say, "What the fuck."

I don't remember driving home.

Michelle actually says, "What if we had it."

I say, "You gotta be kidding."

She says, "We'd be a family."

I start telling her about how there's no way a guy like me can have a baby now, at this age, especially with all the plans I had. I'm thinking to myself, *Can she really be serious?*

I ask her what is she gonna do when I go to California in a couple months and she says, "Yeah, right."

I tell her we gotta get this situation taken care of pronto and she cries and says, "No way," and jumps right out of my car at a stoplight.

I have to roll alongside her in the car for about a mile before she gets back in. With a face like a rock-hard boulder, staring straight ahead, she says, "Fine."

Not long after that, Mrs. Cartwright from the main office pokes her stupid head into my English class and says there's a phone call for me. I figure it must be serious cause no one ever gets a phone call like that at school.

When I pick it up it's my mom. She says, "Come right home after school."

I ask her why and she says to just do it and her voice sounds funny. I'm thinking, *okay, this is weird.*

When I get home she leads me to her bedroom where she's got all my roids scattered out on her bed. She's got the pills and the vials and all the syringes spread out. She's got tears in her eyes and she says, "What's this stuff?"

I smile cause I know what she's thinking. She found my stash. Before I can answer she says, "Well what is it, uppers or downers or what?"

I chime right in, grinning, "Yeah and sidewaysers too."

She doesn't like that and bursts out crying. I tell her to calm down and then I tell her about the juice and how it's really a good thing. That she should be lucky that I'm not doing hardcore shit. And how come she's going through my stuff anyway.

She tells me to just wait until my father gets home.

When he walks through the door my mom tells him the story. He comes to me and as he throws his hard hat onto the chair, says, "Wipe the grin off your mug."

I say, "What grin," and I can see he's had a crappy day.

He says, "You're a fuckup." He starts to swing at me and I duck. The switch clicks.

My head spins and things just happen. I clock him on the side of the head and he falls back into my mom and they both crash onto a desk and end up on the floor.

Shit.

I scoop up the roids and bolt.

I jump into my '76 Monte Carlo and tear down the street, tires screeching.

I don't even know where I'm going.

I slide a Black Sabbath cassette into the player and Ozzy is yelling and I crank up the volume and the speakers are thumping and I can't believe I just smacked my old man.

I swerve onto the main strip near my house and some guy cuts me off. In a fuckin' Pacer no less. He doesn't even wave or anything and this pisses me off. I speed up, getting alongside this guy and he knows I'm right there and he doesn't look at me, just stares straight ahead and we're going faster and faster.

I lean over and crank down the window, almost losing control and the wind is blowing in my face. I yell, "Hey douche bag," and he just ignores me.

I pull closer to him and start running him to the curb and now he starts honking and he slows down cause he has no choice. Then I see him take a sideways glance at me. He's starting to shit in his pants.

We finally come to a halt and I jump out of the car, running around the front toward him. Now he looks like a chicken-shit. He's got a pencil neck. He throws it in reverse and slams a parked car before he speeds away, smashing a couple of garbage cans in the process.

I do a loud, "*Yee haw,*" and yell full-out, "*That's right a-wipe.*"

I slide back in my car, pumped, and decide to go over Stevie's.

When I get to Stevie's I see that Michele's car is parked out front and I wonder what the fuck is going on.

I make my way around to the side door that leads to the basement where Stevie's room is and I let myself in. My head is really hot now and I feel like I got a wicked headache. My heart is racing like never before and my body feels like it's tingling.

When I get to the bottom of the stairs I see the two of them sitting on the bed and Stevie's hugging Michele. What are they, like long-time lovers?

They both see me and turn and jump and Michele starts right in saying, really fast, "We were just talking," and, "I needed somebody to talk to."

Stevie saying, "Hey man, what's up?" And, "It's not how it looks." And he's got that stupid smirk on his face.

It was the smirk that really did it for me.

And the switch goes off.

The switch has a loud bang and I swear, this time, I can actually hear the sound like a sonic boom.

The rest is a blur.

Later, Michele tells people how she never saw a person pick someone up by the neck with one hand, only in cartoons. And she never, ever, saw a look like the one I had in my eyes.

She flew out of the room screaming and got help and nobody saw what happened next, not even me, 'cause I don't remember anything, just the click and then the white flash.

All they know is that when the police came in I was sobbing and had Stevie's dead body draped across my lap.

They say I was mumbling something and rocking him like a baby.

Headless in New York

FRED THOUGHT IT WAS FUNNY the first time his head fell off. He carried it around under his arm for a while like a basketball and giggled and all he could think of was the guy from that movie, *The Re-animator*.

He didn't think that could happen in real life but here he was in his living room, holding his head in his hands overhead, arms out-stretched, looking in the complete opposite direction his body faced. He could see his back and ass in the mirror.

He still couldn't figure out how he was able to breathe but the opening to his trachea was intact at the top of his neck and by the swishy sounds he knew air was getting sucked into his lungs somehow. And he guessed his brain was getting oxygen by osmosis or diffusion or something.

The fact that he could see didn't surprise him since the eyeballs connected directly to the brain via the optic nerves and chiasm. Thank God for his anatomy and physiology classes.

The arteries and veins seemed to just clamp up too, like a zip-loc bag.

Weird.

He could get things back to normal if he pushed his head hard on the top of his neck and gave it a back and forth motion. It seemed to stay in place but he didn't want to take any chances by doing anything that involved any jerky motions. He found he could pop it back off too with the same kind of motion, but with a little more force.

He remembered that first night a few weeks ago. He had gotten home from work and had his usual snack of crackers and cheese and then he went down for a nap. He fell asleep thinking about Esther.

When he woke, there was his head—down by his feet looking up between his legs. What a sight. At first he thought someone else was in the bed with him and that really freaked him out but when he tried to move, the body above him obeyed. He thought about something and it just happened.

And that part he just couldn't figure out, even still. There was no neural connection between his brain and his body, yet his brain, from a distance, could control the body like a remote-control car.

He had watched his body lose its cool as he freaked out. He watched his frantic hands rub their way around his body, grasp at the empty space above his neck, run around in circles a bit and then cautiously step over to the head, cup it in the palms of its hands as if holding a sacred gauntlet, slowly lift it and clumsily put it back on his neck.

Then he laughed.

The next day Fred got up for work and his head was right where it was supposed to be.

He thought maybe he had been dreaming but when he stood in front of the bathroom mirror with his palms against the sides of his head and gave a combination twist and push it happened again—his head popped right off.

He brushed his teeth by suspending his head by a clenched fist of hair in his right hand, right in front of the mirror, and jabbed the toothbrush with the left. He dangled his head real close to the mirror to get a good look and was able to angle just right to get the shadows away, something he couldn't ever do before. So there were some advantages.

He wondered what other advantages there might be to this situation.

Normally, he might discuss something like this with Esther.

Just for kicks he swung his head around by the hair and was able to get a unique view of his ass—a perspective he had never seen before. He didn't realize there was so much hair back there. This new view was definitely *not* an advantage.

He laughed again.

His early morning walk to the subway station on 86th and Lex was uneventful. His head was stuck back in place and he looked like everyone else.

He wore a baby-blue collared shirt with a red spotted tie, snug around his neck.

He was in the first car so that he could see the tracks barreling toward the train in the front window. Since it was Saturday, there was only one other person in the car, mid-way through, face buried in the New York Post.

At 77th Street a homeless man stumbled on. Tattered clothes and double-fisting a load of dirty, ripped shopping bags full of useless debris. He sat down and started mumbling.

Fred decided to sit too, though a good distance away from the smelly guy. He massaged his neck and could see his own reflection in the window across the car. He smiled.

He looked normal.

The train rocked and stuttered around a curve. There was loud screeching of metal wheels on metal track. The lights flickered.

There was an abrupt halt and start and the motion was something like whiplash and before he knew it his head was rolling down the center aisle.

Fred could see the posters and advertisements along the wall spiraling around, alternating with a shoe-level view of the cans and bottles and crumpled newspapers under the seats.

His head thudded against the front door and then started back down the aisle toward his body and he could intermittently see his headless form sitting there and he told it to lean down and reach and it did, scooping up his head like a shortstop in the infield.

He quickly popped it back on—having to loosen the tie quickly with one hand first but there it was, back in place. He pushed down hard on the top of his head and then shot a look over at the homeless guy, who had a weird grin on his face.

Fred said, "Morning."

The guy cackled and smacked his lips. "Lookin' sharp, fella. Yup."

The other guy reading the paper hadn't moved.

Fred laughed.

Fred couldn't concentrate at work. He hated working Saturdays. He sat in his cubicle, pretending to be on the phone, pretending to write on a blank pad. He wished he could call Esther.

He decided to do an internet search to see if there were any other cases like his. He searched things like, "Head falling off," and all he got were a bunch of jokes and songs and some prank videos. Nothing helpful.

He then stumbled onto one of those medical sites with its own search. He tried more medical type terms like "cranial detachment" and "headless" but found nothing at all similar to his situation. Seemed there were no other cases of someone's head falling off at the shoulders and living to tell about it.

He figured it was time to see a doctor.

"So, Fred," the doctor said, "tell me exactly what you're feeling one more time."

Fred sat on an exam table, wearing a gown. The doctor sat on a stool in front of him.

"Well," Fred said. "The other morning I woke up and my head was off. You know, detached from my body."

"You mean it *felt* like it was detached, no?"

"No. I mean it was really off. I picked it up and carried it around."

"Well, didn't it hurt?"

"Not at all."

"And you found you could still breathe? And think and see?"

"That's the crazy thing. I just can't figure that out. I mean, I even move my body from across the room. I was quite frightened at first, but now I think it's kind of cool. Even funny."

"No bleeding?"

"Not a drop."

"Well, Fred. I don't know what to say. I must admit, I've never come across this. You would certainly be worthy of writing up. A definite medical case report."

"I did a web search myself. Found nothing like my case."

"Well, I suppose I should have a look, no?"

"Should I pull it off now?"

The Doctor stood. "*No no no.* Not yet." The doctor pulled a stethoscope from the pocket of his white coat. "Let me examine you first."

Fred sauntered down Third Avenue near 34th Street looking down at the prescription in his hand. The doctor had ordered an MRI of his brain and cervical spine. *Just to check.*

So Fred called the Radiology Center the doctor recommended near NYU and the receptionist had told Fred, sure, come on over now. We're not that busy today and we just had a cancellation.

So off he went.

Fred couldn't believe that the doctor didn't want him to pull off his head right then and there. The doctor told him that he didn't want something to go wrong. He had no experience with that sort of thing and wouldn't want to be caught unprepared.

His caution kind of made sense, Fred thought after a while.

"Fred Tibbles?"

"That's me."

"I'm Steve, the MR tech. I'll be doing your scan. I just need to take some history."

"Okay."

"Do you have any metallic devices in your body? Valves, clips, pacemakers, wires, anything of that sort?"

"Nope."

"Any past surgeries?"

"Nope."

"Wallet, keys, credit cards. All metallic objects in the locker?"

"Yup."

"Why did your doctor send you? What's the reason for the scan?"

Fred cleared his throat. "Well, my head comes off my body and I can reattach it."

Steve the tech stared.

Fred couldn't read his face. There was a smirk blurred together with the slightest hint of anger.

Steve didn't say anything.

Fred finally said, "I'm serious."

Steve said, "Just hop up on the table here."

On Monday Fred got a call from the doctor's office. The message was to call right away and please come over to the office. The doctor wanted to see him.

Fred called and said he'd come by at lunch, around 12:30.

The receptionist said okay.

"Well, Fred," the doctor said. "The radiologist faxed over the report from your MR today and then he followed up with a phone call."

"Yeah?"

"They don't always do that. I mean, he thought the findings warranted a special call."

"That's interesting."

"Yes, that's what the radiologist said."

"So?"

"I looked at the study too. Just because I had to see for myself. Well, there's a band of abnormal signal across your cervical spinal cord. At about the C4 to C5 level."

"Okay. English, Doc."

"Well the radiologist felt that this was related to some kind of trauma. Almost as if the cord had been severed. Said he'd never seen it before."

"I see the case report coming for sure now, Doc." Fred smiled.

"And there was air in the disc space at that level. Really strange. And then he told me that there was this abnormal appearance to the soft tissues in a ring-like configuration at that level. All around the neck."

"Kind of makes sense, no Doc? I mean with what I been telling you and all?"

"Well it just can't be. I mean you must have had some kind of trauma. You must have a concussion too. Have you been in a car accident or hit your head recently?"

"Not at all. Like I told you. Just woke up the other morning and there was my head. At the foot of the bed."

The doctor took a deep breath. "Very well," he said. His voice was crackly and he had a very stern, serious expression. His hairy eyebrows scrunched low over his eyes.

He stared at Fred.

"I can't believe I'm saying this. But, here it goes. Fred, please take off your head."

Fred grinned, satisfied. He sat up straight, inhaled deeply, let it out. He methodically placed his hands on the sides of his head, exaggerating his motions slightly like a magician on stage ready to end the show with a special trick. His fingers fanned so that the thumbs were behind the ears and his pinky fingers crossed his eyebrows.

Fred winked at the doctor. "Ready, Doc?"

The doctor nodded slowly.

Fred gave the old push and twist motion and there was a shucking sound.

The doctor stared, mouth open, slack.

Fred's head came off, and he stood pole-straight, holding it high in the air with both hands, tooth-filled grin still on his face.

The doctor laughed.

After leaving the doctor's office, Fred decided to go see Esther. He got on the subway to Queens.

He couldn't figure out why the doctor thought the whole thing was so funny. He figured that was better anyway. The doctor said he'd probably be a great candidate for a case report, given he was such a unique patient. He needed to be written up so the rest of the medical community could learn from his situation.

The doctor also told him about a procedure, a cervical spinal fusion, he called it. It involved putting screws and rods in the bones of his neck, overlapping the area where his head came off, so that it wouldn't come off anymore. Would just keep it locked in place. The doctor thought it might be best, to prevent any future problems. What if his head came off and ended up too far from his body?

The doctor said he'd discuss it with his colleagues at something called a case conference, then let him know.

Fred got off the subway at 148th Street and he was pleased to find the sun still shining brightly when he emerged from the underground station. He hummed as he walked the four blocks to the cemetery.

He zigzagged along the beautifully manicured paths until he found his beloved Esther.

Excitement bubbled over as he thought about all he had to tell her. He hadn't been there in a whole month. He found it too unbearable. But he felt different now.

He found the new stone. He wiped it with a bare hand. Cleaning off a light layer of dust and pollen. He sat cross-legged on the slightly elevated mound.

He stared at the engraved lettering: Esther Tibbles 1969–2012.

So young, he thought. It was so wrong. So unfair.

"Hi, honey." He mustered up a smile. "Watch this."

He positioned his hands and popped off his head.

His headless shoulders shrugged. "Crazy, huh?"

He placed his head on the ground in front of his legs, to be as close as possible to Esther. He could smell the rich green grass, feel the warmth on his face. He told her all about what had been happening. His head falling off, the MRI, the doctor. All of it.

He waited a bit. Enjoyed the sun, the feel of the damp grass blades on his cheek.

"Oh, honey," Fred's head finally said. "Strange, isn't it?"

A sharp twinge of anger surprised him. "You get a brain tumor and die. Me? I can pop my head off any time." He inhaled and furrowed his brow. He willed his hands to turn his head so the other cheek was on the ground—a whole new view.

"Could you imagine?" Fred's head said. "I mean, if you could've done that? Just pop your head off any old time? Huh? Maybe we could have put a new head on. You never know. Could have been cured!"

He told his hands to lift his head, hold it in front of the stone. He stared at her name. The dates.

Fred tried to laugh at the whole thing. He almost did.

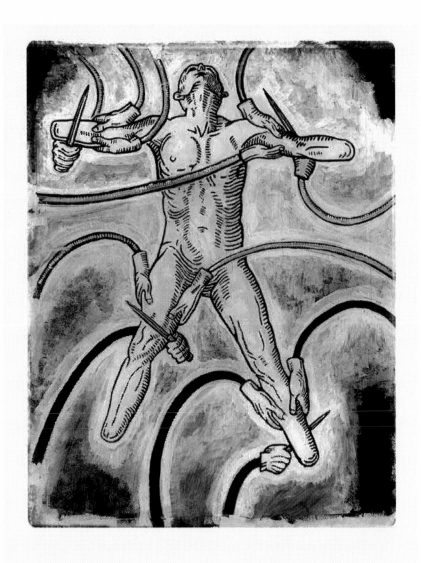

Stuck

Dr. Jed Thompson tried to twist his way out of bed like he did every morning but he couldn't. His right leg was stuck. He managed to twist enough to reach the alarm clock and switch it off before Wendy started yelling. She slept in the guest room down the hall but still, if he disturbed her *beauty sleep,* she turned into a raging bitch. Didn't matter that much anyway given the way things were going, but he still had to play nice until he could figure out how to exit his marriage gracefully. Or any way possible.

All he could think about was Angie. Beautiful, loving Angie.

Jed was just able to reach the lamp, flick it on and it took a few moments for his eyes to adjust. He tried to swing his right leg upward but again, it wouldn't budge. It felt as if a hundred-pound weight was tied to his ankle. Was it asleep? Numb?

He started to undo the tangled sheet and comforter, which were wound around his legs and stomach. He was finally able to expose his legs and he had to squint to see his foot. He thrust his elbows into the mattress, lifted his upper body, then did a full crunch to bring himself into a sitting position.

It looked like something was twisted around his toes. Threads? Jed bent forward and was barely able to reach his ankle. He clutched his leg with both fists, just above the ankle, lifted. The foot rose slightly off the bed, stretching the sheet and tenting the mattress.

Jed let go. He rattled his head and laughed. He scooted forward along the sheets on his butt, bent his knees. He was now able to run his hands over his feet. He felt string-like structures extending off the tip of each toe, infiltrating the material of the mattress.

He leaned and slid the lamp closer across the nightstand for more light. Soft structures the texture of licorice sprouted from each of his toes into the bed. Toenails?

He shuddered and began tugging and jerking at the things. He tried to free them from the mattress. Jed pulled and heaved, giving it his all, straining back, putting some weight into it, and the pressure started to hurt his toes.

He tried a slow, deliberate forceful pull instead of a quick one and they started to give. A little more and then *Pop*. One of the rope things came free. He had momentum and he felt stronger now, beating it, breaking loose. *Pop. Pop. Pop* and then *pop*. He was released and he flopped backward into the pillows.

Jed shot up and hopped off the bed, dragging the five loose structures, each about a foot long.

He hobbled into the bathroom, disgusted, slammed the door to hear Wendy's hoarse voice from down the hall, "Hey! Quiet!"

Jed had his foot up on the counter in front of the sink, staring down at the five odd appendages. At first he was hesitant to touch them but then figured, whatever, they were already touching him.

They looked like thick cords of twine, grayish-brown. The tips were frayed. They definitely were part of the nails. It was as if his nails had grown furiously overnight, achieving a look he had only seen in record books or in the circus—odd people with freakishly long, curly nails.

Only these weren't curly like those nails. And they weren't hard either. These were soft and pliable, like strands of saltwater taffy. They extended to the nail bed and blended with his nails, disappearing beneath skin.

Jed eyed the cup holder next to the sink handle. He lifted the scissors, poked his fingers through the loops. He tried cutting but the blades were dull, resulting in a shallow linear divot across the nail. He needed the heavy artillery—one of those new knives in the kitchen.

He creaked open the bathroom door, looked around, not sure what he expected to see, but making sure Wendy was still in her room. He shuffled across the bedroom rug, awkward due to the ropes hanging from his foot.

He opened the bedroom door, taking extra caution not to make any noise and disturb the beauty queen. He listened for a moment then started on his way across the light-brown hardwood of the hallway.

He half-hopped toward the kitchen, glad he lived in a ranch style home, without stairs to contend with. He made it to the terracotta tile of the kitchen and thumped along to the knife block, swiped one of the smaller steak knives, spun and started back.

The nails scraped along the hardwood and his leg ached from the weird walking motion. He swung his leg out to the side to clear the rope-nails. As he approached the bedroom door his leg swung out a little too much and knocked the wall with a *thonk*.

His bedroom door had swung closed so he grabbed the handle and pushed it open with a creak and Wendy blurted from down the hall, "What're you doing out there, huh?"

"Nothing," Jed said. "Just getting some water. Go to sleep."

He made it to the bathroom, shut the door, locked it, and sat on the toilet, breathing heavily. Then he went to work.

He lifted his leg so he could rest his foot on the counter. He held up the rope-nail of his great toe, pulled it straight, creating tension so it would be easier to sever. He had to slice a few times, hack once or twice and the thing came off. He cut it as close to the toe without slicing his own flesh. He kept hold of the detached nail and went right to the second in line and kept doing that all the way across, his pace picking up a bit, almost working into a frenzy, until he was free of all five rope-taffy-twine nails.

The work sent sweat streaming down his brow. He swiped his face with his free hand and lowered his foot. Leaned back, a bit more relaxed, having rid himself of the freaky growths.

After a moment, Jed stood and looked in the mirror. He pretty much looked the same. No other lesions seen. He lifted the fistful of nails and studied them closely. Brought them to his face to see if they had an odor. Nothing.

What next? He had to get these things examined. Get them to a lab or something. He figured he'd run the story by Lance, and see what his colleague thought. He opened the bottom drawer below the sink, found his travel shaving kit, unzipped it and dropped the five nails inside and zipped it up, put it back in the drawer under an old hairdryer and nose hair clipper.

He felt normal again. He realized he was late for the hospital and patients would be waiting.

After rounds with the residents and then a short time at the Neurology Clinic, Jed was able to find a moment to page his friend and colleague, Lance, in Dermatology. He realized he had actually forgotten about the morning's events for several hours, as if the whole foot toenail fiasco was some kind of bad dream.

He rubbed his toes together in his shoe, feeling the thick cut-off nail stumps, and knew it was definitely not a dream.

Lance agreed to meet him at the Dermatology Clinic, in the minor procedure room. They knew the clinic would be empty for a while, until noon, when the patients for the afternoon session started to file in.

On his way to the clinic, Jed's cell phone vibrated in the pocket of his white coat.

"Angie?"

"Hi, Jed. I think we need to talk. I really need to see you and talk."

"Hey hey. Slow down. How are you?"

"Fine, Jed. I'm just sick of the whole thing. I mean, how much longer can we do this? Huh? You're married, Jed. This little relationship or whatever you want to call it goes against everything that I am."

"Angie, baby. Calm down, sweetie. We'll make this work. Just a little more time."

"I think you're living in a fantasy world, Jed. You have me tucked into some box, a nice separate little compartment. You're good at that."

"No. No, you're right here. Real as can be. In my heart. No boxes. I just have to work things out with Wendy. She's sick with her Lyme disease. It looks like she might have Crohn's disease now on top of all that. And now her mother has breast cancer too. I can't just leave now. Wendy and I got married for all the wrong reasons. I know it. She does too."

"See? What about me? I'm not married, Jed. I never wanted to start this. I knew it wasn't a good idea. I told you that didn't I? And then I fell in love."

"Please, just hang in there a little longer. Until I know Wendy is okay. Then I can tell her. Get this done."

"I don't know, Jed. It hurts so much now. The hurt outweighs the joy. Something needs to happen, Jed. I can't wait much longer. It's not fair."

"Okay, okay. Listen. We need to see each other. I need to see you. I'll call you later."

"I have to go. Bye, Jed."

Jed slipped the phone back in his pocket, realized he had walked into a patient's room. He glanced at the man in the bed, gaunt with the sheet tucked at his neck, IV hanging. The man stared back vacantly and for a moment Jed thought the guy might be dead until he blinked and said, "Who the hell're you?"

"That's looking a little funky there, Jed."

"*Funky?*" Jed sat on the crunchy-papered edge of one of the examination tables in the Dermatology Clinic. Lance sat at Jed's knees, on a low-rolling stool, the heel of Jed's left foot in his gloved hand. "Come on Lance, I need something a tad more medical, buddy."

"Yeah. Hmm. You said you cut these nails this morning?"

"They were a foot long. They weren't like that the night before. I have the nails at home to prove it. Under the sink in my bathroom."

"Looks like some kind of weird fungus. Seems they're already growing back."

It was true. Jed had cut them down to the skin. Now they were about an inch long.

"You gotta do something." Jed said. "They *grew into the bed*, Lance. I couldn't move. I had to rip them away."

"Wow. Really?" Lance had a scalpel now, cutting away a chunk of nail. "I just need a small piece. I'll get it right to the lab, STAT."

"Tell them to hurry. This is a real, bona fide emergency, not like all that other crap sent to that lab as so-called STAT. And it's nasty. You gonna give me something?"

"I have lots of antifungal cream around. Samples. I'll give you a script for some oral meds, hardcore antifungals. Stuff I used to give to AIDS patients. Just in case this fungus decides to go all systemic on you."

"Great. All I need." Jed smirked, tried his hand at some levity. "Hey, there's a fungus among us."

"Funny one, dude." Lance rolled his eyes. "Never heard that before."

When Jed got home, Wendy sat in her usual spot, in bed, pillows propped behind her back, covers up to her waist, TV on.

Jed stopped in the doorway, studying her for a moment. The door opened to the side of the room so he could stand there and watch without being noticed, at least for a while.

Wendy was stunningly beautiful—no question about it. Slender and muscular from dance and yoga, jet-black hair cascading to sexy shoulders, shiny and wavy. The biggest brown eyes, perfect cheekbones. Fake tan. It didn't seem to matter though—he felt nothing.

Wendy's big brown eyes found him in her peripheral vision.

"Hey," Wendy said. "What the hell are you doing? Staring at me like a damn perv? Creepy, Jed. Just a little creepy."

"Just looking."

"Looking at what?" Wendy adjusted her covers. "Get me my wine, will you? You know where."

"Okay." Jed leaned against the doorframe. "So how was your day?"

"Fine, fine. Get the wine and I'll tell you all about it."

Jed shrugged, turned and made his way down the hall. Angie would never talk to him like that. He opened the fridge and found the bottle of Chardonnay. Went back to the room of doom.

"Thank you." Wendy unscrewed the top, poured the wine into a long stemmed glass on the nightstand, placed the bottle next to an empty one with a clank. "So how was work?"

"Okay. Had to see Lance about a toe problem."

"Toe? *Ew.*" Wendy sipped. "What kind of problem?"

"Seems I have a little fungus on my toenails. Made the nails grow a bit."

"Gross. Jed, that's so gross. Toes? Not just one? *Ew.*" Wendy gestured towards his room with the wine glass. "I'm glad you sleep in there."

"Well, he prescribed some medication." Jed sat on the far end of the bed.

"Good. Listen. I've been thinking. You know. I spoke with my mom today. Can you move a little? Can't see my show. So, I spoke to my mom, and like, even though I'm forty-four, we decided it's not too late to have a baby. You know? My parents really want a grandbaby."

"Really? You and your mom decided?"

"Yes. These days. The technology. You know, well, you're a doctor." Wendy pulled a long sip then rested her glass on the nightstand. "You know what can be done if we need to. It would be fun, huh?"

"Fun?"

"Come on, Jed. You used to say how much you wanted kids. *Little stinkers*, you said."

"That was years ago. I'm not so sure now."

"Well. I want one. Come back later and, you know, we'll start the process if you know what I mean. After my show. If I'm not asleep."

"I'm gonna shower."

"Make sure you clean your feet."

Jed showered, ate a ham and swiss sandwich with milk and went back to Wendy's bedroom with ample time to ensure that she was asleep. Sure enough, he peeked in and her head was flopped back, still sitting, snoring. The TV on, spewing forth about some celebrity breakup.

Jed went outside and called Angie on his cell.

She didn't answer.

Jed slept fitfully. He couldn't be sure exactly when he fell asleep but he knew it was some ungodly hour after the birds started chirping.

He was on his back when the alarm went off. His eyes flipped open, fixed on the ceiling.

He couldn't move—like the morning before, but this time both feet were anchored to the bed. And his hands. He couldn't lift his hands.

He pulled and pulled. Tried to bend his elbows, knees. Nothing.

Panic set in. He was pinned to the bed. He had an itch. Great.

He decided to do one full-on pull. Whole body contraction, give it his all. Something had to give.

He braced himself. Took a deep breath. Counted off, then, *uuuuuuugh*. He held it as long as he could, muscles screaming. Then he just gave in, relaxed. His heart pounded and he was winded.

The alarm got louder each passing minute, a built-in mechanism that was supposed to scream, "Hey, get up already!"

He knew what he needed—Wendy. Before he could call out he heard her voice, "Turn that damn thing off already!"

"Help!" Jed said reluctantly, wishing he could handle this himself. "Heeeelllp! Wendy!"

"What?!"

"Come here! Help me!"

Jed heard a loud sigh, some feet hitting hardwood and then the stomping toward the room.

Wendy appeared in the doorway, arms folded across her chest. Hair atypically mussed. "What."

"I'm stuck."

"Stuck? Huh?"

"I think it's the fungus. This happened yesterday but it was only my foot. I was able to pull it out."

"What? The fungus? No way! I'm not touching that stuff. Just get up, Jed."

"I can't, I'm telling you. It's grown into the bed."

"Those sheets are expensive, Jed! They better not be ruined."

"Screw the sheets! I'm sewn into the goddamn bed!"

"Don't you curse at me, Mister or I'll just go right back to bed."

"Please! Can you pleeease help me?"

Wendy stepped closer, cautiously, as if crossing a minefield.

"Pull the covers off," Jed said. "Let's have a look."

Wendy stopped at arm's length, leaned over and gripped a handful of covers and in one quick motion swiped them off the bed, exposing Jed.

Wendy screamed and ran from the room.

Jed took a moment. Didn't bother to yell or make a fuss. He had to regroup and get this situation under control. He could hear Wendy down the hall whimpering.

He lifted his head from the pillow, stretched his neck to get a look. All of his fingernails had those things on them, spiraling into the bed sheets, disappearing into the material. He couldn't see his feet but he knew it was the same. He could feel it.

Deep breath. A plan. "Wendy?"

It took a moment. She was in the hallway. "What are those things, Jed?"

"The fungus I was telling you about. That's all."

"Gross!"

"Listen, I need you to get one of the kitchen knives. A sharp one. Bring it in here. I need some help, Wendy, honey."

"A brand new kitchen knife? Then we have to throw it away. I'll never use it again. And those sheets, Jed. The whole bed. It's gotta be trashed."

"Fine. Fine, Wendy. I'm getting really uncomfortable. I need you to get a knife so I can get out of here. I'll go see Lance and get the medication. I have some cream already."

Jed could hear Wendy pad down the hall toward the kitchen. He heard some drawers open and slam, some metal clanking. Then her footsteps coming back. She peeked into the room.

"Wendy, listen you just need to hack one of my hands free. Then I can do the rest. Can you do that, huh?"

"Do I have a choice?"

As Wendy approached, Jed could see that she was wearing the yellow rubber gloves from under the sink. She held out a long steak knife.

"Here." Jed twisted his head to his left. "Start there on my left hand. Pinky. Just cut through those...cords. Right on through. Ready?"

Wendy came closer with the knife, tentatively. "I can't believe I'm doing this. *Ew ew ew.*"

She got the blade under the pinky nail and pulled upward, both hands on the handle. She groaned until it went *pop* and she squealed.

"Good. Good, Wendy. Next one. Four more times. Perfect."

She went to the next finger. Same thing, got underneath, pulled up and pop. Next. *Pop. Pop. Pop.* Jed's hand was free and Wendy threw the knife on the bed and ran from the room, saying, "I'm gonna be sick, Jed. I'm gonna be sick."

Jed hacked through the cords on his right hand and was working on his feet. Feeling euphoric, as if he was escaping from prison. Freedom was in sight. He hopped from the bed, jagged cords dangling from hands and feet, and shuffled to the bathroom into the bright light. Had to have a look. He pulled his shirt over his head, feeling claustrophobic, his body slick with a film of sweat.

He glanced at his face in the mirror and shook his head. He didn't even look like himself. It seemed as if he had aged twenty years since yesterday.

He opened the drawer beneath the sink and retrieved the shaving kit. He unzipped it, set it on the counter.

He sat on the toilet and began the tedious task of cutting the fingernails and toenails so they would at least look presentable.

All he could think about was looking good for Angie.

Jed showered and got ready for work. He kept all the nail clippings, put them in the shaving kit along with the clippings from the day before. Only this time he stuffed the shaving kit in his briefcase.

He found Wendy in the kitchen in her robe, sitting at the breakfast table with a Bloody Mary.

"I'm surprised you're still up." Jed said.

"Up? You think I could sleep after that nightmare of a morning? I still feel sick."

"How do you think I feel? I'm the one with the fungus. It'd be nice to have a little support."

"Support? Like you support me? I want to have a baby and you act like you don't know what I'm talking about."

"Well. I don't. You wanted to wait and wait. Now you want it just to make your mom happy."

Wendy's face tightened. She took a long sip from her drink. "Fine. Now I'm glad because you have that gross fungus disease."

"Anyone can get a fungus." Jed searched the counter for something to eat and grabbed a banana. "It just happened."

"It never happened to me."

"Well aren't you just the wonderful fungusless princess." Jed headed back to the bedroom to gather his things.

Wendy's voice echoed down the hallway. "Don't start with that princess crap."

There was heavy traffic on the way to the hospital. Jed sat in his car, phone in hand. He punched in Angie's number. Straight to voicemail. He left a message, about how he really wanted to see her, he needed to talk. That he loved her.

His gym bag was on the front seat next to him. Briefcase on the floor. He had his shaving kit. A change of clothes, sleepwear, gym stuff. Wendy said it might be better if he maybe stayed at a hotel tonight. With all the fighting—and especially the fungus—she thought it would be best. He didn't disagree.

Someone honked and he realized traffic had moved and he was a few car lengths behind the next car. Big deal. Everyone was so impatient. Really? What? So I can catch right up to the next car and sit there again for a few minutes? Okay, that good?

Jed punched in Lance's number and he picked up immediately.

"It happened again," Jed said. "Worse this time. Any results yet?"

"I brought it to the lab, told them to please get right on it. They said they would but it's early. I suspect they'll have some results by mid-afternoon. What happened?"

"Hands and feet this time. It was horrible. Woven to the bed like some Boy Scout patch. Had to get Wendy to cut me out."

"Whoa. Sorry Jed. That's sounds awful. We're dealing with a really aggressive fungus."

"We? Sorry, Lance. Sounds like you got up from bed just fine."

"Yeah yeah. Okay, Jed. Got me, buddy. Come to my office at lunch. Let's see if we can make some headway. You use the cream yet?"

"Nah. Forgot. Didn't fill the script either. I'm stressed to the hilt."

"Well get on it, man."

"See you later."

Jed tossed the phone onto his gym bag. Another horn blast and he crawled forward a few feet.

At lunch, Jed went over to Lance's office in the hospital. Lance sat at his desk in front of stacks of papers, flipping through patient files. The desk was a cheap hospital-issue model, pseudo-wood and metal legs. In the corner of the desk, there was an oversized model demonstrating the layers of human skin in graphic plastic detail.

"Sit down, Jed. Got some news."

Jed sat in the metal chair. "Good?"

"Let's say, interesting." Lance studied Jed's face, as if searching for some anomaly. "You look like hell."

"Haven't slept in a couple days. Stress. Hyperaggressive fungus. You know, usual stuff."

"Well. Ted over in pathology called me. You know Ted? Great guy. He tells me his tech came to him asked if he would look at the fungus sample. So he does and he says he's never seen anything like it in all his years. It's like some alien fungus, replicating like crazy with bigger and thicker cells and hyped up organelles. He's gonna send it to the Mayo Clinic to get another opinion."

"I have another full bag of it more in the car if you want. This morning's harvest."

"Definitely bring it in. So, I'm not certain what to do yet. I wrote you a new script for some additional meds. I want you to take all three. And the cream."

"Can't wait."

"You have any other symptoms? You feeling okay?"

"Just stressed. I need some sleep. Wendy kicked me out. We've been fighting. Again. She's freaked out by the fungus."

"Too bad. If there's anything I can do, give me a shout. You need a place to stay? Marcy and I have a nice guest room."

"Thanks, but, no. I need to be alone. Think things over."

"Okay. Here's the script." Lance pushed the paper across the desk. Jed picked it up, folded it and put it in his shirt pocket without looking. "And bring me those other nails okay?"

"No problem." Jed pushed himself up. Straightened his slacks. "Thanks, buddy."

Jed walked into the hall and called Angie. Right to voicemail. He didn't say anything this time.

Jed finished his day at at about five. Dictated some reports. Finished some paperwork. He thought about going to the gym but decided he was too tired. He knew that was when he really should go but he was beyond tired.

He was walking across the hospital parking lot toward his car when his phone vibrated. It was Angie.

"I thought you were never gonna call," Jed said, a little too eager.

"I wasn't, Jed. But that last voicemail sounded so pathetic. I just got a tad worried."

"So what? We're broken up now?"

"Well, like I said. I never liked this and I like it even less now. You're a mess. You need to figure things out. But this situation is complicated, and I don't like the way I've behaved. You know I won't sleep with you until we're married right? I don't care how old I am."

"I know, I know. That doesn't matter, Angie. I'll wait. It's not about that. I want to marry you. You're the person I'm supposed to be with. You know that?"

"Well, you're with someone else. That's all I know."

"Will you see me? Please? Let's have a coffee. You eat yet?"

"I'm not hungry." Angie waited a beat and Jed knew this was her way—not to say yes too quickly. He loved it. He felt like a puppy. He hung on as long as he could. Didn't want to be the first to speak. Finally, Angie said, "Maybe I'll have a coffee."

"Great." Jed blurted. "Usual place. I'm about ten minutes away. I'll get a table for us."

Jed couldn't believe it. The coffee date went wonderfully. Talking a mile a minute, feeling euphoric. Laughing like a child. The physical exhaustion seemed to just disappear. Angie was chatty too. Telling him about her day. Then heavy duty life philosophy. All the things she wanted to do.

Jed told her the whole story about the fungus and she listened, never making a face, just listened. At the end she looked up at him with the most beautiful blue eyes. Her eyes seemed watery, sad, as if she were holding back tears. Angie said, "Oh my God, Jed. That's horrible for you. I wish I was there to help."

When she said that last line Jed thought he would burst out crying right then and there in the coffee shop. He just stared at her in amazement, said, "Thank you, Angie. Thank you."

Then he told her about Wendy and the argument and how tonight he was on his own. She didn't say it at first but toward the end of their little date she said, "So what are you gonna do about tonight?"

They were in the parking lot of the coffee shop, Angie leaning against her car, Jed leaning on Angie. He came close to her and said, "I don't know."

Angie studied him for a long moment. Figuring the whole thing out in her head. Weighing options. "Well. I guess you can stay at my place. Of course you know I won't sleep with you. Right? Maybe we can cuddle. We've never actually had an overnight thing together."

Jed brushed her blonde bangs off her forehead, put his arms around her and held her tight.They didn't need to say anything. It was understood. They went back to her place. They got into their pajamas and Angie made a pot of tea. They sat in the den and talked for hours. No TV.

They finally ended up in bed, pajamas on, Jed holding her close. Angie edged closer then said, "Come here," patting her chest, the place between her breasts. Jed rested his head there.

He listened to her heartbeat, felt the soft thud. He embraced the warmth, the softness of her breasts. Angie ran her fingers through his hair and he began to drift off almost immediately, as if he were floating on some magical green ocean.

He rubbed his toes together, scraped his fingers along his palms. It all felt smooth and good. Normal.

Before he went to bed though, he made sure there was a knife on the nightstand, just in case he needed it.

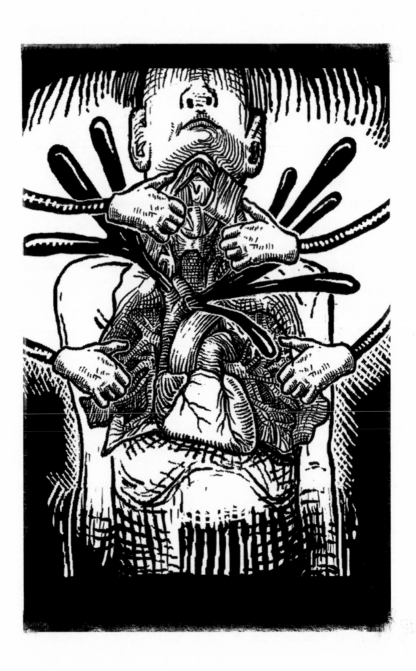

Diary of a Scutmonkey

JULY 8TH: BEGINNING

Wow. First week of internship and I'm wiped already. Exhilarated, really. In a good way. It's been wild. I just got home and it's 10 p.m. Gotta get up about 4:30 a.m., to get to the hospital for pre-rounds at 5 a.m. And I'm on call every third, meaning I'll be sleeping in the hospital every third night. Can't believe it was just a week ago I was a fourth year medical student. I had some easy electives, some time off. I was able to cool down after a busy third year. But internship is a whole different animal. As a student, I wasn't really responsible, just kind of tagged along, observing, learning. Now I'm an official member of the medical team. I'm actually getting paid. Very little but it's something and, hey, it feels good to be a salaried employee! This is the real deal now. I mean, I still have to report to the senior residents but much more is expected of me.

But man, I don't know how I'm gonna keep this journal. Told myself I would. *I should.* Gotta find the time. I think I'll just jot down interesting events, procedures. Maybe some standout patients and unique things they might say. Interesting cases in general. Maybe write them as mini-stories. The pearls of wisdom I learn etc. I'll try to elaborate when I can. I'm starting a vascular surgery rotation next week which is notoriously brutal. Maybe some of the other rotations will allow a little more time to write.

Onward!

JULY 15TH: APOCALYPSE NOW

First day of vascular surgery. The first two weeks were crazy. Just general surgery stuff. Trying to get acclimated. Conferences, some meetings and protocol stuff.

Now I'm in this dinky call room with John, the Vascular Chief Resident and two other guys. There's Rich, a third year and Jaime, a second year transfer from Puerto Rico. It's 6:30 a.m. Just back from rounds.

The Chief Resident, John, speaks in a monotone voice as if he's stoned, in some kind of surgical yogi zone. And he's smoking! He's taking long drawn-out inhales from his cigarette, smoke bending and twisting upward in elongated curling shapes, talking in his deep gravelly voice.

The dim smoky room has two cot-like beds along the wall. It's so small we're practically sitting on top of each other and the lights are off except for a small lamp (John's request). Rich is wired, as if he's on speed, but spaced at the same time. He's looking around like he's got somewhere else more important to be. I think he's slept 4 hours in the past week. Jaime is ready to crack. He's rocking back and forth looking as if he'll bust out crying at any moment. In the dark, with the smoke, John's weird voice and spaced out looks, I feel as if I'm deep in a mysterious humid jungle alongside Marlon Brando in some scene from *Apocalypse Now.*

Like we're all there on some strange medical mission. Ignore pain, block out the outside world. Look to our leaders for guidance. It feels like there's a chance we may not make it. Jaime certainly looks like he'll be the first to fall. I feel like some kind of warrior, organizing an attack on our common enemy—death and disease.

John goes over the list of patient's. Strange thing is, he makes up these weird names for everybody. Usually something that relates to their current medical situation. Like a rhyme or word play that he thinks sounds funny. Like, Prosthesis Prostakoff, Crispy Toe Crispin, Silly Putty Gilberty, Bucky Tridente.

Finally, John tells me to report to OR 7 and scrub in on a fem-pop bypass. Go introduce myself to Dr. Helmet Lugnut, the operating surgeon, who I've heard is the toughest vascular surgeon in the hospital.

AUGUST 5TH: DISIMPACTION

"Hey scutmonkey," the Chief Resident says. "Know what this is?" He's staring at me. There are seven of us standing in a semi circle in front of a view box in Radiology; two interns, two third year students and two residents.

And the Colorectal Surgical Chief Resident.

Mrs. Jacobowitz's abdominal x-ray hangs backlit on the box, illuminated like a work of art.

"The abdomen?"

"Nice shot, smartass...NO." He points at something. "THIS."

It's the first week of colorectal surgery rotation and I haven't seen a heck of a lot of abdominal x-rays. I spent the past couple of weeks looking at arterial angiograms during the vascular surgery rotation.

I stare, eyes squinting, evaluating.

He stabs his finger. "This area of mottled heterogeneous increased density in the midline pelvis."

I rub my chin. The two students and intern study the tile floor.

"Hint," he says, resigned. "Soft tissue density mixed with air. Distending this lumen. Stretching it. Causing poor Mrs. Jacobowitz's problems."

He shakes his head. Finally, "...It's SHIT. Okay, everyone? S..H..I..T. Our lovely patient here is FOS—FULL OF SHIT. She's impacted, loaded to the hilt. Ready to explode. Hasn't moved her bowels in two weeks. Does anyone know what needs to be done here?"

One of the residents straightens up, obediently chirps, like an Army private minus the salute. "Disimpaction."

"BINGO. Manual Disimpaction. Guess what, Altman. You're up. Ever disimpact someone?"

"No. But I watched Dr. Jenkins do it the other day."

"Stellar work," he says, only half serious, whipping the x-ray from the box. "See one, do one, teach one. Go save a life."

I review the chart at the nurse's station: Ida Jacobowitz: 91 year-old female with history of dementia, breast cancer, hypertension, stroke, status-post hysterectomy, cholecystectomy, appendectomy, right mastectomy and removal of benign bladder polyp. A laundry-list of medications. Now presenting with constipation.

Okay.

"Go away!"

"I want to help, Mrs. Jacobowitz," I say. "I'll remove some stool. You'll feel better."

"I don't need any cookies! Go on. Get back to your mother!"

I realize negotiation is out. Move on. I see restraints on her wrists, tied to the guard rails. At least she can't punch me.

"Move your legs apart ma'am." I place a chuck sheet under her legs, help spread her knees, to access her anus. I crunch the sleeves of my short white coat, mid forearm, and double glove.

I gaze down and gasp.

It looks like she's crowning a baby, the fecal head bulging out, pushing, splaying the anal ridges, forcing the mouth agape, like a gasp itself, like Munch's *The Scream*.

I poke and pick at the protruding alien fetus head and nothing happens. It's like soft rock and I suddenly think of a yellow mining helmet, chisel and hammer. I pluck at the rock, flick it, and try to get something off, anything, maybe a crumb.

My finger maneuvers its way around the mound, getting beyond the rim of her anus and then it starts. A small chunk pops off and I'm convinced this project will be a success.

Another chunk. Then another. *Plick plop poop flink.*

I'm making headway, now with two gloved fingers gliding ever so slightly into the rectum, a slight groan from above, and then a solid meaty chunk falls to the sheet. My fingers are bent, forming something of a spoon and now the stool goes from hard to medium soft, the texture of warm clay, like after you've rolled it around in your fist a while.

Now a third finger and a bigger spoon, a ladle maybe, curving, swiping and forcing out chunks and then damn boulders of feces. There's a substantial moist pile on the sheet and I think about getting rid of it, throwing a clean sheet down, but the three fingers turn to four and the hand is sinking deeper and deeper, now up to my knuckles.

I take an arcing swipe and I release something that's the size of a small fetus.

The pile is more like a mountain. The stench is powerful, the simmering smoking Everest of waste having fermented for two weeks, aging, maturing into something hideous.

I enter again, my thumb slides in and I'm almost to my wrist and I wave out a chunk and I'm right back in for another. I'm impressed with myself, like I've mastered this whole process and I smile. A wide satisfied grin.

The stool is getting softer and now it's like tofu and the chunks break off in more of a linear fashion, organized, and I can feel the stool getting warmer, some life coming back, getting deeper, past the rectal vault, into the sigmoid colon.

And that's when I freak out because in my shit-scooping frenzy I realize I can't see my wrist and my forearm is starting to slide in and I think, then cringe, holy hell, I'm almost to my elbow!

I can't get my hand out! I pull, the sphincter choking my wrist and I ease back a little.

The stool has gotten very soft and I wiggle my fingers, push a bit, and I feel as if I've made a chink in the dam wall because I feel trickles of hot fluid running over the back of my forearm and I think I've gotten to the critical level.

I realize I have to remove my hand, reassess the situation, see if maybe she can expel the rest on her own, now with the brick wall violated, and I hear her saying something and her legs start to flail.

I feel a foot hook around the back of my neck and just as I pop my hand out with a *SCHLOP* she's saying, "Get out of there you crazy person! Get! Get!" and I say, "Hold on a minute, Mrs. Jacobowitz."

I hear some gurgling and her other foot wraps around the other side of my neck and I attempt to stand upright and she slams me, forces me, face-first into the mountain of glistening stool, gushy clay smearing and squishing across my cheeks and I lose balance and I yelp a muffled dead sound, tilting to the side and twisting my face toward the gaping, mocking anus as it screams and howls and then there is a massive explosion.

The heavens open up and an angry storm of shit and fluid rains down and gushes onto and into my mouth face eyes nose hair shirt coat bed wall floor TV chair tray railing window...

AUGUST 10TH: AMF YOYO

I spent the day in the ER with this attending I hadn't met before. A real character. Nice guy though. Dr. Alfonso Stockinghaus, or Dr. Al. He's tall, trim and muscular, with slicked-back dark hair and a bushy moustache. Looks like he should be starring in an old-style soap opera.

I'm following him around like a little puppy, getting charts, helping him admit patients. Drawing blood, doing some physicals. Listening to his smooth rap with patients.

We have this one patient, young guy. He's cantankerous and looks sleazy, too smooth for his own good. Dr. Al gets right to the core of this guy's long-winded rambling and confusing story. He's been here before, with a toothache. Today he seems to be feigning back pain. He's a drug seeker hoping to score some pain meds. Dr. Al discharges him, gives him nothing but a script for physical therapy.

Dr. Al scribbles his signature in the chart. He jabs the pen tip into the paper for emphasis as he finishes, says, "Discharged AMF YOYO."

"What?" A new code word I haven't heard.

"Discharged. Gone. AMF YOYO." Dr. Al grins and winks, leans in, says in a low voice, *"Adios motherfucker, you're on your own,"* and saunters off.

August 12th: High Five

"Hey Altman," the chief resident says.

We're in a small group outside a patient's room. I look up.

"One of the high-fivers needs a central line over on Two North."

High-fiver. Another code word from the secret language of medicine. High-five means HIV, postive or full-blown AIDS. Probably half the patients on Two North are dying of AIDS. "Got it," I say.

He smiles. "Make sure you double glove."

Tom is forty-one, has AIDS, history of PCP, and Kaposi's Sarcoma. The chart indicates he has newly diagnosed cryptococcal fungus in his cerebral spinal fluid. I stop in the doorway, a baby blue gown over my scrubs, wearing a flimsy mask with a built-in plastic face-shield. I'm double-gloved and holding a central line kit.

Tom stares into space, a cloudy film yellowing the whites of his eyes. He's sedated, an oxygen mask over his nose and mouth, and incredibly cachectic—hollowed out cheeks with taut skin over bone. He's restrained with straps around his wrists and ankles, tied to the side rails.

His shallow breath sounds sharp and junky. The room smells stale with a faint hint of urine.

I say *hello* but he probably can't hear me, although you never really know. I roll the tray table close and adjust its height, then open the kit, creating a sterile field. I open the packet of betadine and pour the mud-colored liquid into the tray reservoir. I slide the sheet down, move the gown aside at the groin.

His legs are as thin as my forearm, the contour of the femur obvious, condyles at the knee splaying widely. His sunken abdomen is retracted, really, creating a sharp drop-off from his rib cage—muscle attachments and insertions painfully visible.

I push two fingers into the groin, where thigh meets abdomen, to feel for the femoral arterial pulsation. The anatomy plays back in my head, the order of structures inside to out, medial to lateral—vein, artery, nerve. I remember this by *VAN*. I picture it in the groin, front end smashed up against the vein.

I find his thready pulse and ink a line right over it with pen. With the small sponge from the kit, I paint the area with betadine to sterilize it, then unfold a sterile drape sheet, a small hole in its center, and rest it over the area.

The needle is a sizeable gauge with a sort of platform around its upper end. I wrap two fingers under the plastic platform, my thumb on the top of the needle. Ready to jab. Deep breath. Once I hit vein, I'll have to move quickly, thread a thin guide wire through the needle center, into the vein. Then the needle comes out, I dilate the hole, then bury the catheter.

At least that's the plan. I've only done this once before.

Blood will ooze, no doubt. Infected blood, a death sentence if it mixes with my blood. Even a drop.

I touch the needle tip to the skin surface, over the ink line, angle best I can away from the artery. I steel myself, push. The needle pierces skin. Tom bucks slightly. I wait. Push again. I angle this way and that—a little medial, a little lateral, push deeper, and pull back.

Bingo. Dark blood bubbles out of the needle tip onto my fingers. Warm blood. Infected blood. I grab the wire while holding the needle steady with the other hand, feed the wire tip into the bloody needle. The wire staunches the oozing.

When the wire is far enough in, I apply pressure below the needle then start to retract it over the wire, being careful not to let the wire slip out.

The needle comes out and I plop it in the tray as if it's burning hot (well, it is in a way). I thread the plastic dilator over the wire to make the hole just a tad bigger, *in out, in out.*

I drop the dilator back in the tray and grasp the catheter tip in my fingertips. It's like threading a needle and it takes a few awkward tries before the catheter is over the wire. I snake it down the wire and the tip disappears under skin, into the femoral vein. I keep sliding until the catheter is all the way in, *hubbed,* as they say.

Just need to get the wire out, cap the catheter and I'm home free. I pinch the catheter and start slipping the wire out. I put subtle pressure at the needle hole, over the catheter. *Breathe.*

I can't tell where the wire ends and it pops out, wanting to coil back up. The tip flicks, taking a few drops of blood with it and sends them sailing up to splash across my mask and eye shield. I freeze. Don't feel anything on skin. No wetness, no warmth. I turn my lips in under the mask. I want to run but I can't.

I click into automatic. I screw the cap onto the catheter, grab the hemostat and thread with a curved needle. I throw one stitch into skin next to the catheter, faster than I've ever done before, then wrap the thread around the catheter and tie, securing it in place.

I drop the tools in the tray and peel off the bloodied outside gloves. Holding them out front, I drop them in the tray and rush to the mirror above the sink. I stare at my face. Blood droplets form a bloody smile across the mask, beginning by my chin, arcing upward toward my left eye. Nothing in my hair. Nothing on any exposed skin as far as I can tell.

I release the mask straps from behind my ears, slowly and carefully, as if I'm handling a bomb. I hold the mask between thumb and forefinger, take a last look at it then drop it in the biohazard container.

I walk closer to the mirror, face right at the glass. I look at my face, hands. Then again. I check the inside gloves. They're clean.

I'm still standing, searching for blood in the mirror, while Tom stares at the ceiling.

AUGUST 23RD: SIGNS

I learned a new sign today in Radiology. The Throckmorton Sign. A small group of us were looking at an x-ray—75-year-old male with hip pain. It was a frontal pelvic x-ray showing the pelvic bones, hip joints and surrounding structures. The radiology resident says, "Anyone know the side of pain?"

A senior surgical resident blurts out, "Left."

"Excellent," the radiology resident says. "And can you tell the group how you knew that?"

"Sure," he says. A little smile. "The Throckmorton Sign."

"Can you explain for the benefit of those uninformed junior residents?"

"Sure." He strolls up to the x-ray hanging on the view box. His face is deathly serious as he uses his finger to outline the contour of the penis, which is clearly evident on the film, and angled toward the left. "The Throckmorton Sign," he says, "always points to the side of pathology." He and the radiology resident exchange a smile and nod as he steps away.

Of course this is total bullshit.

SEPTEMBER 6TH: AOB

I was in the ER again tonight with Dr. Al. When I arrive he's standing next to a stretcher talking to an elderly patient. He turns as I walk up. "Good, Altman, you're here. You can admit this nice young lady."

"Okay," I say. "What's going on?"

"She's AOB. Been vomiting." Dr. Al says and points to a grungy middle-aged man and woman hovering nearby. "That's her son and daughter if you need any more info."

"Dr. Al?" I say as he starts to turn. "What's AOB?"

That grin again. He leans in. "Alcohol on breath." He walks away.

The son is behind me now, tugs at my white coat. "She gonna be admitted, doc?"

"Yes."

"Good." The son turns, lowers his head to talk into his mother's ear. "Hey, Ma. We gotta go. Can we have car fare?"

SEPTEMBER 18TH: INSERTION

"Well, Doc," Wilma says. "I'm smelling something funky-like. In my virginny."

Wilma's thighs ooze over the edge of the examining table. I'm on a low stool, clipboard in hand, scanning her lab work.

"In your what?"

"My virginny. You knows, my lady-friend there downstairs."

I nod. Rub my chin for effect. "Vagina?"

"Yessiree, Doc."

Another beat. "Something...uh...funky?"

"Yup. Funky-like is what I says."

I'm nearing the end of a short Ob/Gyn rotation. Supposed to get some gynecology OR time. The OR opportunities are pretty limited so I'm on the wards most of the time. It's been an interesting rotation though, exhilarating actually—delivering babies, nothing like it. Little head crowning, grab, rotate, shoulder, shoulder, *boom.* Clamp cord, cut. Baby.

But the call is brutal, every other night, beeped at all hours, screaming babies popping out all day and night. Emergency C-sections, episiotomies, heart monitors, labor, labor and more labor. The OB part I can deal with.

It's the other stuff. Gyn clinic. Yeast infections, PID, chlamydia, syphyllis, vaginitis, warts, herpes, you name it. I guess it has to be a calling.

"How long have you had the...uh, funky smell in your virginny?"

"Coupla weeks."

"Any discharge?"

"Any whosawhat?"

"Discharge. See any fluid or strange material coming out of the vagina?"

"Nope. Not really. Just the usual stuff. But there's this nasty nose-burnin smell-like. Just sayin."

Not a good sign.

"And it's starting to hurt a bit. All crampin' like."

Hmm.

"I'll have to take a look."

"In there?" Wilma's waving a hand now, like a conductor. Leonard Bernstein. Beethoven's Fifth.

"Yes ma'am. Have you had a pelvic exam before?"

"A who?"

"PAP smear? Anything like that?"

"Nope."

Nope? "Well. I'll insert a speculum." I gesture towards the tray table. "One of these. Evaluate the vaginal canal, cervix, that kind of thing."

"Alrighty."

"Here." I nod at the nurse who is wide-eyed, displaying a folded baby blue gown in outstretched hands. I take it from her. "Put this on and we'll get started."

A short time later Wilma lumbers into the room. Blue gown taut. She climbs onto the table.

"Here," I say, "slide your feet in these things."

The nurse helps her get into lithotomy position. She pushes her feet in the metal footrests. The nurse is at my side. I coat the plastic disposable speculum with gel. Angle forward, take a deep breath. I stop short, stunted for a moment. *Is that real?* Wilma's perineum resembles the droopy face of a washed-up old clown. *Really?*

She's right about the odor too, something rancid and bitter. I swear smoke-like fumes are wafting from between her thighs. I lean back, squint. Try to spare the nostrils, looking for a safe zone.

With outstretched arms, stretching to the max, I slide the speculum into the vaginal vault. I look away, twist and lock. Click. I maneuver the light to shine straight in. Twist the lamp a little more. Get the shadows just right. Straight down. Perfect. *Hmmm.*

I make out something that doesn't belong. Hiding in the shadows. It has a lobulated appearance. Weird. I bend the snake-like neck of the floor lamp, try to get a better look, angle the beam of light. Blink a few times. The heck is that? Okay. There it is. Something. Definitely doesn't belong.

Still staring, I ask, "You have any other medical problems?"

"Huh?"

"Any other health issues?"

"Nope. Just got the sugar."

"Diabetes?"

"All my life."

From the tray, I grab the tenaculum, which resembles an elongated ice tong, and insert the metallic claw, figure I'll grab the thing. Bull by the horns. Ease it out. It looks like it has wings. Leaves? Christ. At least it isn't moving. I think. A dead animal? The acrid scent burns. A tear squeezes from the corner of my right eye.

Got it. Slow. Pull back. Easy. The hell is this thing? Jesus Christ. Should I call the CDC? Maybe it's just an old tampon. Yeah, that's it. Is it? Keep pulling. Slowly. Don't lose it. Getting closer. Into the light now.

I wiggle the thing from her vagina, finally free. I hold it at arm's length and stare. The nurse looks confused. Her hand swings to her mouth. It looks like a plant. Pale white roots. Brown stem with crumpled, folded brownish-green leaves. Dripping some whitish material.

I swing round on the swivel chair. Release it from the clamp. Plop it on the table. Push it with the metal tongs, spread it out. See if it's alive. Poke. Prod. Definitely leaves and roots. Tubers?

"So, Doc. You got somethin'?"

I stare at the table. "Ah...yeah."

The nurse glares at me. Questioning—no, *begging*—eyes. She looks pale. I shrug.

I think I see movement. I lean closer. There's a whitish worm on one of the leaves swaying back and forth. As if waving hello. Reflexively I lean back and grimace.

"Doc?"

"Well," I say, startled. The nurse rushes from the room. Both hands over her mouth. "It looks like a plant."

I see another worm, waving. "You ever put a plant in there?"

A long pause. "Plant? Ain't that kinky, Doc."

"Any seeds or anything. I don't think it just *grew* there."

"Hum."

Do I really send this thing to the lab?

She says, "Hold up a minute."

"Yeah?"

Well, Doc," she says, a deep belly laugh. Pleased with herself, a bit proud. "Well, Doc. I just 'membered something."

"Go on."

"Well. Don't know if it means something or nothing."

"Tell me."

"Well, 'bout a few weeks ago. Me and my man. Big ole Clyde. Lordy Lord gotta love the man. We ain't got no birth control, ya know?"

"Yeah?"

"Well I gets this thought about like an idea. Like a diaphragm."

"And?"

"Well Clyde. He can't wait. Crazy man. Won't go to the store or bother to get the prophylactics. When he wants it, boy he wants it. Ain't no stopping 'em."

"Good old Clyde."

"Well. I look in the kitchen cabinet. And then I see it. I gets this idea. A per-tater. I cut it up. Puts a slice in there. A nice thin sliver."

"Potato?"

"Yeah. Cut it nice."

"A real potato?"

"'Bout the same size as a diaphragm."

"A potato slice in...the virginny?"

"An I forget to get it out after."

"A potato plant. Guess that's what we have here then."

"That what the smell is, Doc?"

I nod my head slowly, thinking about the Ear Nose and Throat rotation that starts in a week.

"Yes. Seems to be...ahh...rotting a bit. I'll send it to Pathology."

Another worm. I turn to look at Wilma, stand up, force a pleasant grin. "A potato plant. I'll send it to the lab so they can check it out. Confirm it. That's right."

She laughs.

"Wait'll I tell ole Clyde." She claps her hands. "And he does like them French fries anyway, oh boy. Wait'll I tell him. He'll get a laugh. Lordy Lord."

A beat.

"Hey Doc?"

"Yeah?"

"Can I take that plant with me?"

"Take it home?"

"Yeah." She shifts onto an elbow, wide grin. "Wanna grow Clyde some a them, ya know? He'd jump for joy over some fresh home-grown per-taters."

OCTOBER 4TH: TWO NORTH

I was back on Two North this afternoon. Had to check on Tom's central line. I'm walking along in the hallway when a patient rushes from inside his room to the doorway.

"Doc!" He's a gaunt figure, bones in a gown, dark skin lesions splotching his face and forearms. He's awkwardly dragging a squeaky IV pole at his side. "Get me the hell out of this room!"

I stop, puzzled. He's a few feet away, glaring at me. He looks like a cast member from *Night of the Living Dead.*

Before I can speak, he continues, craning his neck, turning his head back into his room. "You can't get AIDS from being in a room with someone!" He's talking much more loudly than he needs to, clearly for the benefit of his roommate, who I assume is not HIV positive. "I ain't messin' with no one in here and I ain't sharin' no needles! So relax!"

He turns so he faces directly into the room. "I should be worried about *you!*" He pauses. "Who knows what diseases you got!"

He waits for a reaction. Nothing.

"So, fuck off then!" He turns back to me. Then more quietly. "See Doc? See what I gotta deal with?" You gotta get me outta here. I don't think I can take it anymore. The guy hung a plastic tarp clear across the room. He wears a mask and gloves at all times and leaves the window open. It's freezing."

"I'll talk to the Chief Resident?" I shrug.

"Hurry, okay?" he says. "I ain't got much time."

November 24th: Pearls

Today I picked up three pearls of surgical wisdom. This morning I scrubbed on a messy Billroth II resection (Gastrojejunostomy) for bad gastric ulcer disease. Chief was having a tough time achieving hemostasis, the bovie cauterizing away, zapping the bleeders, filling the OR with the smell of burning flesh. Seemed it would never end but Chief took his time, zapping and zapping, vessels oozing, getting one and another popping. Chief sees the look in my eyes, my strength waning. "Surgical adage," he says, winks. "*All bleeding stops eventually.*"

I scrubbed on two more cases and did afternoon post-op checks at about 8 o'clock then found the third year resident, Sammy (aka Scammy!). I was post call and wanted to sleep. We saw a couple of patients. I say, "I think I might go and change." He stops and glares at me, dark circles under his eyes. "Dude, you know the rule. *NEVER change out of scrubs. It's futile.*" I smile. He doesn't. We walk over to the nurse's station. The chief resident, Dale, is there looking at charts. Sammy nods and says he has to go remove a drain.

"What about you, Altman?" I tell him I'm going to hang around, see what's happening, thinking I'll look like a dedicated intern. Dale shakes his head, "You know the old saying, man. *The longer you stay, the longer you stay.* You should always get the hell out when you can." As if on cue, my beeper buzzes. I'm told the attending is looking for an intern to scrub on an acute appendix. They're wheeling the patient into the OR right this minute and get the hell upstairs. I look over at Dale and he's shaking his head again.

This time he's smiling.

JANUARY 1ST: CRAPPY NEW YEAR

Yeah. Happy New Year. More like crappy new year. I spent all of last night in the OR. At midnight Chief and I were tending to a ruptured appy. When the clock hit twelve the scrub nurse said flatly, "Happy New Year, folks."

Chief's eyes darted toward mine above his mask, squinting because of his smile. "Get used to it, champ."

After that it was a small bowel obstruction due to an inguinal hernia. I managed to sleep one hour and then it was down to the ER. I've been thinking. I'm at the six month mark now, halfway. Felt more like six years. Haven't exercised and I eat like crap. So far, I've done general surgery, vascular, colorectal, Ob/Gyn, ENT and ahead there'll be cardiothoracic, ortho, urology, neuro, more ER and more general surgery.

I hardly ever see the light of day, except for a couple of moments when I step out of the lobby to the sidewalk between cases. Many nights I stare out the huge windows of the fifteenth floor recovery room after a surgery, gazing down on the city, watching people carry on with their lives. I feel like a spectator in the sky, my life on pause. Onward.

JANUARY 14TH: PENETRATION

"I got some pain down there, Doc." A patient named Clayton pats his lower abdomen. He's lying on a stretcher, a wrinkled blue hospital gown stretched over his paunch. A thick handlebar moustache hangs from his nose.

"Down there?" I'm standing along his right side in the cramped emergency room cubicle. I'm covering the ER this whole month.

"You know?" Clayton waves the air above his pelvic region. "Down low. Like in the privates."

"I see." I nod my head. "How long have you had it?"

He smoothes his face, twists the curly portion of his moustache with thumb and index finger. "Think since about last night."

"Okay then, sir," I tell him. "We're going to have to do some tests. Blood, x-ray, that kind of thing."

Clayton stares toward his feet. He's wearing thin navy blue dress socks, scrunched down around his ankles. His calves are voluminous and hairy. He takes a deep breath and exhales through tight lips. "Maybe I should tell you."

"Tell me?" I wait. My eyes are heavy. A siren wails outside the hospital's walls. Another delivery. I wonder where we could even fit another patient. Every bed is occupied. The hallway narrowed to single file by stretchers lining the walls. "You'd like to tell me something?"

"No, Doc." He swivels his head, eyes bearing down on me. "Nah. Nothing"

"Okay, then," I say, tugging a stethoscope from the pocket of my white coat. "Let's have a look, eh?"

"Okey-dokey."

I listen to his heart, lungs. Check reflexes. Palpate abdomen. Listen to bowel sounds.

Nothing abnormal.

"Yeah," Clayton says, kneading his gut with both hands like a giant mound of dough. "It's not right. Down below there."

"I'll need to examine that area."

"Well," he says, tilts his head, smiles. He hesitates then turns his palms up. "Okay, then."

I snap on latex gloves. Draw the curtain with a *whiish*, retract the gown to his umbilicus. Genitals, normal. Turn to the side. Gel. Rectal exam. Slightly lax sphincter tone but otherwise normal. Guaiac negative. Nothing significant visually or manually.

"Everything seems pretty good," I tell him, peeling off the gloves, dropping them into the trash container. "I'll be back. Someone'll be by shortly to take you to x-ray. The nurse'll draw some blood."

He laughs, tugging and straightening the gown down at his knees. "I ain't going anywhere, Doc."

He's fifty-two. Vitals are fine. No significant medical history. Labs come back okay. No fever. I get busy with some other patients. About an hour goes by. The x-ray tech pages me over to Radiology. Clayton's films are ready.

We stand gazing at the abdominal x-ray series on the view box. The abdominal gas pattern is normal. No obstruction or free air. No radio-opaque calculi seen. Soft tissue shadows are normal. Bones normal.

What doesn't belong is the penis-shaped dense object overlying the lower pelvis in the midline. The outer portion the density of rubber; the metallic inner casing housing two D batteries, some springs, and metal plates.

A runaway vibrating dildo.

"Second one tonight," the tech says, eyebrows raised, hands in pockets, swaying back on his heels. "Only the other one was a metal torpedo. In some lady's rectum."

"Wow." I nod, massage my chin. "That's the longest I've seen, I think."

"Whatd'ya say, a foot?"

"Yep. At least," I say. "A good footer plus."

"Hope the thing's off."

"Didn't hear any buzzing," I say. "Besides, probably would have felt something."

"I guess that's good," he says. "Huh?"

"Had this guy one time," I tell him. "Had to wait three hours for the batteries to burn out before the GI guys would scope him."

"No shit."

"Yeah," I say. "He was some politician. Never said a word."

"Interesting," the tech says. "Republican or Democrat?"

I glance at the ceiling, rub my chin, smile. "Can't say I remember."

"I seen a big old coke bottle one time," the tech says. "Classic Coke."

"Me too," I say. "All sorts of beer bottles too. We had a contest one time, as a med student. Trying to guess the brands."

The tech laughs, shakes his head.

"Winner got to take the bottle home."

"You're kidding."

"Yeah, I am."

We stand there a moment shaking our heads, staring at the films to the muted din of the ER down the hall.

"Well, it *is* Saturday night," I say. "Everyone's having fun but us."

"You got that right, Doc."

I snap the films off the view box and slide them into the beige manila envelope, hand them to the tech. I shrug. "Guess I better call GI."

The tech nods and flicks off the glaring light of the view box.

I walk back down the hall, toward the escalating noise of the nighttime ER.

February 9th: Peek and Shriek

I was in the cafeteria this afternoon, in line to pay for a bagel and coffee, when this guy, Jake steps in behind me. I remember him from med school. He's a few years ahead of me, in the surgery program. He's a quintessential surgical guy, physical and intense, wearing scrubs that are a little too tight, showing off muscular arms. He's pumped up, I can tell, and he slaps me on the back, "Hey *duuude*. How you been?"

"Pretty busy."

"Me too, man." He downs a small carton of milk. "Check it out. Just got out of a badass case, man. A real peek and shriek."

"Really?" I say, not wanting to admit I hadn't heard of that, though I really want to know. "What's that again?"

"Peek and shriek, man," he says. "Guy had colon cancer. Bad. Mets everywhere. We open up the belly to do a resection and we're like, nope! Nasty carcinomatosis. Close right the hell up. That's a peek and shriek."

"Whoa," I say. The cashier waves me toward the register.

MAY 28TH: INFLATION

"Father Murphy, I'm gonna have to put another catheter through your penis. That'll relieve the discomfort. Urine will flow again."

"Jehyeeesus, hurry boy," Father Murphy says, face scrunched up. "Pains like bloody hell."

"I'll be right back." I go down the hall to the supply closet by room 348 and gather the necessary materials; a fresh tube of petroleum jelly, a 14 French Foley catheter, a twenty cc syringe, a roll of paper tape, a packet of Betadine, a sterile drape, gloves and some sterile gauze. I stuff everything but the catheter into the side pockets of my white coat and head back to room 340.

"Just relax, Father," I say as I set up a sterile field in his lap. "I'm going to inject some gel into the penis."

"Get to it, boy, get to it."

I snap on sterile gloves. I pop the plunger out of the syringe casing, squeeze in clear petroleum jelly, pop the plunger back in.

I insert the plastic tip of the syringe into the urethral opening while applying slight traction with my other hand to keep the penis taut. I push all twenty cc's, pinching the glans to keep the stuff from oozing out. The trick is to lubricate the urethra, especially the portion that runs through the prostate, to allow easier passage of the catheter.

Father Murphy had surgery earlier in the day to reduce the size of his humongous prostate, a TURP, taking it from the size of a softball down to a baseball. The gland is now swollen and seeping blood, which ends up in the urethra. Clots form and block the plumbing.

This is why I was paged at three in the morning. I'm the dick doc. At least for the night. The pecker checker. Part of the Rod Squad. The Stream Team. Urology.

Thankfully, internship ends next month. Thinking about orthopedics. I'd take a bone saw over a catheter any day.

When I got to the floor earlier, Father Murphy had the post-op catheter in place. It slipped out during repositioning as I flushed out the chunky clots with saline. My chief resident told me to never ever let the catheter pop out. Now I see why. I couldn't get the friggin' thing back in.

Urine is building.

Father Murphy is in extreme pain. His bladder is probably the size of a basketball now, seams ripping, wanting to explode. Sweat beads on his forehead. He's writhing. Looking up from his crotch to his pained face is when it hits me.

Father Murphy? That scar on his forehead. The eyes.

"Father," I say, starting to thread the catheter through his shaft, staring at his face, the eyes. "You ever serve in a parish out in Lakewood?"

He's breathing faster, trying not to move. He manages, "Many years ago, yes."

Holy crap. It's him. I wait a moment, then ask, "Our Lady Queen of Mercy?"

"Yes."

Yes, he says. Bingo. The memories flood in. My head hurts. My face flushes. Father Murphy. My ears start to burn. The long summer days at the beach with the other boys. The "outings." The showers after the beach. The long awkward showers. The extra scrubbing to get the sand off. Him saying things like, "Let me help you," while smoothing the lather, and then, "It's okay."

I press on. I say, "My family belonged to that parish."

He does not speak.

"I was part of that parish," I say, louder now. "I used to go to Jones Beach with you."

"You remember the beach," he says, nodding, a grimace. A fake smile. "How...nice."

I wait a second, and then say with force, just to make sure he hears it. "I remember *after* the beach too."

There is a long pause, an awkward stretch, as our minds reel.

"Those years," he says between breaths. "My memory is poor."

I keep poking with the catheter. Back and forth. Push. Pull. Push. It will not pass.

"The showers after the beach," I say, to remind him. "You know?"

"Oh, those years," he says. "A faint memory, they are. Almost there? God bless you, boy. Hurts like bloody hell."

"I'm not your boy," I say though gritted teeth. "But I do remember the showers."

He strains to look down at me, lifting his head slightly. We lock eyes.

"That's right," I say, my face contorted into something between a scowl and a smile. "The *showers*, Father."

"My memory's bad, Doctor," He says, putting his head down, breathing faster. "Forgive me. Forgive me."

I think I see a subtle smirk dancing about his mouth. Smirking now? He arches his head on the pillow, whooshing sounds through pursed lips. He's staring at the ceiling, knobby hands clutching the metal guardrails.

The catheter finally pops into the bladder. There is a balloon on the end of the catheter that is supposed to be inflated when the tip is in the spacious bladder lumen, to keep the catheter from slipping out. When inflated, it is the size of a golf ball. I slowly slide the tip back, out of the bladder, back into the urethra, leaving it at about the level of the base of his penis.

The urethra is a tiny tube with the diameter of a cocktail straw.

I thumb the syringe that inflates the balloon and the golf ball expands in the cocktail straw. I say, "You remember the showers now Father?"

There is a weak groan before the pain is too much. Father Murphy passes out.

I begin to see some swelling at the base of his penis, from the slow deep venous bleeding. I stand in silence, acutely aware of the pungent mixed odor of stale breath, urine, betadine and sweaty ass. I gather the materials off the bed and throw them away.

His sacred priesthood slowly grows thick and blue at its base. It resembles a gnarled miniature tree stump. I gently pull the hospital gown across his thighs. Pat it so it's flat, smooth.

I rub my chin. Exhale.

Urethral rupture.

This will be considered a complication.

An intern mistake.

With my middle finger, I make the sign of the cross.

I walk back to my call room and wait for the nurse's page.

June 3rd: Lucky Strike

I was on afternoon rounds in cardiac surgery today with the legendary Dr. Seltzmann and a large gaggle of residents. Seltzmann is a burly, barrel-chested guy with a booming voice (I thought he was AOB too! It was Saturday after all).

We're in the ICU, huddled around the bed of a woman, a heavy smoker who we're told was caught puffing away in her bathroom by the nurse on the morning of surgery. The patient is day one post bypass and she's sedated with a long endotracheal tube jutting from her mouth, taped to her cheeks."Hey," Seltzmann says, motioning toward the endotracheal tube with a clipboard. "That's the biggest Lucky Strike you'll ever see!"

There were a few uneasy giggles from the interns as we moved on to the next patient.

June 14th: Rupture

"You can do it, boy." Chief is on the phone, miles away. "You're here, what, a year now?"

"Alone?"

"Just watch for now, champ. Get 'em in the OR. Watch the pressure. Get those lazy ass anesthesiologists to put 'em to sleep and if the pressure crashes, which I'm sure it will, you gotta open'em up."

"Then what?"

"Don't worry boy, I'm on my way. Maybe twenty minutes with this goddamn traffic. Just get'em open if you have to, feel around, find the aorta and clamp the sucker."

I hang up the phone. From the ER desk, I can see Paulie the Rug on the stretcher along the wall with his leaking aortic aneurysm and fake hair—IV going, intubated, the nurse bagging him, the transporter and ER doc staring at me. I try to put out of my head the fact that this guy is a prisoner, doing life for murder and racketeering, and hep-B positive to boot.

I remember the Hippocratic Oath.

As I walk up, the ER doc says, "There're two guys wanting to talk to you." He throws his chin at the hall. "There."

Two creepy dudes in suits stand along the wall, smiling.

"You guys wanted to talk to me?"

The taller guy is in my face. His breath reeks of stale coffee. "My boy dies, you die, Doc. Simple as that."

"Excuse me?"

He nods at Paulie. "Let's just say...he's important to us. He dies, you die."

"He's real sick, though."

"Don't matter."

They stare at me.

I see no point in pushing things.

I'm not sure what to say. "I'll do my best?"

"That's good." He winks. "That's real good."

They walk away.

Ten minutes later we're in OR 10. Everyone is scurrying about—a scrub nurse preparing a tray table, anesthesiologist hooking up lines and another nurse prepping Paulie's abdomen. I'm standing with my hands in the air—mask, cap and booties on, having just scrubbed. The nurse finishes prepping, holds out a sterile gown for me. The gloves are next. Double.

"Pressure's plummeting," the anesthesiologist says, behind a hanging sheet.

"We gotta open." I nod at the scrub nurse. She has a puzzled look on her face.

"Don't worry. Chief'll be here in a minute."

She says, "Oh."

I stand along Paulie's right side. "Eleven-blade." The nurse slaps metal into my hand in perfect position.

As if holding a pencil, I rest the tip of the blade under the xyphoid in the midline and push as I slide across skin, watching the abdominal flesh separate easily and the yellow fat globules balloon out. A brand new blade cuts like a boiled knife across a half-melted ice-cream cake.

The adrenaline kicks in.

I slice swiftly, curving around the umbilicus, moving quicker than usual. Normally we would get the small bleeders as I went through fat, then retract before splitting rectus muscle, careful not to poke into the belly. Not now. Now I was pushing hard, cutting through all layers in one shot. With one stroke, I was in the peritoneal cavity.

As the abdominal wall splays open and the nurse hooks a retractor into place, a volcano of blood blasts straight up and seems to stop in mid air before curling and crashing like a tidal wave. Rivers of thick darkness flow over the sides of Paulie's body and like hot lava creep along the drapes in slow motion. Audible splats of blood smack the tile floor like a slap in the face.

Infected blood.

He dies, you die.

I lean back. The nurse gasps, says, "Jesus Mary and Joseph."

It must be his total blood volume, easily several liters gushing and it doesn't stop. The goop pools around my feet, the cloth booties turning dark. Chunks of coagulated blood crawl along the drapes like spiders, hanging and tumbling to the tile.

Loaded with millions of microscopic hepatitis B organisms.

I say, "Holy crap." Toss the scalpel on the tray. "Retractor."

The nurse hands me the instrument. I hook it under the abdominal wall and pull.

I'm in automatic mode.

I submerge my other hand in the abdominal cavity, sinking into the bowl of hot infected soup, blood at the top of my glove, soaking the sleeve. My arm burns. My fingers are under omentum, sliding around knobby mesentery, past sausage-like intestine, smoothing along the posterior abdominal wall.

I can't feel an aneurysm and I realize there's no way I would since the thing is ruptured. I'm in the midline, fingers skimming over undulating spine. I feel something—it's in the correct anatomical location at least. A tubular wad of tissue. The aorta? There is no pulsation.

"Pressure's crap," the anesthesiologist says.

"Clamp." I trade the retractor for the hemostat and sink the tip down. With effort, I secure the clamp at the base of the aorta.

I wait.

The nurse glares at me. The only sounds come from the monitors, beeping and swishing. Blood drips onto tile, slower now. *Blip— Blip—Blip.*

It is eerily quiet after the commotion.

He dies, you die.

"He's crapping out," the anesthesiologist says in a monotone, busy behind the drape.

My forearm marinates in tainted blood.

After a moment, the anesthesiologist is quiet. I hear a sigh. I stare at the wall. The red hand of the humongous clock stutters around, seeming like an eternity.

Chief finally blasts through the doors in his street clothes, grinning, snapping on gloves.

"Damn, champ," he says, looking around. "Looks like a goddamn horror movie in here!"

"He's gone," the anesthesiologist says.

"Figured as much." Chief peers into the abdomen, tilting his head, stepping carefully through the bloody pond.

I pull out my dripping hand.

Chief drops his in.

"Jesus, boy," Chief says, a deep laugh. "You clamped the god-damn mesentery!"

"Well..."

"Doesn't matter, champ." Chief peels off his glove. "Guy was goner from the get-go. You might as well go break the news to his family downstairs. Two guys. Say they're his brothers."

June 19th: Codes

There's an overhead page for a code on Three South so I run over there, just to see if I can get involved. I've only been to a couple and it's always so chaotic. As I jog up to the room there's a senior medicine resident by the door, like a bouncer. "Hold on buddy. This one here's for MRB."

I say, "Oh," and back away and eventually leave.

Later, I ask one of the senior surgical guys what the heck MRB is. He looks annoyed. "Maximum resident benefit," He says. "Patient's already dead so it's a chance for those pansy medicine residents to practice code procedure."

July 13th: Retraction

Last I heard Walsh had fainted right in the middle of a radical nephrectomy, plopping face first into the sterile field before crumbling to the OR floor. And his internship was just starting.

The chief had given him the rest of the week off, something unheard of during an internship. Usually you had to suck it up. But the chief probably knew that this guy wasn't going to make it. Basically the time off meant you weren't coming back next year and you better start looking for another residency, something like radiology.

Walsh is now standing in front of me with a patient, Mr. Logan, between us. Our faces are a foot apart and I see the look in his eyes, one I've seen only once before. It was just last year, a guy named Adam something, a fellow intern, who ended up throwing himself off the hospital roof.

We're midway through a total colectomy, hacking out Mr. Logan's entire colon because of familial polyposis syndrome, a genetic disorder that carpets your colon with thousands of little polyps. The chance that one of those little knobs degenerates into cancer is virtually guaranteed, only a matter of time.

Chief is standing next to Walsh, closer to the patient's chest, abutting a baby-blue sheet draped between two IV poles separating us from the anesthesiologist and Mr. Logan's head. A scrub nurse stands just behind Walsh, next to a tall metallic table scattered with sterile instruments, handing them out on request, like a medical waitress.

Chief says, "Gimme the staple gun," and then, "Godammit Walsh, retract!"

The nurse hands Chief the staple device. In both hands, Walsh holds what looks like a miniature metallic golf club, each end hooked under the fleshy abdominal wall that is spread apart in order to give the real surgeons ample exposure to operate. His left arm reaches across the lower abdomen, pulling away toward my gut, the other pulling toward his own body. He has been in the same position for about two hours.

"Godammit Walsh—pull! Pull it like you mean it boy!" Chief places the end of the staple device around a portion of the rectosigmoid colon. "You should be bloody good and rested after that free weekend. Ready to retract!"

Walsh hadn't spoken since we started the case and even then it was a lame *hello*. All I can see are eyes, vacant and lost, peeking out from between the mask and cap. Probably wondering what had gone wrong in his life to warrant this torture. How he ended up here. I knew the feeling. It had been only a couple of weeks since my own internship ended. But it gets a little better each year, that's what I hear anyway. I wanted to tell him. I guess he doesn't realize that yet.

"Gimme a 2-0 catgut on a curved needle," Chief says to the nurse. "Here Altman." He hands me long forceps. "Run this, I'll get the bleeders."

Walsh's eyes stare straight through me. I pray he doesn't faint again.

"Pull Walsh Pull! We can't see a goddamn thing!"

"Chief..." I say but it's too late.

A freaky cackle pours from Walsh's throat as he whips the retractors across the room, metal clanking against the wall and then on the tile floor. Walsh spins back to the instrument tray and palms a scalpel, 11-blade, and backhands it into Chief's neck, in and out.

Chief doesn't move and Walsh must have gotten the common carotid, probably just about at the bifurcation because the bloodworks are terrific. Chief is like a human lawn sprinkler with spurts coating the ceiling and spraying across my mask in a warm wet splash.

I arch back as Walsh takes a wild swing at me across Mr. Logan and slips on the blood-smeared floor. His face slams right into the gaping abdominal cavity. The nurse screams and instinctively reaches over and whacks Walsh on top of the head with a metallic pan and he goes limp, sliding to the floor in a heap and dragging a portion of the sterile drape with him.

Chief has staggered back and sits on the floor against the wall, holding pressure to the wound, stopping the bleeding but still looking like hell.

July 21st : Limbo

I'm not sure I can do this anymore. Well really, I'm not sure I *want* to do it. This past year has been absolutely wild. A blur. All the stuff I learned and the crazy things that have happened. Not sure if I want to do this for another four years. And besides, after that, life as a new surgical attending would be just as brutal, maybe worse. Who am I kidding? The rest of my life would be like this.

I'm thinking of at least transferring hospitals, maybe even specialties. I used to joke about radiology, but that doesn't sound half bad right now. Much better lifestyle. And that thing with Walsh. Could that happen to me? Could I crack like that? Anyway, Chief is doing okay, and knowing him, he'll be back at work in no time. I think the only reason he made it was because he was smack right in the OR already. They literally threw him on a table in the very next room in minutes and the vascular surgeons went right to work. Turns out his common carotid and jugular were totally transected.

Walsh is in a psychiatric lockup or something, awaiting a hearing and apparently his attorney is going with temporary insanity, you know, under excessive stress. We'll see. In the meantime, the hospital started a minor quality control investigation into the Father Murphy thing. His holiness hasn't said a word yet, probably too worried about himself. Bastard. I'm not even sure if he understands exactly what happened.

Yesterday, I could've sworn I saw those two guys from the ER that day. Those friends of Paulie the Rug. I thought I saw them sitting in a car on my street. It was one in the morning and I was just getting home from the hospital post-call. Got me kind of worried, though. But those guys weren't serious, right? *He dies, you die?* I mean, stuff happens. Out of anyone's control. Who knows, maybe I imagined them. I was pretty spent that night, after coming off a thirty-six hour shift.

Venice Beach Birthday Boogie

So I roll over and there's one of my roomies Marc, huge redneck bastard, looking like a barn silo in a shredded flannel shirt. "Yo, Yankee," he says, square head glaring down, ears jutting like Dumbo, "you trainin' or what?"

I squint. All I see are flaring black nostrils. Hell if that nose don't look like the entrance to the midtown tunnel, Queens side. I laugh.

"Heck's so funny?"

"Nothing." I kick the sheet down like I'm riding a bike. "I'll train when I feel like it. Today's my birthday, ya ugly hillbilly. Twenty-one."

"Ah, who gives a rat's ass."

"I do, you *Deliverance-lookin'* Tennessee blockhead." I rub my eyes and get on an elbow. I take a breath, think about it. "Way I figure it, there're three things I wanna do today. Treat myself."

"Like get a life?"

"Three goals for today."

"Let's hear this crap."

"Eat," I say as I roll to my side, sit up. "Maybe a good steak."

Marc's got a dumbass look on his face, he's playing along, stuffing a turquoise Gold's Gym sweatshirt into his gym bag.

"Get some anabolic agents." I stand, smack Marc's meaty redneck delt for effect.

"That's two, Yankee."

"You can really count, huh?" I step over in front of the little mirror nailed to the wall, swing into a double biceps shot, lock the guns, smirk. "And get laid."

"Ahhh, shit." Marc waves his hand. "Stupid New Yorker. Good luck with that." Marc shakes his head, tightens his weight belt, heads for the door, "I'm doin' legs."

It's been rainy and overcast for weeks now. Usually gets better in the afternoon, sun burning off the haze, but it's still gloomy for LA and it's been going on way too long.

I'm at the second floor window, staring through the Venetian slats, scoping out a wet Pacific Avenue in Venice. The surf shop across the street dim and empty. Ten o'clock in the morning on a Tuesday. Been two years of this crap. Thinking maybe I should head back to the east coast.

Studio apartment, four guys. Was my apartment first, so I got the good bed, a single next to the bathroom. It has a box spring and frame. Marc was here second so he got the mattress with the box spring on the floor. The two Australian guys, Paul and Gary, they each have a thin mattress squished up against the wall. Just needed a place to stay for a few days that turned into a few months. Right. Whatever.

We all manage to scrape up the rent each month. All we need is a place to sleep and keep our shit. Seems there's a lot of shit to step around, the place is so small.

There's a poster scotch-taped to the wall, a contest Marc recently placed in, the Grand Prix, with a cartoon of a jacked-up bodybuilder hitting a most muscular pose, his face contorted into a crazed maniacal grimace. One of the Australians scribbled "Marc" across the guy's chest.

There's a wood desk in the corner, came with the place. The drawers are empty. The top is littered with vitamin bottles, two jugs of amino powder, a container of isopropyl alcohol, a few brown bananas, a blender and a mountain of individually wrapped syringes.

And a telephone.

The telephone rings.

"Frankie?"

"Donna?"

"You wanna talk?"

"'Bout what?"

"Us."

"Go 'head."

"You're an ass."

"A good start, I guess."

"Fuck you."

"Like I said."

"Can't you just be normal?"

"Me? You're the freak."

"Wish you were just a little older. Like twenty-four. More mature."

"Well, happens today is my birthday."

"Yeah, I know it."

"Heck you want?"

"Wanna be with you."

"You told me to fuck off."

"Was pissed. You can be an asshole, Frankie. All your gym shit."

"Nice."

"And Becca wants to see you."

"Don't gimme that shit. She ain't mine anyways."

"Kid loves you."

"She's got a daddy."

"Never met 'em."

"Not my problem."

"I'll come by later."

"You know what? Don't bother."

"Fine."

"Fine."

I hang up, look over at Gary and Paul, both sitting up on their mattresses, one scratching his head, the other his ass.

"The coont?" Paul says.

"Easy."

"That shit I'm taking is pretty powerful, mate," Paul says. "Lookit this boner." He unfolds the sheet, revealing tented shorts. "Christ. Was in the market yesterday, right? See this lady, she's got no bra, pushin' the cart. Nipples like cigar butts. I get this wicked boner, mate. Like instantaneous."

"Hm. Guess I woulda too."

"But Christ, mate," Paul says, half disgusted, "she was like, dunno, eighty years old, jugs hangin' down to her knees."

Gary grunts, heads to the bathroom. "Tits 'r tits."

"That ain't right," I say, pull open the fridge, grab a quart container of keifer, "but nipples 'r nipples, huh?"

"Fukin' right," Paul says and farts.

I climb onto my motorcycle. It's parked in the alley alongside the three-story brick apartment building. It's a Yamaha 650. No big deal. Gets me around. Don't even need a helmet in California.

Cool.

I cruise down Pacific toward Santa Monica, the air thick, moist, starting to come alive. Pacific turns into Neilson Way, take that past Pico, turns into Ocean. It's a little nippy, but I dig it anyway. There's no traffic, it's after tourist season, plus it's a weekday.

I cut it low, angle, take the driveway into the Kensington Hotel parking lot with a jolt. Park. Go to room five. Knock.

The door swings open. Christian fills the frame. Towering mandingo bastard. Looks like he should be in a comic book. Head to toe shredded muscle. He's the real deal though. Just won a national contest and it looks like he might be getting out of the rat race. Going pro. Maybe. If he plays his cards right.

He's also the juice man.

"Fuck's up?"

"Need some shit."

"Ay'ite. Come on."

Christian flops onto a cheap couch. It creaks and bends. There's a cheap coffee table at his knees, a tall green bong on top, smoke billowing upward.

His two roommates are there. Steve, short uptight guy from Florida. He's at the sink in front of a blender, cracking eggs into the glass pitcher. He's got a perfectly groomed pompadour, wearing black spandex bike shorts and a yellow Gold's Gym tank top.

Chuck is lounging in a cheap wood chair next to the cheap couch, head slung back, arms and legs splayed. He's wasted. He's from upstate New York, kind of a hick. He's frickin' crazy muscular huge, training for the Mr. California, his girth crushing the chair. He looks like a juiced-up ape. He's wearing pink posing trunks and white hightop sneakers.

"How the hell you guys train on that shit?" I say.

Chuck moans. "Gets you in the zone, man." He doesn't move. Stares dreamily at the ceiling.

"Kinda shit you want?" Christian says, sucking on the bong.

"Bottle of Decca."

"Shit. Thasit?"

"Yup." I mosey in, peek over Steve's shoulder. "Pay you tomorrow, okay?"

"New Yawk scammer." Christian coughs a furry cloud of smoke, puts the bong down, and reaches for a box on the floor. "Ten."

"No problem."

Chuck drawls, "Did my heaviest squat stoned outta my mind."

Christian cackles, cardboard box in his lap. "Dang farm boy," he says, flips me the Decca. "Used to squat wit a cow over his shoulders. Like Arnold with them tree trunks in Austria."

I palm the vial out of the air, wriggle it in my sock. "Thanky, brother."

"Screw you," Chuck says. "Least I didn't hammer the cows."

"Squeal!"

"Ghetto loooooser." Chuck starts to laugh that uncontrollable stoned laugh.

Steve dumps amino powder in the blender, big scooper thing, revs it up.

I watch.

Steve seems agitated. I'm in his space. He pours, then stops. "You want some or what?"

"Friggin' A," I tell him, snatching the cup and chug the frothy goodness.

I pop back on Ocean, cross Pico and shoot over to the beach. I arc through the parking lot, digging the weight of the bike, down to the walkway, and kill the engine. Push the shades to my forehead. It's still overcast, gloomy fog pushing down on the waves. Not many people out, some bikers, a few joggers and some roller skaters. I can barely make out two dudes in wetsuits bobbing on surfboards in the mist.

I been doing it a lot lately, coming to the beach, usually when it's quiet, night, in the fog. Just to clear my head. Been thinking lately, like what am I gonna do. Go back? I stare at the waves, wonder what the family is doing in New York, haven't talked to them in over a year. A few brothers, a few sisters.

Last time I spoke to my mom, she tells me my father died, finally drank himself to death.

I waited a long time before I said anything. I said, "Yeah, so?"

And then hung up.

After twenty minutes of staring, thinking, I'm back on the bike, cruising down Main Street in Santa Monica, past the Omelette Parlor, Josephina's, some art galleries. Loop down Rose, over to Gold's. I pull round to the rear, so I can go in through the back door. My membership expired about six months ago and as long as I go in the back, nobody asks anything.

I slip into the huge warehouse of a gym, Def Leppard blasting, the familiar smell and sound. Tangy sweat, air heavy, plates crashing, grunting, metal on metal.

Platz is squatting. Fives plates each side, bar bending over traps, head up, intense, each thigh a gnarled sequoia. Shredded. Up and down, easy for reps. Boom Boom.

Dickerson is doing bent over rows, two plates each side, heels on a wood block, weight belt, grunting with each thrust. I nod but he doesn't see me.

The Barbarian brothers are benching, three plates each side, bar thumping off swollen pecs, each rep a scream and a yell. Workboots and cutoff sweatshirts and bandanas and jeans.

I head over to the fountain, take a sip of cold water, look around. Van Halen now. *Running with the Devil.*

I go to the curved overhead bar, hang, start some stretching. That's when I see Pat, he's scrambling over. Wired.

"Hey, dude," he says.

"Hey." Pat's in his mid thirties. A promising bodybuilder, years ago. Won some big shows. Ain't done shit since. Been out here fifteen years, from Canada, now lost, beat up. He's wearing sweat pants, flip flops, and a tank top he's torn up so much his shaved chest and abs are fully exposed, down to his belly button.

"Fuck you been up to?" Eyes darting. "Ain't seen ya."

"Been around."

"Yo. Got a gig for ya tomorrow. Make some money," he says. "Gay bar in the valley, the Steerhead or some shit. Want some bodybuilders to do a kind of pose off. Like have a little contest and shit. Hundred bucks each. You in?"

I take a deep breath, drop from the bar, adjust my shirt. "Gotta work. Workin the door at Josephina's now."

"Yeah? Sure? Easy money, man. Buncha fags."

"Nah."

"Hey, man," he says. "You gimme a ride somewhere later?"

"Happened to your car?"

"Freakin' thing died, dude."

"Whyncha fix it?"

"Cashish, man."

"The hotel?"

"Nailed me rifling through a bag. Some stuck-up bitch. Got fired."

"Ass."

"What? I'm gonna be a bellhop my whole life?"

"Where?"

"Culver City, man. Easy. Just gotta get something."

"Don't know."

"Dude. I helped you out. 'Member? I took care a you."

"That was a friggin' year ago."

"So? Come on, Frankie baby."

"Whatever."

"I'll get over to that shithole of yours later. Eight okay?"

"Whatever. I gotta train."

"Wanna do shoulders?"

After I train, I shoot over to Von's in Marina Del Rey. Walk around, grab a quart of strawberry keifer, open it and start gulping as I wander the aisles. I head to meats and stuff a fifteen-dollar steak in my sweats down front when no one's looking, in my underwear. I pull my tank top low, the meat wet and cold, almost freezing my prick off.

Outside, the sun struggles to break through clouds, not quite winning.

I park the bike in the alley next to my building. Notice the gas is low, make a mental note. Walk round front, steak in hand, there's Gary coming out the door, holding it open for me.

"Hey."

"Got some meat, mate?"

"Yeah. I got some meat for ya, Right here." I cup my groin, pull. "Anyone upstairs?"

"Nah. Meeting Paul for a workout, then going to Westwood. Gonna see the new Arnold flick, *Terminator*. Then we gettin' pissed."

"Heard it's good. And Marc?"

"Came back, then went to see that new bird. Redondo Beach. Said he won't be back till tomorrow."

"Cool."

"Oh yeah. Donna came round. Said she wanted to talk to you."

"What'd you tell her?"

"That you were out, I dunno. Hell you want me to tell her?"

"Okay. That's cool."

"Cheers, then."

Gary leaves. I key the lobby door, take the stairs two at a time, second floor. Inside, I plop the steak in a frying pan, on low, peel open a syringe wrapper, load up the 2 cc's of Decca and slam it in my glute. Wham. Inject. Way I see it, I've already tackled two of those goals.

Now I gotta work on number three.

I eat, then take a shower.

I walk out of the apartment, loop around back and I'm right on Venice Beach Central. Kind of slow today, still gloomy. Usual mix of smells; food, piss, incense, ocean. Few tourists, most of the regulars. That guy in a turban, on roller skates with his guitar, glides by, shows his toothy smile.

I walk over by the weight pit. Got shorts on, flip-flops, fisting my shirt in a ball. I feel good after that steak and Decca lunch, and the workout. Pumped. After the shower, I rubbed an oil and lotion combo on the guns and I'm sweating, the oil beading.

I spot two pretty black mamas hanging around the pit. Watching the tatted up brothers pound iron. They check me out as I walk up, giggling a bit. I smile.

I hang around, kinda loose, like I don't notice too much and sure as shit, they come wandering over.

"Hey." I say.

"You a muscle man?" One says and they trade glances, laugh.

"You a hot piece of ass?" I stay serious. They get serious too.

The hotter one glares, got a cat look in her eye. "I'm LaTonya."

"Frankie," I say and shake her fingertips. The other one might as well not be there the way we're checking each other out.

The other one chimes in, "I'm Vanessa."

"Hey," I say, not taking my eyes off LaTonya.

We chat a while. I tell her I'm from New York and I put the accent on and they love it and they make me say, "ged ova hea" a few times and they're giggling away.

It's not long before LaTonya and I both know we wanna go off for a walk on our own and Vanessa senses this, she's not happy about it, but she ends up saying that she has some friends over by the basketball courts and she'll catch up with LaTonya later.

LaTonya and I walk around, take each others hands, look in some shops, watch a group of kids doing some weird dance moves, a big circle of people around, kids asking for money after, passing a basket. We walk away.

Finally she says she's thirsty and I point over to my building, say that I live right there does she wanna come up and get something to drink.

She swivels her head, looks around at nothing, smiles and says *why not.*

After I tell her it was my birthday, that was it—I was in.

I'm in my apartment, lying sideways across the bed, hands clasped behind my head, feeling like the king. LaTonya on her knees in front of me, head in my lap, working it.

And that's when I hear the knock. *Rap Rap Rap.* A quick staccato. Then again. *Rap Rap Rap.*

LaTonya looks up. I press a finger to my lips. *Shssssh.*

One more time. *Rap Rap Rap.*

We wait.

Nothing.

We wait even longer.

Nothing.

LaTonya gets a little freaked out, so we get dressed, quietly, wait about ten minutes and LaTonya says she has to get back to the beach, find Vanessa. She'll be worried.

I say okay.

I look out the window, down the street. Nothing.

We leave. Down the stairs to the front door.

As soon as I open it I hear, "Who's this nigga bitch?" And there're fingernails stretching across, reaching for LaTonya.

Donna.

Donna's screaming and carrying on and kicking and spitting and I get between the two riled up babes and we spill out onto the street, mangled, and LaTonya breaks away, rushes off, opposite direction, looking at me and shaking her head and I mouth the words, *I'll call ya*.

LaTonya makes a funny face, hurries along.

I grab Donna's shoulders, try to calm her down and she's kicking and I have her locked at arm's length. My back is flush against the brick wall of the building and she's thrashing and I'm telling her to calm the fuck down please and that's when some long-haired blonde dude hops out of the surf shop from across the street. He's got no shirt and puka beads drape his neck.

I guess all he sees is some guy strong-arming some chick but he can't see me because Donna's pretty much blocking his way.

He rushes over, says, "Hey! What're you doing to her, man?"

Something clicks in, like a little juice rage and I thrust Donna to the side and I step towards this dude and that's when he sees me for the first time, shredded and raged, and I'm in his face and I yell, "None of your freakin' business!" and he steps back saying, "Whoa whoa, man, it's okay I was just wondering," and I raise a fist and he quickly backs up, backpedals a few steps, turns and jogs back to the surf shop.

I go back over to Donna and she's not there and I look to the alley and I see her running to her little car and see her mom is in the passenger seat and baby Becca is in the back, in a car seat, wailing.

Donna reaches into the car and comes out with something in both hands and briskly walks toward me, with a purpose, and I can see what she has now.

A cake.

She rushes me like a ninja, lifting the cake overhead, two hands, yells, "Happy birthday, asshole!" and whips the block of icing at my head and I duck and it misses and slams into the brick wall and this pisses her off and she actually screeches and runs back to her car. Gobs of cake and icing crawl down brick.

She gets in her Datsun and I hear the car revving and I wait and then I see the car go forward, pitch, reverse, forward again, pitch, reverse.

I sprint over and see that she's hit my bike and it's on its side and keeps hitting it and her mother is screaming and the baby is crying and I yell, "Hey!" and she backs up one more time and then screeches wildly down the alley, out of sight.

My bike is okay, no major damage, just some scratches and dings. I lift it up and wipe it off. Head back up to the apartment.

I sit on the edge of my bed and shake my head.

Laugh.

I end up taking a shower, finish off what LaTonya didn't get a chance to, lie down. I guess that counts for goal three. I have both windows open, blinds up, the beachy breeze coming in smells good.

The sun is sinking behind a haze, low in the sky, and there's that feeling of the day turning to night. I hear the occasional car rumble by outside, some music playing in the distance, down by the beach, the sporadic loud cackle. A motorcycle.

An apartment door opening and closing. Footsteps on the stairs. Another door. *Whoomp.*

And then I'm out.

"Frankie!"

I hear my name, like in a dream. Open my eyes.

"Frankie!"

Outside. I get up and go to the window. There's Pat. He's pacing back and forth, looking around, hands to his mouth.

"Yo!" I call down.

"Hey hey," Pat says. "Let me in, man."

"A second." I put on a tank top, flip flops. Head downstairs. Open the door.

"Hey man, you gonna gimme that ride?"

I wipe my face, turn up the stairs. "Where again?"

"Culver City." He's following me up the steps. "Two minutes. In and out."

I stop, mid stair. "Fuck for?"

"Just pick some shit up." He stops on the steps too. "Drop off some money. Is all."

"Shit you pickin up?"

"Some crystal, man. Great shit. Hypes you up bigtime."

"You need something to hype you down, dude."

"Yeah yeah. We goin?"

"Let me piss," I say. "Gotta get my keys, some sneakers. Meet me by the bike. In the alley."

And he's off.

I'm cruising east along Venice Boulevard wondering what the hell I'm doing. Got this thirty-five year old loser on the back of my bike— one I never bothered to register or insure, previous owner's plate on the back.

I'm twenty-one, still have a chance. I realize as the wind is slapping my face, damn, I don't want to end up like this guy—lost in Venice beach, getting some younger guy to take you to pick up some crystal on some random weeknight because you don't even have a friggin' car.

And then I laugh at the stupidness of it all. How ridiculous we must look. Pat's about two-twenty and I'm like two-thirty. So we have five hundred pounds on this Yamaha 650, cruising up Venice Boulevard.

Must look like two idiots.

I figure I've had about enough. Maybe it really is time to go back to New York. Who the hell knows, maybe go to college or something.

"There," Pat says, pointing at a yellow house. "That one."

I swing over in front. A stucco cheap looking piece of shit house, right off Venice Boulevard, bushes ragged, worn roof, garbage cans tipped over on the side. A dented garage door.

I click off the engine and Pat says, "Better leave it on."

"How come?"

"Just you never know." He heads up the walk.

"Hey."

Pat turns.

"It's my birthday, you know."

"Yeah?"

"Twenty friggin' one, man."

"Whadaya want, a kiss?" Pat says and walks, but quickly turns. "Only jokin', dude. Just a kid, huh? I'll give you an extra blast of this shit. Okay?"

I shrug and turn the ignition.

I'm sitting there about three minutes, engine humming, before Pat comes flying from the house, yelling, "Go! Go! Go!"

"What?" Reflexively, I downshift to first, click, grip and turn my wrist while Pat is running alongside, hopping on.

I hear a *WHAP*, a door slapping open and there's some yelling as I make a wide wobbly arc in the street, a truck just missing us—gust of wind, horn blaring.

I look back and see three gangbangers spilling out of the house, across the lawn, the glint of metal in one of the guy's outstretched hands. Another guy is jumping into a low rider at the curb and there's yelling and howling and Pat is screaming, "Go! Go! Go!"

I kick up the throttle and pick up speed and I hear three sharp reports, *CLACK CLACK CLACK* and the car is screeching around in the street.

I gun it.

I hear three more CLACK CLACK CLACKS and Pat thrusts and I feel Pat's head on my shoulder, heavy, like he's decided to take a nap and his arms go slack from around my waist and I feel his whole body, his being, just give, a final exhalation and I see the car gaining in my mirror.

Pat's arms flop to his sides, dangle, and there is nothing left, he's just a flaccid body and I feel him start to fall away as I accelerate and then the bike is lighter as I see Pat in my mirror, almost in slow motion, sail backward as if he's just parachuted from a plane, and it seems as if his arms are reaching for me.

And then there is impact, slap, flat on his back, with a sudden spring upward, as if he met the rubber of a taut trampoline, his feet flailing upward, puppet-like, unwilling, back around, just in time to meet the grill of the low rider.

The car screeches, angles, but this is futile as Pat hits, face first, upside down, and the car spins wildly, its back end slamming a parked van and then quickly swinging back round the other way into an oncoming pickup and there is a loud shattering and shrieking of glass and metal as I gun the throttle and soon I can't even see the car, or Pat.

I'm lost.

I zoom down Venice Boulevard about a mile before I turn off onto a side street, then turn again and again and again. My chest is tight and I realize I'm breathing in short jabs and my arms are locked and my fists are crushing the hand grips.

I slow it down, just coasting.

I'm aware of my surroundings again. Coming out of it. A neighborhood, houses and parked cars, someone walking a dog, looking at me funny.

It's getting dark now, cool and misty.

I pull off to the curb and straddle the bike, leave it running and I notice a splotch of blood on my right shoulder.

After about five minutes, running the scene over and over in my head, I pull away slowly, making my way back toward Venice.

I end up on Washington Boulevard and from there I know where I am. I shoot down toward my apartment, thinking about what the hell should I do. Nothing. The bike is not even registered to me, the plate old and barely visible. Nobody knows I took him there, right? Poor Pat. Damn. Least the guy went out shit-faced and freaked out.

Poor Pat. Damn.

He didn't feel anything. Right? Was dead before he fell.

Pat.

I'm definitely gettin' the hell outta here.

Don't want to be another Pat in ten years.

Damn.

Going back.

Poor Pat.

When I ride past the front of my building I see someone lurking in the shadows by the doorway.

Donna.

I pull the bike round the side, park it in the alley. She comes ambling over as I climb off.

"Frankie."

I wipe my face. "Hey."

"What's wrong?"

"Nothin," I say quickly, trying to be cool, shaking a little. "Don't got any cakes do ya?"

"Funny, ya jerk." She moves closer. "I don't care you hangin' with some brown sugar bitch. It's my fault anyways. I drove you to it."

"Donna."

"No really." She tries to rest her arms on my shoulders, sees the blood stain. "What's that?"

"Nothin." I take her hands. "Listen. I don't know. I'm all shook up. I'm thinking like I might be going back to New York. Ya know? I think I did my thing here."

"What? No, Frankie." She gets closer. "You can't. I love you."

"Yeah, love you too. But we ain't so good together. And I don't wanna end up some loser here. Ten years later doin' the same shit."

"We can be good together if we want." Donna rubs my cheek. "We can make it."

"I dunno."

"Well, Frankie?" She looks at me a long beat. "Got something to tell ya."

I look at her. "What."

"I'm havin' your baby."

"No way."

"I'm pregnant," she says, looking in my eyes, serious as all getout, but smiling. "And you know me, my beliefs. I'm havin' it, Frankie."

"Really."

"Love you, Honey. We gonna be in each others lives now, forever."

I stare down the dirty alley, head spinning a bit, notice some bent garbage cans spilling broken bags on the cracked pavement, an old Jeep, faded graffiti on the brick wall, a cool breeze smelling of salt, the sound of a wave crashing in the distance. Some faraway music.

"Frankie?"

Crap.

"Honey? We'll do it, ya know?"

Poor Pat.

"Let's go inside, Frankie."

I shake my head, half smile on my face. Wonder if the bike would make it cross country. How much gas would it need? Bet it would be brutal on the ass.

"Come on, baby," Donna says. "We'll talk it ova."

"Whatever."

We start toward the door. She hooks her arm around mine, pulls in tightly.

Happy birthday to me.

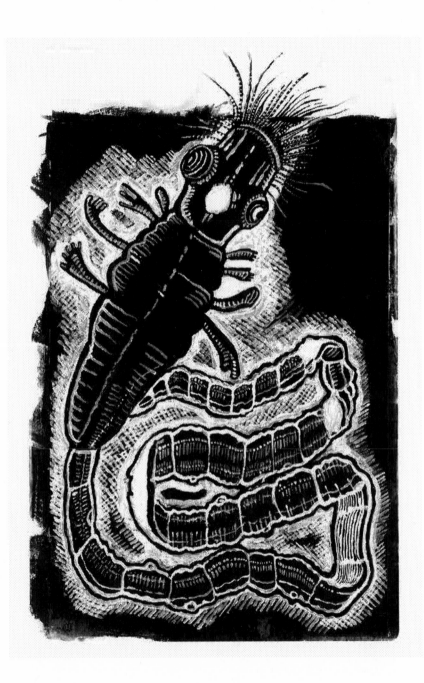

Expulsion

STEVE PUSHED HARD, STRAINED, but the bowel movement wouldn't come. He made sure not to hold his breath, didn't want to valsalva and have a heart attack right on the bowl. What a memorable way to be found dead, curled on the bathroom tile, pants around your ankles, feces crusted on your ass.

Steve took a break, wiped his brow, inhaled deeply then exhaled smoothly through pursed lips, letting the muscles relax. He sat upright, realizing he was hunched over, figuring this would help elongate the colon, let the sigmoid stretch, get ready for the final expulsion. But damn did it hurt.

With three fingertips, Steve massaged his abdomen. A doctor, Steve knew his anatomy. He pushed proximal to distal, starting in the right lower quadrant, at the level of the ileocecal valve. Right where feces began to take shape, exiting the small intestine as a water-logged slushy material, then entering the colon to begin the process of water removal, the end result a semi-solid paste.

He worked his way around, upward towards the transverse colon, across the midline to the splenic flexure, then downward along the left colon, across into his pelvis, deep, to get the sigmoid toward the recto-sigmoid junction.

He'd done this before, massaging along, jokingly calling it the *poop-guiding maneuver* or *colonic-cupping* or some other term that would momentarily amuse him. Usually it helped. This time though, it was slow going, feeling as though he was guiding the stool along as an oversized solid unit, sluggishly sliding along the haustral-folded mucosal surface of the large intestine.

He braced himself once more, inhaled and exhaled, getting in the zone. His abdomen gurgled, and he could feel contractions, spasms, and his gut caught. A dart of pain. Bloating. He twisted his torso, first to the right and then to the left, creating some postural and anatomic elongation and foreshortening.

This was it. Showtime. He felt something settle deep in his pelvis, engage. Home stretch. He flexed a little, felt his muscles tighten, his anal sphincter starting to relax and widen.

Something started to pass. A last deep slow protracted inhalation. The mass slid along his anal canal, bridging the anal verge, feeling prickly, almost painfully stretched. Then a building pressure, a feeling of evacuation, turning the corner, on its way, half in, half out now. The final push and a splash.

Steve realized his eyes were closed. He came to as if from a dream, droplets of moisture beading his brow, total muscle relaxation, settling back to homeostasis.

He rested his hand on the toilet roll, started to spin it, tissue paper descending to the floor.

And then another splash.

Again? He hadn't passed anything else. At least he didn't think he had.

His senses sharpened, alert again.

Splash.

Steve twisted off the bowl in a svelte dance-like motion, one hand on the bowl, the other on the cool porcelain of the tank. He nearly slipped back onto the tile at the site of the thing.

Steve didn't move. He froze, thinking the smartest tactic was to stay still. Human instinct. He felt as if he were outside his own body, an observer looking down, maybe via camera over his shoulder. He wished he wasn't there. But he was.

He waited.

The thing in the toilet, the thing that just slid from his very own abdomen, falling from his ass into the water of the bowl, was alive. It seemed to be looking at him.

Black and glimmering with a slimy sheen, it was about a foot long and thick as Steve's wrist. There was a head-like region and a pointed tail. Small protrusions dotted its sides. There were two dominant protrusions on the head that looked like eyes, and there were cilia-like structures sticking from its head, which undulated in the water. The eye protrusions stared at him.

Steve couldn't take it anymore. He knew it had been only seconds but he felt as if he were standing there for hours. The cold hard tile bore into the soles of his feet. He snapped back into his body, out of the camera and into his head.

Flush it.

His mind raced. *Flush it flush it flush it.* Steve glanced at the thing, hoped it couldn't jump, spring forth and latch onto the meaty flesh of his arm. He avoided eye contact for fear it might sense a challenge. He eyed the toilet handle. Then the thing. Then the handle. The thing.

Steve's arm shot forward, surprising even himself, stretched fingers reaching for the metal, then contact and a forceful push downward.

Water gushed onto porcelain, the familiar sound and spinning. He arched back and rolled his eyes downward to peer into the bowl.

The thing was surfing around the edge. *Go, go, please go.*

The wide hole at the bottom of the bowl began to suck water. He watched the spinning fluid and black thing rotate around and around.

A sharp squeal and the bumpy protrusions on the thing's side elongated slightly, shot out, like mini arms reaching for their lives, tiny suction cups on the ends. The thing braced itself to the sides of the bowl. The water kept sucking and the splashing sounds diminished until the bowl was empty.

The thing remained still, then relaxed slowly as the bowl filled with water, releasing its grip, started to float once again.

A whip of its tail and a splash.

Steve realized he was breathing rapidly, his pants still down around his ankles. He looked into the bowl and the thing looked back.

It seemed to be smiling.

Steve stared the thing down. He took two cautious steps back, just enough space so he could keep an eye on the slimy creature. He slowly bent his knees, squatting, and reached for his pants. All the time with his eyes on the bowl. He clutched the material of his trousers, yanked them up, buttoned, zipped.

Think think think.

Steve needed a weapon. A knife? That might work. Would create a mess though. Maybe just poke it? Give it a little nudge? Stimulate it. See its reaction. Yeah, that's it. He needed to get to the kitchen, maybe the garage for heavy duty tools.

Steve eyed the trash can on the floor. He picked it up. Could use a little more weight. He carefully turned, opened the glass door to the shower, picked up a big plastic bottle of shampoo. He dropped it in the can. Then the humongous bottle of designer conditioner. He realized it was Sherrie's. Guess she left it here when she moved out. Hadn't noticed that for a month? Whatever. The bottle had some good heft.

Steve stepped to the toilet, peeped in and saw the thing floating in the water. Its tail flicked and he jumped. Steve quickly reached and slapped the toilet cover and it slammed shut with a thud. He whipped the weighted trash can on top and hopped back.

He heard some muffled splashing.

Steve rummaged through the kitchen drawer. Spatula, ladle, pizza cutter? Nope. Hmm. Knives. He turned to the wood block on the counter that housed the fancy-occasion cutlery. He slipped out the longest knife, the carver. Held it out front, jabbed it a few times like a sword. Feeling satisfied, he rested it on the counter. Next.

He turned his attention to the cabinet under the sink, swung it open. The bucket. He pulled it out, set it on the counter, examined its contents, taking each one out and placing it on the granite top. Sponges, window cleaner, wood polish, rags. He headed for the garage with the empty bucket in hand.

His mobile phone vibrated in his pocket. He pulled it out, saw the number, hesitated, then pushed a button. "Yeah."

"Steve?"

"Yes, Sherrie."

"Hi."

"Ah. Hi." Steve made a weird face. He retreated back into the kitchen, put the bucket on the counter and leaned against a drawer. "Whaddaya want?"

"Don't know."

"You don't know. Wonderful. You wanna call when you do?"

"I said I was sorry."

"So?"

"So can't we talk?"

"I'd rather not. I'm...kind of busy anyway." Steve looked at the knife on the counter. "I have a little situation here."

"You need some help? Can I come by?"

"*No no no.* Nope. Listen. I'm in the middle of something. Why don't you call that guy you work with. What's his name...Clarence? Something like that?"

"Very funny. It's Clay. Listen. I said I was sorry. I made a mistake. I know it. Please. It's been a month. I really want to see you."

"I'll call you tomorrow. How's that?"

"Promise?"

"Yeah." Steve smirked.

"Okay."

"Bye." Steve ended the call, slipped the phone in his pocket. "Right."

He headed for the garage.

Steve studied the garage wall. Took in the musty garage smell. Shovel. Clippers. Hammer, screwdriver, drill, weedwacker. Lawn chairs, umbrella, rake, hoe.

Steve had an idea and turned to the opposite wall. He looked around, behind some boxes, propped-up wood planks, sheetrock. Cans of paint on the floor. Metal shelves. Bug killer, lighter fluid, work gloves, more cans of paint. Bingo. There it was. Propped next to the shelves against the wall. Behind stacks of cardboard boxes. The boxes that had belonged to his late mom.

A pang of sadness rippled Steve's gut. Thinking of his mom, passed now for over a year. He picked up the device. It had been one of her favorite things toward the end, when she had a hard time getting around, moving in general, weakened from rounds of chemo. Plus, her bones were riddled with metastases and she had a lot of pain with the slightest movement.

It looked like an extension of an arm. A three-foot long silver metallic pole. One end a black handle to squeeze, the other a grabbing device, like an elongated lobster claw. Steve slipped the contraption from behind the boxes, held it at arm's length, squeezed the handle and watched the claw-like end open and close, a big grin on his face. *Perfect.*

Steve was glad the thing didn't flush away down the toilet. It was kind of a reflex action, see something nasty like that, heck, just get rid of the darned thing, make it disappear, make believe it didn't happen. Get back to normal.

But it did happen. It was there and what if it did flush and it populated the sewer system? The CDC would have to get involved and he could be responsible for a worldwide invasion of those things. He wasn't even sure what the thing was.

Steve's mind scrolled through all the worms, eels, and parasites he could remember from med school. It had been years since he thought about infectious disease. Seventeen years since med school graduation. An Ophthalmologist, he'd gotten pretty rusty in that department. His world revolved around eyeballs.

He really needed to figure out what this thing was. He practically gave birth to it and he felt some kind of bizarre parental responsibility. Steve smiled. It really wasn't that funny though.

Steve walked up to the covered toilet and looked at it with a new determination. He yanked on the heavy-duty utility gloves he retrieved from the garage, squeezing in, getting ready for war—his mother's gripping device in his right hand, the bucket on the tile next to the bowl.

He took a deep breath, put one foot on the toilet cover as he carefully lifted the weighted trash can and silently rested it on the counter next to the sink. He pumped the handle of the gripping device, forearm muscles flexed. Removed his foot from the toilet, arched over and pinched the edge of the toilet cover.

One, two...three.

Steve flipped the cover open, jabbed the gaping claw into the water, opening and closing, opening and closing. The thing flicked its tail, coiled, straightened, coiled, straightened. Steve finally got purchase on its midsection and held tight.

Steve leaned, lifted the bucket with one hand, brought it up alongside the rim of the bowl and in a twisting, flipping motion slammed the thing into the bucket where it made a *schluuuck* sound.

He threw the empty gripping device aside with a *clank* against the wall and let out a moan, a half grossed-out, half freaked-out sound. Almost like a squeal and even in the midst of the commotion he felt a wave of embarrassment at the noise and was glad no one else was around to hear it.

Steve made a beeline for the den, toward the hundred-gallon fish tank. He nearly tripped on the rug and stumbled toward the tank, almost knocking it over, bucket in outstretched arms. He flipped open the cover with one hand, a quick twist of the other wrist and the thing splashed into the tank. He dropped the bucket and slammed the hinged cover to the tank, sealing off the watery world.

Steve went to the bookcase against the wall and starting stacking thick medical texts on his arm, back to the tank and stacked the tomes on top of the cover, using three piles of two books across for maximum safety.

He stepped back and watched the thing sink like a weight till it almost hit bottom, then suddenly coming to life as if startled from shock. The several fish in the tank scattered under rocks, hid within plastic plants. It twisted slowly like a corkscrew, making its way into the center, then coming close to the glass, the two prominent protrusions on its head seemed to look at Steve. It pressed itself to the glass and stopped, a subtle undulating throb coursing through its body.

Then Steve felt the cramp.

Steve was back on the toilet, his abdomen slightly distended, crampy pain building, pants crumpled in a heap at his ankles. His fingertips pushed along his abdomen, performing the stool-guiding massage technique again.

Steve couldn't believe it. He hoped that this was just some left over stool backed up in his colon behind that thing. The cramping increased. The mobile phone in his pants pocket buzzed. He reached down, a sharp pain, and fished the phone from his pocket.

"Steve. Good, you're there," Sherrie said. "Listen, I've been thinking. I really want to talk to you."

"Not a good time. "

"You okay? You sound funny."

"Not really. I'm having some GI issues. I can't even begin to tell you."

"You need anything? Soup? I can come by."

"No." A bolt of pain. Something fierce. Worse than before.

"I'll bring some soup, okay?"

Steve couldn't answer. The pain stole his breath. He grunted without exhaling. He felt pressure build in his head and his gut.

"Steve?"

"Uhh."

"You okay? Steve? I'm coming over. I don't care what you say."
Click.

The bathroom turned fuzzy. The light dim, the small picture on the wall blurry. He placed the phone on the counter and forced himself to breathe, again, not wanting to valsalva.

He couldn't help it. The pain was unbearable. He forced a huge inhalation, tried to push, felt the dizziness come, rocked his head back.

"Steve! Steve!"

Steve roused, still on the bowl, Sherrie standing in front of him, shaking his shoulders.

"Huh?"

"What the hell is going on?" Sherrie looked around, taking in the gripping device on the floor, puddles of water on the tile.

Another cramp tore through Steve's gut and he groaned.

"Steve, tell me!"

"Fish tank," Steve mumbled. His head started to clear. He felt he could speak again. "Look in the fish tank. And you know what? The bucket on the floor? Bring it back. Okay?"

"What are you talking about? The fish tank!"

"Go look."

Sherrie shook her head, headed for the den. He counted off the seconds he knew it would take before she would see it.

Bingo. A loud gasp, then, "*Ewwww!* What the hell is that?"

The pain was building. He felt something brewing in his pelvis. "Sherrie?"

Sherrie appeared in the doorway holding the bucket, put it on the floor. "What in God's name is that thing?"

"I shit that monster out."

Sherrie stepped back. "What!?" She could tell he was in agony.

"Something's happening. Again." Steve felt razors in his rectum. He tried to arch down and look between his legs. He could make out a black tail protruding from his anus, about three or four inches long. Another creature, bigger this time.

The stretching started, the pain amplified. Steve groaned.

"Steve. Please tell me what's going on here! Should I call an ambulance?"

"No! Not yet!" Steve spotted the gripping device on the floor. Nodded at it. "Pick that up."

Sherrie was on automatic pilot. Things were too weird to stop and question. She just acted. She picked up the device and stood there, a bewildered look on her face.

Steve massaged his abdomen. Took slow deep breaths, twisted, bent. The ache escalated exponentially.

He looked between his legs again, the tail about six inches. Its body tapered upward and the thickest part was yet to come. Steve noticed that Sherrie was angled over too, looking between his legs. She screamed.

"Steve!"

"I know! I know!" Steve screamed back. Steve had an idea, a kind of do-or-die decision, one that throws all logic and dignity out the window.

Steve slid off the toilet onto the cold tile. He got on his back and lifted his legs. "Pull my pants off!"

Still holding the gripping device, Sherrie ripped his pants off and threw them in the corner.

Steve lay on his back, knees bent, feet on cold tile, pelvis arching skyward. Sherrie understood, got in front of him, knelt down and looked. Steve could see the flash of horror on her face.

"Grab it!" Steve shouted, his body convulsing in spasm. "Use the *thiiiing!*"

Sherrie took a moment to figure out the device, see how it worked, then started to claw at the thing until she got purchase.

"Pull!" Steve yelled, the pain exquisite.

"Push!" Sherrie yelled.

Steve had both hands on his abdomen, pushing downward for all he was worth in a wave-like motion.

The device slipped and Sherrie lurched back, got the device between Steve's legs again, got a tighter hold on the tail and pulled back, getting her weight into it.

Steve breathed, pushed. Breathed, pushed.

Sherrie pulled. "Come on, Steve!"

A blackness crept around Steve's peripheral vision. It felt as if his insides were being torn to shreds. Pins, needle, spikes and fire.

At this point, all Steve could do was groan. His heart rate was off the charts, respirations out of control. Sweat beading. He stared at the air vent on the ceiling, needing to focus.

Concentrate.

"*Arrrrrrgggggghhh!*" Steve pushed and felt the expulsion and with the release he heard Sherrie cry out as she flipped backward into the wall, the device arcing high in the air, still holding the humungous creature, which escaped the device, slammed the wall above Sherrie's head and flopped down in her lap, flipping.

Sherrie screamed and bolted upright, thrusting the thing onto Steve's legs.

Steve shot up, grabbed the device and clawed at the thing. He grabbed it hard, realized it was too big for the bucket then ran from the bathroom toward the fish tank holding the thing out front, screaming all the way.

"Steve, what the heck is going on?"

Naked from the waist down, Steve stood in front of the fish tank, panting. The gripping device in his right hand, its claw now empty, rested on the hardwood floor. He had just stacked the last of the books and was watching the massive creature he had just expulsed from his bowels. It squirmed around, seemed to check out the other smaller creature then brought its head to the surface of the water, its body hanging down in a straight line.

"I honestly don't know, Sherrie." Steve turned to look at Sherrie, as if to display his seriousness, his face blank. The sight of her gorgeous eyes overwhelmed him, as they often did, and something tingled in his heart despite what he'd just been through. He stepped closer and brought a finger to her cheek, something he hadn't done in a month.

"You okay?" Sherrie followed his lead, relaxing. "That was for sure the craziest thing I have ever witnessed in all my life."

Steve held her eyes, physically exhausted, his body ravaged. "Thank you."

"I'm really scared Steve. I think I should take you to the ER, no?"

"You saved my life, Sherrie."

"What are those things, Steve? I'm really worried."

"Some kind of parasites, I'm guessing. I was gonna call Eric after the first one. Figured a GI guy would be perfect. Then the pain came again. Thank God you came over."

"I had a feeling. Like something wasn't right. I could tell. Why don't you let me take you to the hospital?"

"I feel better now. I think I'm clear. I must be after that. I'm gonna call Eric. He'll know more. This is right up his alley."

Steve rubbed his eyes, took a breath and then remembered. *Dammit.* He was happy for a blissful moment and then reality rushed in. He recoiled and glared at Sherrie, visualizing her staring lovingly into what's-his-name's eyes.

Sherrie sensed this. "What's the matter, Steve?"

"Nothing." Steve spun and stomped toward the bathroom, to get his pants, his phone, all of a sudden feeling exposed. He couldn't help himself. It just bubbled out. "Don't you have to get back to what's-his-face?"

Sherrie chose her words carefully. "Let's not talk about that now. We have some serious medical issues going on here. Let's get you taken care of, huh?"

"Let's?" Steve found his crumpled pants, started to hop into them, his back to Sherrie, feeling uncomfortable. "Like us? I'm taken care of now, Sherrie. I'm fine. Really."

Sherrie stood, hands on hips.

Steve buttoned his pants, grabbed his phone off the counter, turned and walked past Sherrie back towards the den, to the fish tank. "Why don't you just leave?"

"Leave?" It came out louder than Sherrie expected, somewhat abruptly. "After I delivered that...that...that goddamned THING?"

"I said thanks."

Sherrie turned to follow Steve. "Thanks?"

"I didn't ask you to come here."

"You're lucky I did!"

"Lucky?" Steve was back in front of the tank. "Lucky to have you come by? Screw that. I could've handled it myself."

Sherrie came up behind him. "Right."

"Just go, Sherrie. You and that butt-ugly Clap dude are really pissing me off."

Sherrie stared at Steve's back. She took a moment. Breathed. Decided to pull back. "Okay."

"Okay?" Steve whipped round, his face red. "Just like that, eh?"

"Well. You said go!"

"Go then."

"I will."

They locked eyes. All the years of relationship bursting between them like fireworks, sizzling in the silence. All the moments, whispers, holidays, vacations, laughs, touches. Steve's eyes pleaded for things to go back to the way they were, Sherrie's eyes searched for understanding or meaning.

"Steve?" Sherrie was looking at the fish tank.

"What?"

"What the hell are those things doing?"

The larger eel-thing had just broken apart into four separate segments. Each segment dropped away and floated to the gravel at the base of the tank. The original head portion began to elongate. The smaller segments started to jiggle with movement, a new head on each slowly sprouting forth from one end, a tail from the other. After a moment, they too floated around, as if awakened from a long slumber.

"Wow," Steve said. "It's as if they're regenerating. Freaky."

"I don't like this, Steve."

"That other one there." Steve pointed to the corner of the tank, at the first creature he pooped out. "Looks twice the size, no?"

"Bigger, definitely. Steve, we have to get you to a hospital."

"I want Eric to see these. He has to." Steve pulled his mobile from his pocket and punched in some numbers.

Waited.

"Eric. Steve here. Listen, I need you to come over right away. I have a GI problem. Serious stuff."

"Like what?"

"You're not gonna believe this. Ready? I just crapped out two live eel-like creatures."

"What? Seriously? What do they look like?"

"One's a foot long, the other longer. And fat too. Serious."

"Really? Give me more, man. Distinguishing features?"

"Two eye-like things on the head. And some cilia-like stuff on its head. Segmented. Grayish-black."

"Sounds sorta like some kind of tapeworm, buddy. That scolex and sucker stuff. Just finished morning procedures. I'm coming over. Gotta see this."

Steve ended the call, put the phone back in his pocket and felt a subtle cramp. He didn't want Sherrie to see and he tried to hide it but his hand grabbed his gut and she saw.

"You feeling it again?"

"No." Steve lied. "These here bowels have been through a lot."

"Sit down."

"Eric thinks they might be some kind of tapeworms. Biggest damn tapeworms I ever heard of. I want to do an internet search."

Steve walked to the nearby study, sat at the computer. Typed in "tapeworm" and hit "images."

Sherrie stood behind Steve, hands on his shoulders. She gasped.

"Hm. Kind of looks like a tapeworm but not really." Steve studied the many images, big and small, color, black and white, lab photos and cartoons. "Ugly bastards though, huh? Up close. Damn. None are that big though."

"Where the heck they come from?"

"Who knows? Undercooked meat maybe. Fecal-oral route. Could have picked something up at the hospital."

Steve hunched in the chair, still trying to be stoic. But Sherrie saw.

"Steve, I can see you're in pain. Soon as Eric gets here we're all going to the hospital."

Steve could tell that the pain was not just a passing cramp. It was happening again. How could it? What could be left in there? He got up, knowing he should be close to the bathroom.

"Come in here," Sherrie said, waving her hand.

Steve heard her but it sounded funny. His head was fuzzy. A little dizzy. He needed to sit. Or lie down.

Steve went back to the den, in front of the fish tank. He knelt on the hardwood, sat, got on his back. He took deep breaths and admired his prized collection of worm things and in a weird way felt a pang of material pride for having carried and then delivered those wonderfully odd creatures.

He heard Sherrie say, "I think Eric's here," and she scurried away. He angled his head to look at the worms and he could see the first one, bigger and fatter now, break away into four segments, taking the total to eight.

He smiled and heard Eric say, "Where are those worms?"

"Steve, you okay man?" Eric knelt at Steve's side, rocking his shoulders.

"Guess. Yeah." Steve opened his eyes, saw Eric. He drew up his knees up and grimaced.

Sherrie stood behind Eric. "He's having pain. I think it's happening again."

"Okay," Eric said. "Steve, take slow deep breaths. We'll help you to the bathroom."

Eric started to reach for Steve's hand, then looked over at the fish tank. He sprung up. "Those are the worms?!" He said, almost shrieking. He ran to the tank. "You put them in there?"

"Yup." Steve said. "Didn't know what to do. Cool, huh?"

"Man, these are the biggest damn worm things I've ever seen or even heard of. *Holy crap,* Steve. They're like hybrid something or other." Eric thought about his comment and laughed out loud. "We gotta get them to the lab! There's a ton."

"They're growing by the minute," Sherrie said. "They break apart then grow again."

"I know!" Eric said. "That's how cestodes reproduce. They're hermaphrodites. Segmentation. Gorgeous, huh?"

"Eric," Steve said in a weakened voice.

Eric looked over, having forgotten Steve in the excitement, saw he was in pain. "Come on, Sherrie, let's get him to the bathroom."

Eric and Sherrie helped Steve up, pulled under his shoulders, guided him to the bathroom. Steve groaned and undid his pants, let them fall and got on the bowl.

"Go for it." Eric walked toward the den. "I'm gonna take another quick look at those fascinating wormy specimens."

Sherrie knelt at Steve's side. Wiped his forehead with the palm of her hand.

Steve curled his body in spasm. Winced. Then sat up again.

"I still love you, you know." Sherrie said, smiled. "Mr. Worm Man."

Steve's head was foggy. He looked into Sherrie's gorgeous eyes. He had no idea what was about to pour forth from his insides. Still, Sherrie's words sounded angelic. He tried to put Clay out of his head. Sherrie was here with him right now, at possibly the worst moment in his life. That's all that mattered. He felt the connection. That had to count for something, didn't it?

Steve's abdominal musculature tightened—rectus abdominus, serratus anterior, obliques. They clenched like a huge fist of muscle. He felt something shift in his pelvis. *Here we go.* "Back away," he said to Sherrie.

Sherrie stood, stepped into the doorframe and watched, fingertips pressed to her lips.

Steve pushed his lower abdomen, felt the pelvic muscles relax, sphincter widen. It didn't feel the same as before. Maybe not as big. Please. The pressure built. Then the release.

There was an explosive blast and loud splash. He waited. That was it? He twisted around and looked. Sherrie bent in to have a look too and she gasped.

The bowl was half-full of mini-worms. Like little babies. Maybe a hundred. They squirmed around and the mass undulated as a single unit.

"Dear God," Sherrie said.

Steve bent to pull up his pants. Eric yelled from the other room, "Guys, Come here!"

Steve and Sherrie rushed to the den. Eric had his hands on his head, fisting his hair with excitement, standing in front of the tank, as if at an altar. "Look!"

The tank was stuffed with worms. Water spilled over the sides, trickling down the glass, the books shifting position. There was no more room for the packed tank of worms. They squished against the glass, twisted and interlocked. They broke apart and regenerated rapidly even in the cramped space. Water started to pour over the sides of the tank in small waves and the cover lifted. The books started to topple over with wet clunks onto the floor.

Steve tried to catch the falling books and slipped on the hardwood. He reached out to Eric, grabbing his shirt. Eric in turn grabbed Sherrie, trying to balance, and the three of them slipped in unison and tumbled to the floor. Eric laughing. Sherrie screaming.

They tried to get their footing, slipping around, and the glass at the front of the fish tank started to splinter. Jagged cracks starbursting along the front then sweeping across the sides. It made a high-pitched sound and then the glass exploded apart under pressure to release the mass of slithering worms and water to the floor among the shards, gravel, rocks and plastic plants.

Sherrie, Eric, and Steve pawed each other, trying to get a hold of something solid, slipping and sliding, contorted, awkwardly dropping back to the floor. Water and worms rose around them, soaking clothes, turning them waterlogged and heavy. Worms flipped and flopped along their legs. Eric sat in the middle of the mess, resigned. Steve knelt, one hand on the floor, the other reaching out to Sherrie, eyes and mouth open wide.

All they could do was laugh.

Jacked

As soon as Marco emptied the dufflebag onto his old mattress he knew he was gonna have to do a blast.

The Russians were really coming through for him, sticking to their word, getting him all the gear he wanted, and at a good price too. He was gonna make some serious coin off this stuff.

The bed was littered with hundreds of bullet-sized glass vials of Deca, Primobolan, Winstrol-V, Depo-test, Dianabol, Equipoise and even some growth hormone. Stanko and his boys had also thrown in a case of D-bol tabs and some designer shit, as a kind of bonus.

Eyeing the mountain of juice, Marco stood in his posing trunks, rubbing a mixture of baby oil and skin lotion onto his shaved, bloated pecs. He smoothed the goop over his coconut-like delt, pushing some onto his twenty-inch arm, flexing his elbow which forced the bicep to peak into what looked like a chiseled triple-scoop ice-cream cone.

Staring into the massive mirror he had secured to the wall above his bed, he hit a double biceps pose, arms flexed overhead. He and his boys had stolen the mirror from a cheap motel on Long Island, sliding it into Ronny's van one night, making sure they didn't crack the thing on the way back to Brooklyn. He admired the slab of muscle in the mirror and he couldn't get over how awesome his legs looked in that particular pose—like goddamn sides of beef, he thought, the light glistening off bronzed skin.

He hit a most-muscular pose—*the crab*—forcing the veins to surge with blood, distend under pressure, and snake across his upper chest, traps, and neck. His face swelled and turned red, puffing out his eyes. He let it go, muscles starting to cramp, and savored the tangy smell of baby oil as it mixed with sweat.

He gathered the necessary paraphernalia into a neat circle at the edge of the bed:

A 3cc disposable syringe with a 22 gauge, one and a half-inch needle.

A 2cc ampule of Primobolan.

A plastic container of rubbing alcohol and some tissues.

Marco slid a wooden desk chair in front of the bed, popped the glass top to the vial and sucked out the 2 cc's of juice into the syringe. He raised the dart overhead to the light and flicked the casing, getting the air bubbles to rise, then flushed them out.

Marco stood and stepped out of the skimpy trunks, kicking them off so they ended up hanging off the dusty lampshade. He swiped his ass with alcohol and with a swift backhanded motion, buried the harpoon in his glute. He pushed the plunger, feeling the tight knot of oily goodness deep in his muscle, his head getting light.

A drop of blood followed the needle out. He dabbed at it with a ball of tissue and tossed everything onto the bed.

The rush stormed his skull, pressure building. Happened every time after a blast. He started posing again, this time with greater and greater intensity, each shot ending in a grunt, holding it, veins on the verge of exploding, blood flooding his dense muscle. Endorphins started to kick in, euphoria on the horizon.

Swinging into a back lat spread, he heard the banging.

He shuffled to the closed door, breathing deeply, a good pump going.

Marco listened for a second, said, "Fuck is it?"

"Marco Serrano?"

"Who wants a know."

"DEA.... Open up."

Marco thought he felt the room shift.

Freakin' DEA.

The Russians.

A set up?

With this much shit he would go away for a long time. Not to mention the weed in the dresser.

Looking around. "Hold on."

"Open it." The voice louder, serious. "*Now!*"

His head spinning wildly, Marco thought he could feel blood vessels absorbing the juice, sucking it up hungrily, distributing it to the far reaches of his body, heart pumping and pumping, tiny cells gobbling up the shit. His girth felt like glazed armor. He wondered if bullets would bounce off. Muscle was thick as hell, right? Maybe he should bolt, make a run for it. That meant leaving the juice behind, wasting it.

No way.

Running his hand through the top drawer of the desk, Marco found the 9 mm Beretta with a 15 round magazine and undid the safety catch.

He kissed the barrel.

The banging was louder now—people yelling, his head screaming, hot blood coursing through hammering arteries and distended veins. No way was he going back to the joint.

Now the bullhorn from a distance, a siren, some car doors slamming.

A helicopter?

Stepping in front of the mirror, Marco hit another double biceps pose, narrowed eyes focusing on the Adonis-like body in the glass— tanned, shaved, perfectly symmetric. Goddamned lines everywhere, shredded. Peaking out perfectly with the diet. Paper-thin skin. Knobby abs like concrete—obliques good enough for a medical textbook. A goddamned freak of nature, he thought and howled.

Marco's greasy hand slid around the doorknob several times before he was able to get purchase. He flung the door open to glaring light and an army of gun-wielding cops.

He heard nothing.

Feeling like Mr. Olympia on stage at the pose down, Marco stood rigid, naked and oiled, palming metal at his side. The hot light felt good, soothing. He flexed his lats, giving the crowd a good show, trying to please the judges. Now he thought he heard applause. The crowd started to roar his name. Chanting now. He took a deep breath and swung the pistol round front, aiming into the blue crowd, all the while keeping his abs tight and lats wide, curling his toes to harden the calves, figuring it was best to get in the first shot.

The Wood

"Woolly what?" I say.

"Adelgid. It's actually an insect, Doctor," the arborist, Stan, tells me. "What you see on the branches are the eggs."

He lifts a knotty segment of hemlock and holds it up for display. It's dotted with white bubbly things, following a linear pattern along the branches. They look like miniature cotton balls.

"Rather fascinating," I say. "Like tiny parasites?"

"Those bugs got a little spike on their head. Stick it at the base of the needle. Suck out all the nutrients."

"Nasty little buggers. What's the prognosis then, Stan?"

"These here trees'll all die. They're dying already. Might take a couple years. But after all the needles fall, the tree'll just die."

"That'd be a shame. They provide all my privacy."

"The needles fall out at the bottom first, then work its way up. Like yours."

"Gosh. I really need this coverage around the yard."

"Sooner or later they'll just be skeletons."

"I have to save them, then."

"We can spray 'em."

"That kills it?"

"Might work, might not. Might be too far gone. At least it'll slow it down a bit."

"What if I do nothing?"

"Just be quicker."

"I have many many hemlocks here, Stan. Three acres worth."

"We can handle that, Doc."

I survey the fifty-foot hemlocks. Once majestic, now thinning and anemic. Going bald, as if they had some sort of shrub cancer. Those skeletal trees were once full, thick, densely green. They stood like armed guards on my property and kept the world at bay. Now they were dying. All sustenance being sucked away by tiny bugs, sapping the life out of my sentinels.

I felt like crying.

"Okay then," I say. "Let's spray them."

"Righty, then," Stan says. "Mind if I ask you something?"

I shrug.

"Why you have all those sheds?" He twists his head, looks toward the backyard.

"They're not all sheds. That one there is a shed." I point. "That one is a cabana for the pool. Couldn't get it closer because of electrical and pipe issues. That one there's a home lab."

"Lab?"

"Research," I tell him, not really wanting to get into that discussion. "I analyze the molecular aspects of fracture healing. Test new surgical hardware, like fixation devices. Sometimes I practice new surgical techniques."

"Yeah?" He keeps looking at me, puzzled.

"On rats and pigs."

"Oh," Stan says. He looks goofy in his hat, the words: *LEAVZ N' TREEZ* emblazoned across the front. "What kinda doctor are you?"

"Orthopedic surgeon," I say. "So how about this spraying?"

"Sure, Doc," he says, flipping papers on his clipboard. "I'll send one of my guys over tomorrow."

As soon as Scully Dunwoody swung his truck into the driveway he knew what kind of client it was going to be. Damn driveway a mile long outlined with pristine Belgian block. He was sure the owner was gonna be an asshole.

Bingo. Sure enough, he's not in front of the mansion for three seconds when the guy comes prancing out from the house, swinging a robe in front, tying it in a big bow like a fairy. Scully thought for sure this guy must be taking it up the ying-yang, married or not.

"Good morning."

Scully snuffed the butt in the ashtray and stepped down from the truck. "Sup."

"You're here to spray the hemlocks?"

Scully thought, like, what the hell? I got a big truck with four huge containers of horticultural soap on the flatbed in full view and enough hose to wrap around this guy's little Taj Mahal twelve times and he's asking me if I'm here to spray the hemlocks? A definite asshole. All Scully could manage was, "That's right."

"Excellent. Like I told the gentleman yesterday, your boss I suppose, I have three acres worth of hemlocks and I'm quite upset about this woolly adelgid infestation."

Scully scratched his butt with one hand, smoothed back his hair with the other, almost simultaneously. He liked to do this little combination when his nerves were getting a little shot. Like when he had to deal with assholes. Sort of gave him a moment to gather his thoughts and keep the lid on things. Scully had been spraying trees for twenty years now, ever since he dropped out of tenth grade and there was no way that this skinny guy in front of him was gonna go walking around in an orange robe talking about woolly adelgid like he was some arborist or something. Probably just read about this stuff on the internet.

"Well, miiiister," and he liked to drawl in these situations. "I'm here to spray every last one of those hemlocks of yours. I got hoses that'll reach the next town over."

"Actually, that's *doctor*, not mister."

Oh, how he knew it. "Sorry, Doooctor." Scully said, like he had a marshmallow in his mouth. And then for kicks: "Well I'm Scully Dunwoody. Some people call me 'The Skull,' others, 'The Wood,' if you know what I mean." Scully winked.

"Well that's very nice Mr. Scully Dunwoody," the doctor said, furrowing his brow. "I'm Dr. Tobias Finkelstein."

Scully did everything in his power not to bust out laughing. This guy was a real piece of work. *Tobias Finkelstein.* Holy crap. Scully mumbled with a cough: "Pleasure Mister Finkelfart."

The doctor hesitated a moment before continuing. Squinted his eyes, cocked his head ever so slightly. Scully figured he better slow it down just a bit.

"That's *Doctor* Finkelstein."

"Yes sir."

"Now," Doctor Finkelstein said, cleared his throat. "Should I walk the property with you? You know, give you the lay of the land?"

"Sure, Doc." Scully smiled to himself, figuring he'd take the stupid walk. The clients never knew it didn't make one bit of difference. They all got the same crap job. He wasn't even sure if he mixed enough soap with the water in the tanks this morning, as hung over as he was.

"I wanna make sure I see everything good," Scully said, crunching his eyebrows. "Get all those hemlocks. You know, give you a real *deluxe* spray job."

"So that's the property, Mr. Dunwoody." I can tell he's half listening. The whole time this Scully guy is looking around like he has somewhere really important to be. Giving me all this wise-cracking stuff. He must really think I'm a fool.

"Sure, Doc," he says, scratching his buttocks again. Scully looks like a hobo that has just fallen off a train. Ruddy complexion with speckled freckles and liver spots under scraggly red hair. Green company polo shirt stretched over a bulbous gut, stained jeans and boots half-untied.

"Any questions," I say, "I'll be inside doing some work in the library."

"No problem, Doc," he says in the same sarcastic tone. "Think I'm good."

He lumbers to his truck.

I walk back into the house and head straight for the back window. I already see him dragging a long hose along the back path, spraying as he goes, not even reaching the tops of the trees.

I dart over to the dining room window to get a better angle and see him spraying and walking, barely getting the trees at all. He keeps looking back at the house. I figure he probably loops around a couple of times, progressively soaking the trees.

I sprint up the stairs off the study, heading up to the second floor to get a better look, ducking a little so he can't see. He sprays and walks, sprays and walks, looking back at the house more than the hemlocks.

By the time I make it to the guest bedroom across the hall, he's already heading to the other side of the property, passing behind the cabana and then the lab. I can tell there's no way he can be soaking the tops of the hemlocks with the force and projection angle of the hose.

I jog into the master bedroom in time to see him pulling back and angling around the front of the house to the other side of the property, where there are a greater number of slightly taller hemlocks. He's still looking back at the house, pulling and swinging the hose, making wide white foam arcs across the hemlocks, barely coating them. Looking like a little spritz.

I run back downstairs and over toward the gym area and squat down and peer through the window. I duck quickly because he's right outside. He's peeking through an adjacent window, into the house, as the spray shoots out in front of him. I reflexively get on a knee and finger a slat of the Venetian blind and see him moving away, hose off now as he swings around the Japanese garden and pond. He starts the hose up again and heads up toward the front, the last place I showed him. Where the hemlocks stop.

I exit the room and head over to the library and look through the front foyer out the door and see him spooling the hose back on the truck. I figure it couldn't have been more than fifteen minutes since he started spraying.

I sit at the desk in the library and see him walking to the front door, scribbling on a clipboard. I wait a moment and then head to the front foyer in time to see him walking briskly toward the truck.

I crack the front door. A slip of paper sails to the ground. "Mr. Dunwoody?"

He stops, turns. I meet him halfway on the red brick walkway.

"Doctor?"

"That's it?" I blurt, a little abruptly. My heart is racing. He has a weird look on his face.

"Gave'em a good soaking, I did."

"You were able to get the tops?" He scratches his behind again, runs a hand through his greasy red hair. "Soak all the hemlocks well?"

"Why yes, Doctor," he says, really putting an edge in the word 'doctor.' "I wouldn't lie to ya."

I realize it's just me and this Scully character standing there, alone. Something tells me to leave it be, handle it another way. No telling what this guy might do.

"Great." I force a smile. "Hey, when can I expect to see some results?"

"That stuff's working right now, Doc. Killing those little pesky insects." And now an oily grin on his weather-beaten face. "Those hemlocks should spring back to life. Fill out good in a few weeks. We'll probably have to spray'em again in the fall."

"Very well, then." I say as he walks away.

I go back into the house, my mouth is dry and my ears are red and burning.

Scully had a wise guy grin on his mug when he turned out of the driveway, hanging his head out the window, managing to plaster the mailbox handle square-on with a gooey spit wad. He cut the turn sharp, coming up on the corner of lawn, leaving a nice tire track in the plush grass. He even thought he saw one of the Belgian blocks twisted out of place.

He checked himself out in the rearview mirror and said out loud: "Later, Finkelfart!"

He cranked the radio full blast and headed to his next job.

Later in the day he dropped the truck off in the company lot and drove his baby-blue Pinto back to Flushing, Queens.

He still couldn't get Finkelfart out of his head, thinking about that asshole all day, even when he got back to his one bedroom apartment, throwing his keys and wallet onto the table by the door. He grabbed a beer from the fridge, took a long gulp and looked around at the apartment. It wasn't a mansion but it was his home. Good enough for him. Who the hell needed all that property anyway? For what?

He took a piss, grabbed a few more beers and the bottle of Johnny Walker and sat in his recliner. Scully had a new flatscreen TV, 19 inch. He was doing okay. He finally got himself hooked up to the internet too and the quality of the porn he could get now was unbelievable.

No more sneaking *Hustler* and *Swank* out of the magazine shop. He had it made. He thought maybe if life hadn't thrown him a few curves early on *he* could be the one living in that mansion. That's how life was. Couple little things and it could go a whole new way. Maybe that Finkelfart woulda been showing up at his house to spray his fucking trees.

Scully figured he got about eight more years with Leavz and Treez and then that was it. Retire and maybe set up some business of his own. Why not? Maybe Finkelfart would be his pool boy. Scully had to smile at that, seeing Finkelfart in his mind, prancing around the pool in a Speedo, saying, "Yes Master Dunwoody, what should I do now?" And then telling him to get on his knees and massage King Scully's aching feet.

Things were getting a little blurry now after the fourth shot and a few beers, feeling good, smoothing out. Scully reached in his pocket and pulled out the rock he had picked up from Finkelfart's driveway. One of the thousands that formed the gravel his truck crunched over.

He brought it to his nose, inhaled good and deep and then licked it, tasting the dirt of the mansion's driveway. He could imagine the good doctor's Mercedes driving over this very rock at some point in the past.

Now he cupped it in his fist.

He fingered the rock and aimed it at the oversized flower pot in the corner of the room. The pot that contained hundreds of rocks from hundreds of driveways. Scully flung the rock which hit the edge of the pot and bounced off into the kitchen. He figured he'd get it in the morning.

A few minutes later Scully was snoring loudly in the recliner, strands of drool draping his lips. The snores started like a purr and then turned to monstrous sounds that intermittently stopped when his breathing sucked in sharply. The noise didn't really matter though.

There was no one around to hear it.

"I would just let it go." My wife Marcy pours another glass of merlot. "What's the big deal? He sprayed the hemlocks, didn't he?"

"That's not the point," I tell her, sitting down at the dinner table and placing a napkin across my lap. "The guy did a poor job. Just sprayed like he was giving the hemlocks a little misting. I won't stand for that. He was a real wise-guy too."

"What do you expect from a tree sprayer?" Marcy says. "I'm sure you don't need a college degree for that."

"I guess. So what, though? I just say okay? Do what you want to me?" I was getting angry again. My heart speeding up. Thinking about some guy like this Dunwoody coming to my home, trying to take me for a ride.

"Well, complain then. Call the company. Tell them you want someone else to come by. Redo it."

"Yeah, but then this guy gets angry. Who knows what he'd do."

"Well, then don't call. But then you can't complain anymore. What if some hospital employee didn't do their job properly? Cutting corners and whatnot. We'd want to know, right?"

"What do you mean, we? You're a pathologist." I was smiling. "What do you know about patient care? Or clinical medicine for that matter?" She knew I was being facetious.

"Well, do what you want then. What could he do anyway?"

"I'm just so darn irritated. All I wanted was the trees sprayed well. Get those hemlocks back. Is that too much to ask? Jesus, I'm paying top dollar for this stuff anyway."

Marcy continues to eat in silence. This means that this topic has run its course.

"Okay," I say. "I'm going to call first thing in the morning."

Scully had a headache all day. He woke up in the recliner right where he fell asleep, a crick in his neck and his ass and back of his legs numb. He did the first few jobs in a daze. Luckily, there wasn't even anyone at home in the first two houses.

All he did was spray a couple of big bushes in front of the houses, then give a spritz along the front door and mailbox, to give it the insecticide smell like someone did a full spraying. How the hell were they gonna know anyway?

He was at his last job of the day when he got the call.

"I need you to swing into the office before you head home, okay Scully?"

"What for?"

"Just need to talk to you."

Scully said okay but he had a funny feeling. The way Stan's voice sounded all professional. Usually his boss kidded around a little more.

When Scully walked into the office Stan was sitting at the desk with his hands peaked in front of his nose. Looking all serious.

"Sit down, Scully."

Scully sat and tried to get a professional face on. Bracing for whatever the heck this was about.

"Scully, I got a call today from a Doctor Finkelstein. You remember him?"

"Yeah." Okay, now he knew. The asshole was being a true-to-form asshole. He'd been through this before.

"Well, he called to complain, Scully. And he said you didn't spray the hemlocks enough. But worse than that, he said that you had a real attitude."

Scully knew enough to keep his temper down in these situations. Play it cool. "Sorry Stan, but you know how these rich people are. I mean, I don't think he liked me as soon as I got out of the truck. He looked at me like I was a piece of crap. I could feel it."

"Scully, we've been down this road. Not to mention you been coming in later and later to get the truck. You're looking a little, how should I say, a little tired, Scull."

"I'm fine, man. Yeah, I been burning the candle a little, but hey. I been here twenty years. Doing a good job."

"I don't know about that, Scull. I don't know how you get through all those jobs so fast."

"I do my job good, Stan."

"We've been trying to land accounts in that neighborhood for years. Finally we tap into a great client and he's calling the next day complaining. That ain't gonna fly."

"The guy's a primo asshole, Stan."

"I don't give a crap. The guy's head of Orthopedic Surgery at Mercy Memorial. He knows a lot of potential clients in that area."

"He's still an asshole, Stan."

"Scull, Scull, Scull."

"Yeah?"

There was a long silence.

Stan looked at the ceiling, inhaled, shook his head slowly. "I'm gonna have to let you go."

"What?"

"I'm sorry, Scully. This comes right from the big bosses. Right from the top."

Scully was looking at Stan but Stan's lips were moving in slow motion. The words were coming out but he heard some underwater sounds like he heard when he went snorkeling in a pool a long time ago.

Stan kept talking and his head was nodding and his hands were waving around but Scully didn't hear anything now. Scully looked down at his own hands and they were glistening with sweat, shaking.

When Scully finally looked up, Stan was walking away, entering the big office in the corner, the door swinging closed.

Scully stood up, looked around, then left.

I was between the second and third hip replacements of the day. I figured I'd let the chief resident start the next case so I could get something to eat. I went down to the hospital cafeteria and was standing on line with my tray when I saw a flash of red hair.

It was only a glimpse because he was walking out of the cafeteria but I could have sworn it was that character tree sprayer from the other day. I paid for my food quickly and hurried into the hall but there was no one there.

I headed back to the seating area. Put my tray down. I pulled out my cell phone.

A woman's voice: "Leavz and Treez."

"Hello," I said. "I'm looking for a man. Scully Dunwoody. Is he around?"

"May I ask who's calling?"

"An old friend. John."

"Hold on please."

A minute or so passes.

"Mr. Dunwoody no longer works here."

"Really? Can you tell me what happened?"

"I'm sorry, sir. I can't release that information."

"Well that's okay. Thanks."

I sit and stare.

Scully was having fun now. He decided he'd screw with the good doctor. Teach him a lesson or two about the real world. What the doctor didn't get was that, yeah, their worlds were separated by money maybe. But there were no actual walls. Someone could walk in and out of someone else's world *just like that*. There was no physical barrier.

He took the railroad out to Long Island. Figured he'd see the doctor at his place of work. Walk around in his world. Get a feel for it. Get real close.

After he was sure the doc saw him in the cafeteria, he was gonna head for the house. Take the train out there too. Blend in. No car. Nothing to pin him down. Like a little ghost.

Mixing worlds. Jumping boundaries.

Wait for him and teach him a thing or two about the real world. Scully's world.

After the hip replacement I had an anterior cruciate ligament reconstruction and then late rounds with the residents and then it was time to head home. I took my time because Marcy had left that morning for a Pathology conference in Atlanta.

The incident with the tree guy started to bother me again. I had forgotten about it for a few hours. The fact the guy wasn't working at the place anymore. Was he fired? Because of me?

No way. Someone doesn't get fired because of one complaint. But what if he had a history? The guy seemed like a seedy character, though harmless.

But you never know.

Scully got to the house about six-thirty. Walked right up that driveway like it was his own house. No one saw him. Hell, the houses were so far apart a bomb could go off and no one would hear it.

He gave the mailbox a good kick before coming in after looking side to side. It felt good. The mailbox plopped over like Mr. Fairy Finkelfart was gonna plop. That was gonna feel good too.

When he got to the house it seemed like there wasn't anybody home. Perfect. No lights. No cars. No activity. He skulked around the house a few times, peeking in the big fancy windows. Nothing.

It was easy to get in through the back porch. Goddamn door might as well be made of paper. Pushed the thing open with one shoulder slam.

When I got to the house I knew something was wrong. The mailbox was damaged. The base was cracked and the whole structure was on the ground.

Instead of driving in, I glided past and parked the car about fifty feet beyond the driveway, along the grass shoulder. The sun was setting, and a light breeze kicking up.

I cut into the hedges along the driveway and walked along the bushes, out of sight. When I got near the house, I stopped and crouched on my haunches and watched a minute.

I couldn't believe I was doing this. A grown man, a doctor, hiding in the bushes of my own house. Worried about some sleazy tree sprayer. I was glad Marcy was away. The nerve of this guy. Showing up at work. Knocking over the mailbox. I'm sure he was just trying to scare me.

Who the hell did he think he was dealing with anyway?

Scully made himself at home, helping himself to some of the doctor's good Scotch. He made a sandwich and had some fruit too. Something he never ate. He even took a nice crap in the big-ass bathroom that was bigger than Scully's whole apartment.

He got a little bored so he went outside and went over to the shed. He had an idea.

I watched for about ten minutes and didn't see anything. I decide to approach the house. I walked around the back and that's when I heard it.

It sounded like electric hedgers. Off in the back.

I slowly stepped along the path to the shed. The sound got louder and I saw a fluttering of hemlock branches. I ducked in again and moved closer. Finally, I saw him.

Scully.

Cutting branches off the hemlocks in great arcing sweeps. This guy was out of his mind. At my house, cutting my hemlocks. My heart pounded my sternum, my breathing quickened. My palms were moist.

Goddamn asshole.

"Hey!"

The hedgers stopped.

Scully poked his head out from behind a branch, started to walk over, about ten feet away now.

"Evenin', Doc."

"The hell are you doing here, huh?"

"Don't get nervous, Doc. I'm helping you out. That goddamn spraying is worthless. Nothing saves those hemlocks. Best thing to do is cut them all down. Replant. Usually something like a Leyland cypress. Heard of those?"

"I don't give a crap what the best thing to do is. I want you out of here."

"Well I got nowhere to go, Doc. See, I got fired."

"That's not my problem."

"Yeah, it is. See, I was told you called and complained about me. That wasn't nice."

"You did a crappy job. You think I'm stupid? Some clueless doctor?"

"Well actually, I do."

"You had better leave." I fished the cell phone from my pocket. "NOW! Before I call the police."

"No police are coming, Finkelfart. You know that. Put that away. No one knows I'm here. I even took the train. I'm on foot. I'll slide in and slide out. Look like a random home invasion."

He started to walk toward me. Turned on the hedgers. I stepped back and stumbled on a root. He lurched and swung the shifting blades, cutting across my forearm. My operating arm. The phone flew into the bushes.

The shirt sleeve billowed open and there was blood.

I twisted back and crawled on hands and knees, hearing the hedgers again. Close. I started to stand and the blade caught me across the lower back and I let out a scream.

Adrenaline flooded in and mask the pain.

I rolled onto my back and kicked up and smashed his arm, flinging it back and the hedgers fell to the grass with a thud, still going, grinding in the dirt. Scully jumped on top of me screaming and swinging fists, catching me in the head. Yelling, "Hey doctor asshole! How's that now, huh? Your money gonna get you outta this now, bitch!"

I twisted my head back and forth trying to avoid the blows, bringing my hands to my face. But they kept coming. I lifted my pelvis, arching my back, sending him off balance, and when he wound up for a big slam I pushed him back and quickly slid to the side, getting out from under him.

I climbed to standing position as he reached for me, his hand snatching some fabric momentarily then sliding loose. I was up and running, as he screamed, "Get back here, bitch! Asshole Finkelfart!"

I stumbled toward the gardening shed. I got in, looked around, and lifted a pair of large pruning shears off the wall, like giant scissors. I darted from the shed and slammed into Scully shoulder to shoulder on the way out, sending both of us apart, him on his ass.

I bolted to the lab shed fifty yards away and managed to get in and flattened my back against the inside wall. I was gasping, chest heaving, tight. I heard his labored breathing as he approached. He slowed down. I could tell he was trying to be furtive. I pointed the shears ahead of me, waist level. Scully threw open the door and barreled into the shed, screaming and I leaned and thrust forward, sinking the foot-long blades deep into his upper abdomen.

He stopped short and grabbed the shears, a contorted, confused look on his face. I knew this wound was not immediately fatal. He sat down on the floor, legs crossed, almost gingerly, still staring at me, unable to speak, his wind knocked out.

I took a step back, wiped my brow, and caught my breath.

I stood, half in shock, cut and bruised, trying to get my bearings.

He finally spoke, more like a groan, "Help me, asshole."

"The hell were you thinking?" I felt like giving him a lecture. How it's bad to do bad things to people. I knew it was silly. Thoughts raced. I felt tingly.

He just shook his head, got on an elbow, then onto his back, still breathing, still alive.

He weakly pulled at the shears.

"Don't do that," I said. "You'll be dead in a second."

"Hospital," he whispered.

"Hold on," I said. My head was starting to clear and grasp the reality of the situation. There was a guy in my lab on the floor with shears protruding from his abdomen. A guy who a minute ago was trying to kill me. A guy who would kill me in a heartbeat right now if he could get up.

If I start treatment and call 911, I'll have some explaining to do. I'll say he attacked me, like he did. But if he makes it he'll have his own story. He'll twist it another way. His lawyer would, at least.

And what if he was set free? I'd have to look over my shoulder forever. Not to mention the media would have a field day with this. Doctor stabbing someone in his home lab. Who knows what people would really think? That I had a double life, some kind of freak? They'd look into my past, try to dig stuff up. They might even uncover those trysts with that male nurse a couple years ago.

Or it could be a lot easier.

"Let me get an IV in you, start some fluids before I call."

I rummaged through some drawers and found a small IV, one I use for the pigs, to keep them sedated during the experiments. I wrapped a tourniquet around Scully's arm, started the IV. Taped it down. I rummaged through another drawer, found a small bottle, got a syringe and quickly drew up the solution.

"What's that," Scully managed.

"Don't worry." I examined the syringe, flicked out some air bubbles as a matter of habit. I sunk the needle into the rubber stopper on the IV, pushed the liquid. "It's succinylcholine."

"Wha'sat?"

"You'll be paralyzed in a matter of seconds."

Scully's eyes popped in terror. His body went flaccid, as if someone pulled a plug on a blowup doll, letting the air fizzle out.

"Every skeletal muscle in your body has been paralyzed, including your diaphragm. It'll be over soon. You won't be able to breathe."

Scully stared.

"But your mental faculties are perfectly fine. You'll be aware the whole time. Isn't that a pleasant thought?"

I grinned. I concluded the chances were low, even if I got him to the hospital, that he would survive. The damage was done. But who knows? And what if he did make it? The thought horrified me more than the injection. I'm sure the piece of dirt would be back to get me. Or someone else. It was obviously his nature. I figured it was akin to involuntary euthanasia. For a good cause.

"You're a piece of dirt, Mr. Dunwoody," I said. "It's my civic duty to get rid of you. Yes, that's what I think. Sorry. You brought it on yourself. I have a large vat of hydrochloric acid here." I nodded my head toward a metallic ribbed drum in the corner.

"I use that for pigs and rats. To dispose of them after experiments. Dissolves soft tissue beautifully and effortlessly, like dropping a sugar cube in hot tea. After that, I'll run your bones, grind them up nice in this machine here. Remember? I'm an orthopedic surgeon. This is my specialty, Scully. So you kinda lucked out, don't you think?"

I thought of the shears, the punches. I smirked and held the zinger for last. Just as he started to fade a bit.

"I'll take that bone dust. Spread it at the base of these here hemlocks. A nice fertilizer. Compost of the *Common Man*. Sounds good, no? See if that works, nurse these suckers back to life, eh?"

One last smile.

Scully was turning blue.

"No one will ever know, my friend." The thought of his evil eyes flashed in my mind. The hatred in his heart.

I tilted my head, got close to him, winked. "Just you and me, Scull." Something came over me, a bizarre euphoria. I couldn't help myself. I grinned, said, "Or do you prefer *The Wood*?"

Adhesion

CHUCK FIRST NOTICED THE STRANGE PHENOMENON the first time he was getting ready to head to the yoga studio. He went to slip on his sandals in the hallway outside his apartment door and the right one wouldn't go on. His foot just nudged it away.

He stepped over to the displaced sandal, turned it right side up with a twist of his foot and toes, and tried it again, a bit more forcefully. *Wham.* It sailed across the hallway, almost down the stairs.

Inside his pint-sized Greenwich Village apartment, Chuck sat on a kitchen chair and tried to force the sandal on with his hand. The leather piece would not slip between his first and second toes. He bent forward and looked closely. Fleshy material filled the space between his first and second toes. He tried to spread the toes apart with his thumb and forefinger but they wouldn't budge.

They were fused.

Chuck pulled a second chair closer, bent his knee, and rested his foot on the chair to get a better look. He tried to separate his big toe and the toe next to it with his fingers but the toes didn't move. He tried harder. There was a slight give, a bit of a stretch, but that was it.

Now the other toes were getting a little sticky, as if there was maple syrup between his toes, drying. Chuck splayed the remaining toes. There was a tiny bit of resistance but after a moment they popped apart. He brought his left foot up on the chair too, so his knees were tucked at his chest. Those toes seemed a little sticky too, though he was able to part them.

Did he step in something? Or maybe spill something on his feet this morning? That was silly. He would have noticed.

Chuck ran through the morning in his head. It was Saturday, so he and Todd had slept in till about ten. No rush on the weekend. He made eggs for Todd, finally talking him into at least eating whites only and not those disgusting yolks. Chuck didn't eat eggs at all. His goal was to get Todd on a fully vegan organic diet like his own. He knew it would take time. Todd was still puffing away at cigarettes and also drank beer. And he wanted more tattoos. Todd was going to be a challenge.

After breakfast, Todd went to the gym over on Houston while he went to the organic market, taking his time walking along Bleecker Street on a glorious Saturday morning. They met back in the apartment after about an hour or so. Todd showered then went over to the bar to start his shift. He'd be gone all night.

Chuck was supposed to teach his yoga class at 1:30 and *boom*, fused toes. He began to wonder if he should get someone to cover his class.

He stared down at his feet. He lowered his left foot back to the floor, then with thumb and index finger, grabbed the right big toe with his left hand and second toe with the right. He pulled apart hard, steady but firm. He kept the pressure up. His forearm muscles cramped and his thumbs started to hurt.

The tissue between the two toes stretched, fanned out, started to look like a web. He kept the pressure on and it started to give. The tissue fissured at the top then he really ramped it up and then *riiip*. The rest of the tissue came apart in one shot.

Chuck froze. Waited. Expecting blood to pour forth or incredible pain to set in. There was no blood. No pain. He took a breath and saw that the rest of his toes on that foot were fully fused now.

"Yes, *fused*." Chuck was on the phone with Todd.

"Chuck," Todd said. "I don't know what to tell you, babe. Maybe you should go to the ER."

Chuck had called the yoga studio and asked one of the other instructors to cover him. He stood at the kitchen counter, scooped a tablespoon of green grass extract into a blender, mixed with flax seed powder, spring water and some other organic supplements.

"Well, at this point I think it might be silly," Chuck said. "They won't think it's an emergency. Hold on." Chuck revved the blender and let it run for five seconds. "They'll probably give me a hard time. They usually make you wait unless you're bleeding to death or standing there cradling an armful of your own intestines. Or someone else's."

"That's gross, Chuck." Todd had the phone pressed against his ear and shoulder while he filled a pint glass slowly with Guinness. "You're probably going to have to see someone at some point."

"Don't you know some doctor guy who comes into the bar there?"

"Think he's a cardiologist. Haven't seen him in a while anyway. If I do, I'll ask."

"You're the best. Love ya. I'm gonna take a bath." Chuck poured the contents of the blender into a tall glass. "Think I need a good soak."

"Sounds good. Call me after."

Chuck drained the last bit of his green concoction with a long swig and immediately washed the glass, drying it and putting it in the small cupboard, positioning it upright, being careful not to touch any adjacent glasses. He couldn't stand the way Todd put dripping wet glasses back in the cupboard, rim down, which certainly made it dirty. All the glasses scattered haphazardly. He told Todd to just leave the dishes for him to take care of. He wiped the counter, folded the dishcloth neatly and set it down. He dried his hands on the separate hand towel hanging on a hook.

He hobbled over to the bathroom, taking note of how difficult it was to walk without flexible toes. Chuck was always reminding his yoga students that the human body was a fascinating, intricate machine. That's why mind/body harmony was so important. Honestly, it was a wonder that more things didn't go wrong more often. Chuck hoped the bath would loosen him up.

Chuck loved baths. Especially in his old-fashioned clawfoot tub. This was certainly one of the best things about the apartment and he was sure it was an antique, probably worth some money. The tub practically filled the tiny bathroom. A sink and toilet were stuffed against the opposite wall, facing each other, so small that your knees would touch the cold metal pipes under the sink when you sat on the toilet. But hey, he had the apartment of his dreams, right on Mac-Dougal Street in the heart of the Village.

Chuck spun the faucet handles, a little cold and a lot of hot. He added a pinch of bath salts and poured in a healthy dose of lavender oil and organic bubble bath. Chuck undressed, folded his yoga gear into a neat pile and rested it on top of the small bamboo shelf tower.

He stepped into the water, savoring the hotness enveloping his feet. After a moment, he squatted and splashed some water on his face and shoulders. He smoothed back his shoulder-length brown hair.

Suds began to rise and he lowered himself into the bubbly warmth. He reclined, the skin of his back meeting metal, legs outstretched, water splashing down on his feet. The water level rose slowly. After a minute, satisfied with the chest-high water and suds, Chuck spun the faucet handle with his feet. The water tapered off to a trickle then stopped. He rested his arms across the smooth top of the tub edge, tilted back his head, took in a prolonged deep diaphragmatic breath, exhaled slowly, and moaned. *Ahhhhhhhh.*

Apart from an occasional car horn or siren, there was peaceful silence in the bathroom. His muscles fully relaxed in the tub. Eyes closed, body encased in warmth, Chuck let his mind open, attempting to enter a meditative state.

He tried to wiggle his toes and they weren't moving much yet. He decided to give it some time. Let the soothing bath water perform its wonders.

He thought about Todd at work, chatting with all those people, laughing, serving drinks. Being all funny as usual. Star of the show.

That was Todd. He was so much younger and Chuck really hoped that he looked at the relationship as seriously as he did. Full commitment. Life long.

It did bother Chuck that Todd didn't want kids. *Yet*, he said. He figured he'd come around eventually. Get all the bullshit out of his system. Adoption was so difficult these days and it was probably better they waited, when they both were a bit more settled, emotionally and financially.

They were kind of opposites, weren't they? But opposites attract. And they did have some common ground. They both liked Thai food. And they both just loved the movie *Dirty Dancing*. Nobody puts Chucky in the corner. He loved when Todd said that.

Chuck felt himself drifting off.

He gave in.

Chuck's eyes flew open and for a moment he didn't know where he was. Bathroom. The bathtub. Yes. The water had cooled a bit. Using his elbows, he slid his butt back a few inches.

He bent his elbows, put his hands on the top edge of the tub. Pushed and went to stand but he couldn't. He couldn't bend his knees.

He let go of the tub, sunk his hands in the water, rubbing and feeling over the top of his legs. He couldn't believe it. No way.

His legs were fused together from crotch to toes. Chuck frantically swiped at the suds on the water's surface, trying to get a look, he couldn't see anything. He leaned so he fell into the familiar seated forward bend position, whispered, *paschimottanasana*, and tried to focus. Feeling around the tub base, he found the little chain and pulled the plug and the water started to drain.

Chuck tried to spread apart his legs, couldn't. Bend his knees again, couldn't. Ran his fingers along the valley between his legs, felt a fleshy connection. Pushed at his legs with his hands. Nothing.

The water level lowered to the tops of his knees. Some sudsy remnants rested on top of his thighs, like sea foam.

Then the water was gone. There was a slurping sound as the last bit of water was sucked into the drain. Chuck sat in the empty tub, a chill setting in, staring at his legs.

The phone. Where was the phone? He needed to call Todd immediately. He kept trying to push his legs apart. Nothing. *Where the hell was the phone?* He reached and whipped a towel from the rack on the wall. Patted down his body. Dried his legs, swiping away small patches of suds.

He had to get the phone. In the kitchen—yes, that's where it was.

Chuck tried to push up and stand but every time he pushed his heels slid along the slick tub. He twisted his body so his chest faced the right side of the tub. He closed his eyes for a moment and thought, *modified Ardha Matsyendrasana? Forget it, go on.*

He draped his left arm over the side, hugging the tub. With some effort he managed to flip his lower body over, so he was facing down. He clawed and pushed with his hands, coming up on his chest, then dragging his stomach over the side so that he was angled over the tub.

He got his hands on the floor, palms on the throw rug. He swiped the rug away, got better purchase on the cool tile.

Chuck wriggled himself over the edge. First the thighs, his knees, then shins. The pressure on his shins hurt. He moved a little more onto the front part of his ankle. In one quick motion he flipped his feet off the edge and his lower body slapped down onto the tile. That hurt. But he was free now.

Kitchen.

Chuck thought for a moment, about the best way to move. He pulled his way through the bathroom door out into the carpeted hall on his stomach. He thought about pulling himself to a standing position but his feet were pointed down and wouldn't bend. Would be hard to hop like that. He sat up, his back toward the kitchen. In staff pose position. *Yes of course, Dandasana.* Using his hands, he pushed his body up and shifted his butt backward.

Push slide. Push slide.

Chuck thought that this was one of the few times when having an apartment the size of a closet was an advantage. He tried to laugh at the thought. He slid into the kitchen, rested there a moment, then pulled a chair alongside the counter.

He turned on his side, then stomach. He stuck his feet in the space between the lower counter edge and the floor. He did a push-up and walked his hands back. He bent at the waist, forming an inverted "V," mimicking the downward-facing dog.

He balanced on one hand and lifted the other onto the chair top. His hand was a little too close to the edge because when he pushed off with the other hand the chair flipped to the side and he came down hard on the wooden chair leg. He thought he heard a rib crack.

He took a moment, regrouped, felt his ribs and figured it was probably just bruised. He turned the chair upright, this time wedging it against the table and the counter. He repeated the hand walk maneuver, wincing in pain, and got both hands on the chair, finally.

He pulled himself forward, twisted in one quick motion and got into a sitting position on the chair, only his legs were sticking straight out.

He could see the phone on the counter, within arm's reach.

"Slow down Chuck. Tell me what happened."

"It's not just my toes anymore Todd it's my legs now too they're fused together just like the toes were and I'm stuck together and I can't walk and I'm crawling all over and I look like a goddamn mermaid!"

"That's crazy Chuck. This whole thing is crazy."

"Yes! My legs are stuck together!"

"*Jesus.*"

"You really need to come home, Todd. Now. I don't know what to do."

"Okay okay."

"Now!"

"Okay. It's gonna be tough—we're getting slammed. But I'll be there. Let me talk to Ron."

"Hurry. Please hurry."

Chuck sat in the chair for a few minutes, legs out like two by fours, but his muscles cramped and he lowered himself to the floor.

He sat there waiting, cold, naked and alone. He teared up once, just for a moment, out of frustration and confusion. *What was happening to him? Did he have a disease?* He kept trying to push and pull the legs and toes apart but they wouldn't move. Even the toes he ripped apart earlier he couldn't budge. Even after the bath.

Todd came barreling through the door like a tattooed bull, looked around and saw Chuck sitting on the kitchen floor. Naked. He ran over to him and knelt at his side.

"Oh my God, Chuck."

"I know. Can you get me some clothes? I'm freezing."

"Sure." Todd jumped up, went into the small bedroom and rummaged around. Ran back to the kitchen with an armful of clothes.

Chuck pulled a T-shirt from his arms and swung it over his head. He realized that underwear and pants were useless.

"Crap," Chuck said. "Not going to be able to get any pants on. Get that big towel we use to sit on in the park. It's in the closet."

Todd darted to the closet, found the oversized striped towel, grabbed it and unfolded it as he walked, shook it out. "Here." He draped it over Chuck's legs. "You look so uncomfortable. I'm so sorry."

"Sorry for what? You didn't do it." Chuck started to wrap the towel around his waist. "Help me."

Todd bent over, lifted Chuck a little to get the towel around and tucked under. "Should we call 911?"

"Don't think so. This is weird but it's not a life or death emergency. At least not yet. Let's cab it."

"St. Vincent's?"

"Yeah. How we gonna do this?"

"I'll carry you, come on." Todd dug both his hands into Chuck's armpits and lifted him up. Put him on the counter. He turned around, his back to Chuck. "Get on."

"Seriously?"

"Better idea?"

Chuck shifted forward on the counter, legs straight out.

"Here." Todd shimmied back. "Just swing your legs to the side."

Chuck wrapped his arms around Todd's neck. Todd hooked his arm around back, got under Chuck's legs.

"Let's rock," Todd said.

"You're choking me," Todd said after the first of five flights of stairs.

"Sorry." Chuck eased his grip.

Chuck was as awkward to carry as a mattress, stiff as box springs. The staircase was narrow and creaky. At the bottom of the second flight, Todd slipped on a loose piece of carpet and nearly fell. They had to stop a moment to rest.

Half way down a couple was walking up the stairs and they just smiled as Todd and Chuck squeezed by, keeping their eyes on the stairs.

Todd was huffing and Chuck couldn't help himself. "This would be a heck of a lot easier without those cigarettes." He immediately regretted it.

Todd stopped in his tracks, drew in a deep breath but decided to say nothing. Chuck thought he heard a growl.

After a minute Chuck said, "Sorry."

They finally made it down to the first floor landing. Todd leaned back, put Chuck down on the steps for a few minutes to get his breath. When Todd was ready again, he said, "Let's go."

Chuck got back on and they clumsily angled their way through the front door and down the two steps to the sidewalk. Todd carried Chuck to the corner of MacDougal and Bleecker.

The streets were crowded. Most people passed by without so much as a nod. It was the city, after all. Finally a cab came down the street and slowed, took a look and kept driving.

"Jerk," Todd called down the street.

Another cab followed. This one slowed then stopped.

Todd pulled open the door, said, "Sorry. We have a medical thing here." Todd backed Chuck into the rear of the cab. Chuck sat long way across the seat in his multicolored towel.

Todd got in the front, next to the driver. "St. Vincent's."

The cab sped off.

"Jesus," Chuck said from the back seat after several blocks. "Look."

Todd craned his neck. Saw Chuck holding up both hands. All the fingers were fused. His hands looked like little flippers.

Chuck could see the cab driver's small dark eyes in the rearview mirror, darting from the street to the mirror, over to Todd, back to the mirror and then back to Chuck. When Chuck held up his hands the driver nearly veered off into a parked car on 6th Avenue.

"Whaaas that?" the cabbie said.

"Just my hands," Chuck said.

"A medical thing," Todd said.

"A disease like?" The driver slowed.

"I don't know!" Chuck yelled, surprising himself.

"You don't yell at me, son!" The cab came to a screeching halt. "You get out now! Go on, get out! No good!"

"Wait!" Todd yelled. "We're just a few blocks away!"

"Pleeease!" Chuck smacked the top of the seats with his flippers.

"Don't touch!"

"Come on!" Todd said.

"Out!" The cabbie ripped the keys from the ignition, opened his door, and lurched out. "I'll call police!"

"You suck!" Todd smashed his fist on the dash, swung open the door and got out. "You're gonna burn in hell!"

"Out! You bad disease!"

"Get me, Todd!" Chuck hammered the inside of the door with both feet.

Todd threw open the rear door, backed up toward Chuck. "Come on." Todd yanked Chuck across the seat by both feet.

Chuck was able to get his flipper-hands around Todd's neck but it was more difficult without bendable fingers. Chuck's legs jutted along the side of Todd's body. Todd hooked his hand under, lifted and stood.

Todd stepped forward and the towel snagged the door handle and as Todd and Chuck moved away the towel ripped off completely.

"The towel!" Chuck said.

Todd spun to see the towel dangling from the door into the street. Todd also saw the contorted face of the cab driver, glaring over the roof of the cab at Chuck's legs. He dove into the cab.

"Bad disease!" The cabbie gunned the engine and the cab roared away, dragging the towel. Todd stood there looking down the street, a small crowd watching them. "Asshole!"

"Come on Todd!" Chuck said. "Just go."

Todd started to gallop up 6th Avenue, Chuck naked except for the T-shirt, popping up and down on his back as if on a horse, his flipper-hands wrapped around Todd's neck.

Todd knew he had to get Chuck to the hospital. He leapt off curbs, side-stepped pedestrians and darted across streets. He heard a few shouts as he passed and pushed at the crowd and he wasn't sure if they were calls of support or horror. He did not care.

He stumbled through the automatic doors at the hospital into the waiting room of the Emergency Department. He went right to the woman at the window. She bolted up at the sight of them, buzzed the door and called for help.

Another woman, a nurse, met them at the door and ushered them to a small cubicle with an empty stretcher. She asked questions along the way. *What happened? Are you in pain? Has there been trauma, loss of consciousness?*

Todd backed up to the stretcher, panting heavily, let Chuck's butt rest on the sheet and went to let him go but he couldn't. Chucks forearms were fused to the skin at the front of Todd's neck, and Todd's right forearm was fused to Chuck's knees.

"I can't move, Chuck."

"I know, I know. My hands are stuck to you. Your arm. It's stuck around my legs."

"Just pull a little."

"I am. It won't go. Pull your arm away."

"I'm trying."

"What's happening?" the nurse said.

"I'm fused to Todd," Chuck said. "Same thing that happened to my legs and fingers."

"Let's pull, Chuck."

"I'm trying!"

"Wait, wait. Concentrate on the arms first."

"Should I call the doctor?" The nurse said.

"Yes! Now!"

The nurse left.

"Come on, Chuck. Let's do the hands. You push out and I'll keep the skin down with the other hand. Ready?"

"Go."

"Pull!"

They pulled and pushed. Nothing happened.

"Wait wait," Chuck said. "I did this with my toes. Just push and hold for as long as you can. Go."

Chuck angled his arms up and away. Todd lifted his chin in the air, leaned back, flattened the skin of his upper chest.

"I feel it."

"Keep going."

Todd's skin tented away from his neck and sternum, then a sound like Velcro splitting apart.

"Pull!"

They held tight, both huffing and turning red. Finally, something gave way, then came the sound of shredding apart.

"ARRRRRGGGG!" Todd yelled as Chuck's hands came free. Todd sunk down, ducked under the loop of Chuck's arms, fused at the hands, one on top of the other.

Todd angled away, anchored to Chuck's legs by his fused arm. He swiped at his neck and chest, chin-tucked to have a look. "Oh, man!"

Chuck looked too. "I'm so sorry, Todd."

"Not your fault, Chucky, but *ouch.*"

Todd had lost the top layer of skin where Chuck's hands came away, leaving marks that looked like burns. Tiny flecks of blood speckled the rawness.

"Let's do the arm before I change my mind," Todd said.

Todd twisted so he had a better angle to pull. "Ready?"

"I guess."

"Push your legs down."

Chuck pushed his fused hands down on top of his fused thighs. "Okay."

Todd pulled his arm and hand away, pushed down on Chuck's thighs with his free hand. The skin of his palm and undersurface of his forearm stretched.

They had a better angle than with the neck. They both held pressure and felt the skin start to yield. They held tight, pulled harder and *riiiiiip.* Freedom.

Todd backed away, breathing in forcefully, trying not to let Chuck see the pain. Chuck flopped back into the pillow, his looped arms overhead.

The nurse and a young doctor rushed into the small cubicle, swinging the curtain away and noted Todd and Chuck.

"*Whoa,*" the young doctor said.

When the chief of surgery walked in, Todd was sleeping in the chair next to Chuck's bed.

Chuck could sense the doctor, but couldn't see him. The thin layer of skin over his eyes allowed for vague shadows only. The doctors wanted to leave that procedure for last, given the delicate nature of the surgery.

Chuck could hear, although there was slight muffling due to the small tubes that protruded from his ear canals, to prevent further fusion. Small tubes also crawled from his nostrils, to prevent closure, and the mouth guard kept his lips apart and he could speak, awkwardly, but he could get his point across. He had eternal cotton mouth and Todd fed him ice cubes all day.

He had a urinary catheter and a rectal tube in place to prevent occlusion and keep a direct connection between his insides and the world outside.

He looked like a starfish, lying in his bed. Chuck's arms and legs were wrapped and separated. Fingers and toes were wrapped individually to prevent contact. The surgical team had spent hours slicing and separating his body, almost as if they were sculpting him from a giant ball of flesh.

"Good morning, Chuck." The doctor stood at the foot of the bed. Todd stirred and sat up.

"Heddo," Chuck said.

"Any news?" Todd said.

"Biopsy results are in and it seems your collagen is in overdrive," the doctor said. "It's something we've never seen before. The molecules are much more metabolically active and replicate at a phenomenal speed. And each time they are disrupted, the process of healing results in an even stronger bond."

Chuck mumbled and it sounded like, "Why?"

"Not sure," the doctor said. "Seems to be an autoimmune response. Some kind of rare connective tissue disorder. Your sedimentation rate is off the charts and some other blood work is abnormal. We're hoping that by discontinuing your organic diet and extensive intake of herbal supplements, we can bring you back to normal."

"You think all those pills and powder he takes might have something to do with it?" Todd said.

"Possibly," the doctor said. "Interestingly enough, test results have improved slightly since Chuck has been here, on good old hospital food and IV hydration."

Todd tried not to but he couldn't help but laugh.

Chuck gurgled something incomprehensible.

Balls to the Wall

"THE HECK IS IN THIS STUFF?"

"Yo," Tank Top Tony said. They were in Tony's Bensonhurst third floor walk-up. "Like I told ya. The best juice around, brudda."

Joey threw his arm up, fist clenched, the twenty-one inch bicep popping. He admired it as if it were some object, some sculpture, just presented to him for evaluation. "Cause I ain't never made gains like this. Not even with growth."

"Hell yeah, bro," Tony said. "The Russians makin' this wonder drug in some lab. From scratch."

"Cool," Joey laughed, said, only half-kidding. "Make sure you throw an extra box in there, huh?"

"No friggin' way." Tony counted the last of twenty boxes of myovar. Each box was slightly smaller than a pack of cigarettes, held three glass vials, each vial containing two cc's of myovar. "These guys're all over me, Joey baby."

"Man, I'd kill for the recipe. 'Specially with all the shows coming up." Joey swung both arms high, hitting a double bi shot. Checking himself out in the full-length mirror on Tony's closet door. "Stuff's expensive, bro."

Tony shrugged. "The hell you want me to do? Get yourself a gay-ass sponsor."

"Yeah right, man." Joey said. "I got a better idea."

"Can't wait." Tony lifted the cardboard box loaded with myovar off his bed, plopped it on the hardwood floor against the radiator under the window.

"Dude. You know these guys. Where the lab is. Hook me up. You don't have to do a thing."

"Huh? No way." Tony raised a blender full of frothing white liquid to his mouth, took a swig. "They find out, I'm a dead man."

"Tell me where it is. How to get in. I do it myself. No one else involved to screw it up. I get caught it's only me—gimme a sip a that crap."

Joey pulled a long swallow from the glass pitcher, taking his time.

"I don't know man. Don't sound too good."

"Come on." Joey rested the pitcher on the wood dresser top, smoothed back his hair. "I make it look like a big job. Looking for money, the whole thing. They'll think it was a bigger job than it is. Maybe even an inside job. Just get me in."

Tony reached, plucked a box of myovar from the pile on the bed, twirled it around his fingers.

"I gotta win that show. Tony baby, whattaya say?"

"Why should I risk it?"

"One paisan to another."

Tony shook his head. "You're Sicilian. My family's from up North."

"So what?"

Tony took a deep breath. Started stuffing boxes of myovar into Joey's gym bag, staring ahead hard.

Joey leaned on the dresser, regarded Tony.

The D train to Coney Island screeched the elevated subway tracks three blocks away. They waited for it to pass, the sound peaking out, then fading.

"Queens," Tony said finally. There was a sharp edge to the word, like he spit it out before he could change his mind. "And I don't know you. We never talk again."

"Serious?" Joey's face lit up like a lamp, big grin on his mug. "Youdabest, my man."

"I'll give you the security code, the time to go. Directions. It's over by the Queensborough Bridge."

Joey spun to the mirror with his grin, fists pinching hips, hit a lat spread, back flaring like pterodactyl wings. He released with an exaggerated exhalation, slapped Tony on the back. "The heck is your name again?"

Joey cruised the BQE north from Bensonhurst in his white 78 Corvette. He clamped the wheel hard with swollen fists, rode the speed limit, steady, not wanting to attract any attention. The flickering Manhattan skyline to his left always got him revved up. The city that never sleeps, baby. It was 2 a.m. He was in game mode—just like a contest.

He checked the directions he had scribbled on a piece of paper, then tossed it to the passenger seat, thinking the whole score should be quick and easy. After all, he knew the code and where the stuff was stored. He knew Saturdays were the one night operations shut down early at the lab, giving people a chance to enjoy themselves for a change. The lab should've been empty for hours by now.

He looped onto the LIE and headed west a short distance, toward Manhattan. He got off on Van Dam Street in Sunnyside, Queens. He crawled along 31st Street, crossing over 48th Avenue, digging the hum and strength of the engine. Navigated his way through empty backstreets, mostly factories and storage places, finally finding the street.

He drove the length of the block, wanting to drive by for a look, nothing too obvious. He spotted the address, a freestanding building next to a carpet warehouse.

Joey read the sign out front, CYTOHEME, INC. Trying to come off as a real lab. *Riiiight.* Supposed to be a place for standard blood work, pathology and routine lab tests. Joey grinned as he rolled by—knowing what really went on in there.

He parked the car two blocks away, walked, an empty gym bag slung over his massive delt.

He punched the security code at the back door, looking around, thinking this was so easy, candy from a baby. He'd get himself stacks of myovar. Mountains of it. He'd be good for a year, maybe two. Hell, the Russians might not even notice any missing if there was as much in the joint as Tony said.

The door sprung open right on cue. He glanced around, stepped in, gently closed the door. He was in a small anteroom, a place to hang coats, drop stuff off, he guessed. There was another door in front of him, just like Tony said.

He opened it, peeked in. It looked like the business end of the operation, but smelled like a doctor's office. Even though it was dark he could tell there were desks, computers, cabinets and some bookshelves. Just like Tony said. He stepped in, let the door click shut, dropped the bag on a table.

And that's when the lights blinded him.

It took a second for his vision to clear. Wouldn't you know it. There was Tony standing in the center of the room, smirking, three other guys with him. Two of the guys fisted black shiny pistols.

Joey took a breath, felt some adrenaline kick in. Figured, dang, all I did was stroll in. I didn't take nothing yet. I'll tell 'em Tony was just foolin' around. A gag.

"Tony," Joey said. "What up, bro?"

"Hey, Joey."

"What the heck's goin' on?"

"You know what's goin' on."

"Not exactly. Tell 'em we were just foolin' around, bro. You dared me to come, right? I said, no way. I wasn't gonna steal nothing from these guys. Tell 'em, man."

"Joey Joey Joey." Tony shook his head. "You're a dumb bastid. Always were."

"The heck you talking about? Tell these guys who I am, my paisan brother."

The serious-looking guy in a suit stepped forward, cigarette dangling from his lips. "No. Let me tell you who *I* am." The cigarette dropped to the floor, mashed it. "Stanko Vasilev. This is my lab you apparently stumbled into. I am the owner and founder of this great company. I make myovar. Lots of it. I understand you like my myovar, yes?"

"Yeah." Joey relaxed a bit. This wasn't sounding too bad. Yet. "The stuff is great Mr. what? Vatsolef? Yeah, your stuff is the bomb and I love it. That's why I came here. I'm crazy about it. The best shit ever. I was just out of my mind. Crazy. Don't know what got into me. I apologize, sir."

"I see," Stanko said. "Then you meant no harm? You just wanted a great steroid? You would go to great lengths to get it, no?"

"That's right. Yup. I wasn't in my right mind. Tell em, Tony. I forced Tony to get me in. My fault all the way."

Stanko circled Joey. Studied him up and down. "What are you, six-foot, 240?"

"Close. Five-eleven, 245."

Stanko rubbed his chin.

"I'm sorry, Mr. Vatsolef," Joey said. "I'll just buy the myovar like I'm supposed to. Maybe I gotta get a sponsor, huh?" He shot a stupid look in Tony's direction. "Right, Tony?"

Stanko stopped in front of Joey, eye to eye, about two feet away now. The two guys with pistols stepped around, flanking Joey. They reeked—a combo of crappy cologne, smoke, and liquor.

"I have a deal for you, Joey," Stanko said. "Because you like myovar so much. See, the reason it is so good is because extensive research went into designing it. It's not like other anabolic agents. It's very unique. We have done our homework. And the research never ends as we fine-tune this phenomenal drug. It is not exactly perfect— yet. But close."

"Yeah, I'll take it," Joey said. "I been on your myovar a couple months now anyway. I'll let you monitor me. Just like a lot of docs do. That's cool. I even got a big show coming up, Mr. Tri-State. Gonna need a lot a juice."

"Perfect," Stanko said. "Only the monitoring is a little more involved than blood work. My scientists need more. They'd like tissue samples of subjects in various stages of usage. We need to look at certain bodily responses, histologic changes, the gamut of endocrine interactions."

"The heck does that mean? Tony? What do you mean, sir?"

"For starts," Stanko said. "My head investigator indicated he needs a sufficient sample of seminiferous tubules, and as a bonus he'd like some epididymal tissue."

"Freakin' what? Semitubes?"

"Joey." Stanko was dead serious. "He'd like a testicle."

Joey backed up. The pistol guys got close, had the metal at his head now.

"Come on, guys," Joey said. "I'll give some blood, that kind a thing. I'll work with ya. That's all you'll need, right?"

"Relax, Joey," Stanko said. "We're not complete barbarians. We are going to do this the proper way. The way a good controlled experiment should be done. There is an operating room downstairs. We have a complete staff—nurse, anesthesiologist, urologist. And guess what? We'll even give you a prosthesis."

"A who?"

"A fake testicle. Only it'll be better than that. It will be complete with tracking device. So we can be sure you don't miss any of your follow-up appointments."

"No way!" Joey squirmed, pumping fists, veins rising on his neck.

"Yes, Joey. And this is just the beginning. I don't know what my scientists may need next. They were saying something about pituitary tissue. But don't worry—we have a good neurosurgeon on staff too."

"Get me outta here! Tony! What the hell?"

"And you won't think about seeing another doctor. The prosthesis is a deluxe model. I will have the capability to detonate the testicle any time. Remotely. At my leisure."

"Screw that!" Joey swung wildly at Stanko, missed. One pop with the butt end of a pistol sent Joey to his knees, head spinning. The other guy clocked him once more for good measure, bringing Joey to his stomach, unconscious.

Stanko stepped back, glanced down at Joey, fished in his pocket.

"Tony...." Stanko lifted a cigarette to his mouth and fired it up. "Tell them we're ready downstairs."

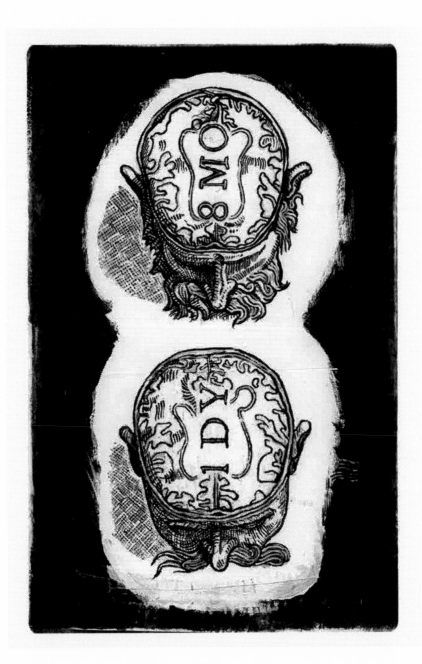

Gyrographia

ALAN STARED AT THE NUMBER AND LETTERS formed by the con-
voluted gyri along the surface of Mr. Bloomfeld's cerebral hemi-
sphere. He shook his head, squeezed his eyes shut, and massaged
them with his thumb and forefinger. He had a minor headache,
something that was happening more and more frequently lately.
Stress? Dehydration? Fatigue? Maybe he just needed new glasses. Or
was just exhausted.

It was late afternoon and Alan had been reading MRI's and CT
scans all day. Earlier he performed three lumbar punctures—two
for myelograms and one for drainage in an 86 year-old woman with
hydrocephalus. The drainage was challenging and took twice as long
as usual. She was osteoporotic and he couldn't make out any land-
marks given she had a spine like a pretzel. A half eaten pretzel practically made of stone.

He scrolled through Mr. Bloomfeld's brain MR images again.
Whipping the mouse up and down, the images scrolling so fast it looked
like a movie. He stopped on the key image. *Yes.* There it was again.

The swirling patterns of grey matter perfectly formed the
number *1*, followed by the letters *DY.* The involved gyri also appeared
a shade darker than the surrounding tissue, making it stand out even
more. He could only discern the number and letters on the sagittal
images, from the side, although when he cross-referenced it with the
other planes, he could see the darker gyri sliced perpendicularly and
top to bottom, so he was convinced it couldn't be an artifact.

The MRI machine was new. Well, new to the hospital, installed two weeks ago, but it was purchased used, a refurbished unit from St. Louis, at a significant cost savings to the department.

Alan knew that seeing images within images is not that unusual in Radiology. Some of the big journals even dedicated a special section to this, presented in a lighthearted manner—a puppy or sunset or spider within the images of an MRI, ultrasound, or CT scan.

But those images were different, rendered by a curious accident of lines. Shadows and curves of normal anatomy arranged to create something else by chance. An illusion.

How many times has an image of Jesus or the Virgin Mary been reported in something like a grilled cheese sandwich, a potato chip, in a window or even on an iron?

What Alan saw was different, evident over several images in different planes. The odds that perfectly formed random numbers and letters were created by chance? No way.

Alan decided to get some history. All the tech note said was, "r/o mets." The scan was just completed so he was certain Mr. Bloomfeld would be over in the holding area, waiting for transport back to his room.

Alan headed to the reception desk out in the hall, saw a few charts stacked on the counter and several patients waiting in the holding area. Two stretchers and one wheelchair lined in a row. He opened Mr. Bloomfeld's chart—82-year-old male with lung carcinoma. Alan checked the labs and doctors notes and concluded Mr. Bloomfeld was pretty sick. At least his brain was normal, well, except for the 1DY.

He scanned the holding area. Only one patient was male, on one of the stretchers. From the desk, he could make out an emaciated man with an oxygen mask. Thick tangled and matted silver hair. IV hanging, snaking under the white blanket tucked up at his chin.

Alan walked over, held out his hand. "Hello, Mr. Bloomfeld. I'm Dr. Jacobs." Alan noted Bloomfeld's hand. A slight tremor. Knarled, knobby joints under paper thin skin, a roadmap of light blue veins.

Bloomfeld narrowed his eyes. "Must not be good."

"Nothing like that, sir." Alan reflexively adjusted his tie. "I'm a Radiologist. I was looking at your MRI. Looks fine."

"Well that's something."

"Sure is."

"You know I'm a retired neurosurgeon?"

"Seriously? No. I didn't know that. Know your way around a hospital then."

"Yes." Bloomfeld looked away in thought. "Been inside thousands of brains too."

"I bet. When'd you retire?"

"Five years ago."

"Really? Impressive."

A transporter came by and wheeled one of the patients away. The conversation halted until they were gone, Alan having to step aside for a moment to make room.

"Now I'm awaiting my death," Bloomfeld said.

Alan laughed, thrown off a bit.

"May seem funny to you. But it's true."

"No. Not funny, sir. Just caught me off guard."

"Yeah, well. No one here gets out alive."

"Huh?"

"An old song, I think."

"Yes. You're right."

"*Five to one. One to five. No one here gets out alive.*"

"That's it. The Doors, I think. I remember it now." Alan nodded, imagining the withered old man in front of him listening to that kind of music years ago. "True, I guess."

"Guess?"

"Nope. You're very right. True for sure."

"Don't kid yourself. You're on your way too. Everyone is. Just when you're in the middle of it, you forget. I did."

Alan stood there, thinking. Yes. Old Doctor Bloomfeld was spot on.

"When my doctor first told me. That I had advanced cancer. I was calm. Kind of euphoric really. All of a sudden the pressure was off."

"One way of looking at it."

"The only way. I said screw chemo. Just ride it out. You know? It was the first time in my life that I was truly happy."

"Wow."

"My wife and I went to Tahiti. That very next week. She always wanted to go. I was admiring this beautiful sunset, thinking, normally I'd be trying to commit it to memory. Something to take with me for later. You know what? I was like, what the hell's the point? There is no point. For the first time in my life I was truly in the moment. *That* moment."

Alan didn't know what to say. He smiled and rocked his head gently.

A transporter walked up behind them. "He ready to go back, Doc?"

"Sure," Alan said. He reached to shake Dr. Bloomfeld's hand. "Be well."

"In the moment, son." Dr. Bloomfeld winked. A wet cough. "In the moment."

Alan went back to the reading room. Dr. Bloomfeld's brain image was still on the monitor. So was the 1DY.

"Hey, Sundeep." One of his colleagues was in an adjacent reading room. "Can you come here, look at something for me?"

Sundeep walked over, stood behind Alan's chair.

"Check this out." Alan scrolled through many images, not saying anything, not wanting to be obvious. He wanted to see if the finding would jump out to Sundeep. Alan kept coming back to the image with the 1DY on it. He would linger on the image then scroll a little more. "Anything?"

Sundeep scratched his head. "Brain?" He laughed.

"This." Alan outlined the 1DY with his fingertip.

"What?"

"This." Alan made it obvious this time, circling, outlining. "Right here."

"Um. Guess. If I squint."

"It's a different shade, no?"

"Not really, dude. I mean I guess I see what you're saying. I can almost make something out. A little bit of a stretch though. I see gyri."

"Okay. Okay. Look." Alan used his finger on the monitor again. "Here's a *1*, and this is a capital *D* and a capital *Y*. See?"

"Barely."

"Well it's clear as day to me."

"That's why you're the neuro guy." Sundeep laughed and slapped Alan on the back.

"Well, I see it. I'm trying to figure out what it means. If it's real. One day?"

"Yeah. Maybe how many days you have left at this job?"

"Ha. Ha. Maybe it's how many days Dr. Bloomfeld has on this earth."

"Seriously? First off I don't see it. Secondly, how the hell would an MR know that?"

"I know, I know. It's not the MRI. It's his brain. Maybe we're pre-programmed."

"Dude. I think you need a break. I can't believe we're even having this conversation. It's just a fakeout, Alan. Artifact. "

"Fine."

"Now read some more cases, buddy. We're getting backed up."

"So I ask Sundeep to look at it and he laughs." Alan rested a napkin on the table, leaned back in his chair, having just finished a salmon and rice dinner. "Doesn't really see it. Thinks it's a fakeout."

Melissa sipped her pinot grigio and set the glass on the light blue tablecloth. "But you see it clearly?"

"Yes. I mean, whatever. I know what I saw. I'm gonna look again tomorrow. Ask a couple more people to check it out."

"Maybe you're just tired."

"Maybe. I mean, sure, I'm tired. I've been tired a long time. Where are the kids?"

"Upstairs doing homework. They ate earlier. You're stressed maybe? You know, you still haven't decided what we're doing for your 50th."

"Don't know yet."

"Well we gotta figure it out. Get plane tickets, that kind of thing."

"Yeah, I know. I'm not sure I want to spend all that money, though. Go away somewhere. Maybe we should do something local, a little quieter. Dinner. A small thing maybe."

"What? *Dinner?*" Melissa stood and went to the sink with her plate. "Here we go again."

"Here we go what?"

"You're impossible." She scraped the plate into the trash, ran the faucet. "When do you *want* to spend the money? Huh? Actually do something fun, crazy."

Alan reached and grabbed the bottle of wine, poured some in his glass. "I like having a nice savings."

"For what? We have enough. I'm so sick of this." The dishes and silverware clanked in the sink, a bit louder than usual. "Twenty years of waiting. Thinking. Planning. Sometimes you just have to do, Alan. If I had it my way we'd be traveling any chance we got."

Alan knew he was treading thin ice. He chose his words carefully. "We've traveled."

"Seriously?" The water stopped abruptly. "What? Upstate NY? Pennsylvania?"

"What's wrong with that? We've had fun."

"Sure we did. I wanna see more. More of the world." Melissa was now standing at Alan's side, looking down. "We always said we wanted to do that."

Alan looked up. "I do."

"When?"

"When the time is right."

"When?!"

"Soon!"

"WHEN IS SOON?!"

"I don't know!"

"Great." Melissa walked out of the kitchen.

Alan finished his wine. He cleaned up the kitchen and went upstairs. Melissa was getting the girls ready for dance class. She said she was going to take the girls for ice cream after dance and they might do some shopping.

This gave Alan some time alone.

He took out his clothes for the morning, hung them up on the closet door. Chose a tie. Laid out socks and underwear. He sat at his desk, read a journal article about decreasing radiation exposure with new multidetector CT protocols.

He then worked on a PowerPoint presentation he had to give to junior medicine residents in two days on the basics of head CT evaluation.

He showered, letting hot water massage his scalp for many minutes. After, he stood naked in front of the bathroom mirror. He wiped a thin layer of condensation away with a towel. The light seemed extra bright, harsh. He moved his face closer to the glass, studied the image.

Who is that guy? It looked like him, some version of himself. Deep grooves snaking from the corners of his eyes. Several weird purple skin blemishes he hadn't noticed before. Fleshy bags squatting above his upper eyelids. He put a fingertip at the top of each eyebrow and pushed up. His eyes became wide. Like they used to look. He let go and the bags sunk down again, threatening to sag in front of his eyes, blinding him.

He had seen a recent photo of himself in the hospital newsletter. An Alzheimer's fundraising event he attended. When he first saw it he was appalled. It took him a minute to really believe that it was him. He had to find features that he knew were his own. Yes, that nose. The hair. *It's me.* He felt like he used to, when he was younger, but he did not look how he envisioned himself. Denial must be a built-in survival technique.

What really got him were the jowls. The draping skin clutching his chin. Where the heck did that come from? It looked like he was melting. In a way he figured he was. We all are, he thought. Bloomfeld was right. *When you're in the middle of it, you forget.*

The thick streaks of gray hair. Thinning, brittle.

And it wasn't going to get any better.

Aging was a catabolic process. Maybe he knew too much. Ignorance is bliss. Contiguous breakdown. Cell death. Cartilage wears thin. Collagen weakens. Skin sags. Teeth chip, break, fall out. Gums recede. Vision fails. Vitreous humor thickens, coagulates like cooling fat. Lenses cloud, warp. Hearing fails. Ossicles move sluggishly, tympanic membrane less elastic. Brain atrophies. Neuronal loss. Metabolism slows. Blood vessels accumulate plaque. Calcify. Muscles weaken. Vertebral discs loose water. Bones lose calcium. Spinal column shortens. Vertebral bodies collapse.

Alan shook his head. Pulled on his pajamas and crawled into bed.

Alan couldn't sleep. No position was comfortable. The pillows felt lumpy. Thinking. About life, money, his birthday coming up. His jowls. He got up much earlier than usual, decided to head over to the hospital and get a head start.

He went down to the cafeteria and got a cup of coffee. He was still early, so he decided to pop up to the sixth floor to see Dr. Bloomfeld.

He passed the central nursing station, nodded at the two young nurses huddled together over charts at the counter, signing out to one another. Change of shift. This was Alan's favorite time of the day in the hospital. Probably the quietest. Night ending, morning getting started, day shift people arriving, fresh. Wouldn't last though.

He turned into Dr. Bloomfeld's room and halted. The window bed was empty. On the other bed was a motionless figure, sheet pulled over the head. The sign on the wall above the bed: BLOOMFELD.

One of the nurses stepped in behind him. "Saw you come in. Didn't know you were here to see Dr. Bloomfeld."

"He's not mine. Radiology. Just came in to say hi."

"Oh, really sorry. Overnight nurse found him at 4 a.m. No code. He was DNR. He was cold already. She had answered his bell at 3, got him some water. He seemed fine. "

Alan went to the foot of the bed, rested his hands on the cold silver rail. "Probably threw a PE."

"Yeah. Probably."

Silence.

"I'll just be a minute," Alan said.

"Okay."

The nurse left.

Alan went to the bedside and lowered the sheet. No matter how many times he saw a dead body he was fascinated. Dr. Bloomfeld's eyes were half closed, the whites opaque. His lips parted. Skin the unnatural color of recent death. *Where was Dr. Bloomfeld now? Anywhere? Could he see me? Hear me?* Alan smiled. Dr. Bloomfeld looked quite peaceful.

"No one gets out alive." Alan nodded his head in a final gesture. "Guess that'll be me someday, huh? It was nice knowing you, sir. However brief."

Alan started to pull the sheet then stopped. "One day, huh? Just like your MR said. Did you know? Did your brain somehow register that?"

Alan dragged the sheet to cover Dr. Bloomfeld's head and rushed from the room.

Alan sat at the computer workstation. He logged in, got into the PACS system. He used a search filter, allowing him to find all the brain MR's done in the past two weeks. These would have been done on the new MR machine.

He was ramped up, he could feel it—hyper-alert, hands trembling ever so slightly. He was aware of his respirations and the firm accelerated thudding of his heart.

It took a moment for the computer to generate the list. Alan nervously tapped the counter with his fingertip. The little wheel spun around and around on the screen while he waited and then it stopped.

The list.

Sixty eight brain MRI's.

He clicked on the first name. The five panels popped up—sagittal T1, axial T1, T2, FLAIR and diffusion sequences. He clicked on the sagittal T1 window so that it expanded to occupy full screen. He started to scroll.

He stopped abruptly on one image.

No way, there it was. He couldn't believe it.

He wiped his eyes, adjusted the contrast settings. This maneuver only enhanced the appearance.

There was the number *8* followed by *MO.*

Eight months?

Alan noted the age. Eighty-six-year-old female.

He looked around and shook his head. Exited the study. He clicked on the second name on the list. Set up the images. Scrolled.

11YR.

He noted the age. Fifty-five-year-old male.

Exited the study. Next on the list. Opened it, scrolled. *6YR.*

Noted patient's age. Thirty-year-old female.

Alan clicked his way down the list. His breathing turned urgent.

Each brain had numbers and letters: *3DY, 25YR, 6MO, 32DY,* and on and on and on.

Time of death?

He realized he had gone through all sixty-eight cases. Alan backed away from the computer, exhausted.

After a while Sundeep strolled in. In his usual cheery morning voice said, "Hey Alan. You're here early. Getting a head start?"

Alan turned, forced a smile, "That's right."

Alan walked around the hospital feeling like a victim of head trauma. Foggy-headed, distant. The hospital, always its own world, seemed foreign, unfamiliar. He could hardly concentrate on his work. Sundeep had asked him how he was feeling and was he still seeing the numbers and letters on the brain MRI's.

Alan told him no, he was feeling better. Told him he had gone back to the scan early that morning, looked again, and he didn't see it. He told Sundeep that he agreed with him, that it was artifact and what was wrong with him anyway—he must've been tired.

Sundeep laughed and told Alan he was glad, because he was starting to get worried about him. He was about to go to the chief.

Alan went out for lunch, something he typically didn't do, but he had to get out of the hospital. He took his time, had a turkey sandwich, an apple and some water. He sat on the wood bench in front of the hospital and thought things over.

He knew what he wanted to do and finally decided, yes, he would do it. But he would wait until after hours.

"Thanks for doing this, Dennis."

"No problem, Doc," Dennis the MRI tech said as he secured the coil over Alan's head as he lay on the MRI table. Headphones were in place. "We had a cancellation anyway. And you know, you're kind of like a VIP."

"Well, thanks. I know how busy it can get at night though. You don't need me adding to the craziness."

"All good, Doc."

"And again, let's keep this between us, okay? I've been having some pretty intense headaches. I don't want the department getting all concerned."

"No sweat." Dennis held his index finger on a button on the side of the machine and the table moved, sliding Alan inside the tube. "Classical music okay?"

"Fine." Alan could see Dennis via the two small angled mirrors. A painting of the sun setting over a mountain hung on the wall behind the MR scanner.

Alan closed his eyes. He didn't have a problem with claustrophobia like many people did. But he could definitely understand. It was tight. And dark.

Alan tried to relax. He breathed deeply and smoothly, not wanting to move. He felt relaxed. Built in earphones pumped in light classical music but he could still hear the jackhammer knocking, humming and buzzing of the MR.

He thought about all those other MR's. All the numbers. Time stamp of death etched into all those brains. They all had one.

Forced to lie still, he realized how tired he was. He had hardly slept the night before. He felt himself nodding off, drifting into a wonderful haze of sleep. As if in the womb.

Alan was jolted awake by Dennis' tinny voice in the headphones. "All done, Doc."

The table started to move.

Alan slowly entered the world again. Light.

Dennis undid the head coil, removed the top half and Alan felt the fresh air.

Dennis helped him into a sitting position. Alan massaged his eyes, scratched his head.

"I burned it to CD," Dennis said.

"Thanks, buddy." Alan slid off the table. "You can delete it from the system. I'll handle it from here."

"Done."

"And just between us, okay?"

"You got it, Doc."

Alan went to the reading room. He sat at the workstation and popped the CD into the drive. The room was soothingly quiet in the evening. It was dark outside with no light seeping through the windows. No ringing and ringing of phones, everyone with a question. Peace.

The viewer appeared on the screen. His study was the only case on the disc.

Alan inhaled deeply, moved the cursor over his name.

He hesitated, let the cursor hover there for a long moment.

He clicked, almost as if his finger knew that if he waited any longer his mind might not give it permission.

His study filled the screen. Five panels. He dragged the cursor over the sagittal T1 sequence, waited. Then clicked.

He adjusted the contrast, started to scroll. He scrolled and scrolled then stopped abruptly.

He stared at the screen.

Alan did not know how long he had been staring before he clicked and exited the study. The CD popped out. He lifted it from the holder, placed it firmly in his palm and sat there for a moment gazing at the silver disc.

Alan took out his cellphone and called Melissa. She didn't answer. He left a rambling message about wanting to book a trip to Europe. Paris probably, like they always talked about. Could she find the passports.

It was time to go.

Obstruction

JAVIER SANTANA WAS DEAD.

Doctor Mitchell Ross gowned up, clicked a shiny new blade on the scalpel, shook his head thinking how young the guy was.

Ross leaned and pushed. Sliced. Parted skin overlying the left pectoral muscle. Shoulder to xyphoid process. With another smooth cut opened a deep gash from the right shoulder, connecting the other gash at the xyphoid. Continued the incision down midline, carving a semicircle around the umbilicus to the pubic bone, ending up with a crude "Y" gouged into Javier's chest and abdomen.

Ralphie Gomez strutted in, late again, set a cup of coffee on the counter next to the sink, saying, "Hey, Doc. You know you really gotta try the Salsa thing man cause I get so much ass. Know what I mean? I mean, I get ass anyways but when you dancing so sexy and you get that puta so close, man oh man, give em the eye and they melt, man. Telling you."

Ross lifted the V-shaped breast plate, angled it over Javier's face, exposing neck, heart, lungs. He started to hack through abdominal wall, tearing fat and rectus musculature, exposing lumpy omentum, mesentery and bowel loops, which glistened like loose coils of wet Italian sausage in the overhanging light.

"That's fine, Ralphie." Ross half-smiled, only mildly annoyed. Ralphie did provide much needed daily amusement. "About the ass and all, but we gotta get through this autopsy. Gotta give a lecture to the first year med students in an hour. Get that tray over his legs. I'm gonna yank this stuff out, see what the hell's going on."

"You want me a give 'em that talk, Doc?" Ralphie snapped on latex gloves, smirking. He slid on a mask with a clear plastic shield, protecting his eyes. Grabbed a tray off the floor that looked like it could be used for a breakfast-in-bed thing, dropped it over Javier's legs, providing an elevated workspace below the abdomen. "I know this medical stuff like anybody."

"Don't doubt it, Chico." Ross had his hand buried under intestine, pushing it aside to see the attachment. "I think these students want a professor who's actually been to med school."

"Whatever." Ralphie shrugged. "I serious, man. I take you to the club uptown. You see what I mean. Spanish chicks with big bootie, man. You like that, eh?"

"Don't think the wife and kids would appreciate the club. Eh?"

"Let me know you change your mind," Ralphie said. "Who this guy anyways?"

"Javier Santana. Twenty-nine. Found dead in his room. Marriott Express by Kennedy Airport."

"Sucks." Ralphie pulled apart layers of the abdominal wall, helping Ross, getting into the flow of things. "The hotel's shit anyways."

Ross splayed the pericardial sac, slit the pulmonary trunk, slid a finger into the main pulmonary artery, checking for clot. Nothing.

The abdomen exposed, Ralphie busied himself on the neck, tying off the carotid and subclavian arteries as they tunneled out of the thoracic cavity, coursing toward the head. Cut the larynx, esophagus, wriggled them downward. "What do you think happened?"

"Probably drugs, this kind of story." Ross cut and pulled, got the heart, lungs and mass of abdominal organs detached. Flopped the whole mess onto the tray, dripping, sliding. "But who knows. Room was clean. Could've been an aneurysm or something."

"Where he coming from? Colombia?"

"Don't know." Ross reached for the scalpel. "Had no passport or tickets. Just a New York State driver's license."

Ross severed each lung at the hilum, plopped them on the hanging scale, read off the weight. Ralphie jotted it down on a sheet of paper, put the heart and lungs onto a separate tray on the counter. Next to Ralphie's coffee. With a sword-like silver knife, Ralphie started cutting the lungs like a loaf of bread. Ross got busy with the abdominal organs on the tray.

"These lungs lookin' juicy, Doc." Ralphie pushed on a thick slice of lung with a gloved finger. "Like a soaked sponge."

Ross craned his neck, got a glance at the tan tissue. Nodded. "Edema."

Ralphie continued slicing. "The heck that lecture on anyways?"

"Ovarian tumors. Radiologic-pathologic correlation." Ross held the stomach, snipped with scissors. He abruptly stopped, whistled.

Ralphie tabled the knife. Looked over.

"Well lookie here." Ross flicked at the stomach contents with a finger. "Goody bags."

Ralphie got alongside. A better look. "Holy crap. That what I think it is?"

"Yesiree." Ross stretched the stomach walls, parted them. Better exposure. Looked like a wet leather purse stuffed with soggy cigar butts.

"Coke or smack?"

"Gimme that basin," Ross said. "Probably heroin, given the pulmonary edema."

"*Mierda.*" Ralphie presented a silver metallic bowl. Ross grabbed it. "How many are there?"

"Don't know. Twenty, twenty-five." Ross plucked out the oblong capsules with forceps and plopped them into the basin. "Bet there's some in the small bowel too."

"Look like them stuffed Greek grape leafs," Ralphie said. "I like them shits."

"They're okay. Wouldn't want to eat one of these suckers, though."

"The high of your life, eh?"

"Last one," Ross said. "Stomach looks pretty distended. These here are all lodged in the duodenum. Guy obstructed at the gastric outlet."

"Ate too many, huh?"

"Not just that. Check this out." Ross held up a flattened baggie between pinched fingers. "Ruptured."

"Damn," Ralphie said.

"Got a huge blast of heroin. Gastric mucosa sucked this stuff up like a starving vacuum. Straight to the bloodstream."

"How many grams each a those things?"

"Think about ten."

"They packed with condoms?"

"Usually. Seem more advanced, though." Ross fingered a capsule close to the light, squinting. "Some sort of latex. Sometimes they layer it with cellophane, maybe put on a wax coating. Whatever Javier did, it failed."

"Stupid chico. *Pendejo.*"

Ross slid the basin on the counter, cupped the colon, massaged gently. "Sigmoid feels a bit lumpy. Probably has some stuff packed in there too."

"Man, he loaded. Still gonna crack his head?"

"Sure. Gotta be complete. You know that."

Ralphie crammed a stained wood block under Javier's neck. Angled the head up and forward. Got a scalpel. Put metal to hair and skin. Sliced the scalp from ear to ear around the back of the skull. Peeled the tissue forward with force, tearing connective tissue, twisted it upside down over Javier's face. Pulled the Stryker saw from a drawer, plugged it in.

Ralphie clicked a button. The saw whirred to life. The sound dropped a pitch as it sunk to bone.

Ross continued clearing the stomach. After a moment, Ross chopped a hand at Ralphie. "That the door?"

The saw stopped whirring. Ralphie threw a questioning look. "*Que?*"

"Thought I heard a knock."

"Didn't hear nothing." Ralph clanked the saw to the table. Pulled off his mask. Floated it to the counter. Went to the door. He peeked through the small square tinted window at eye level. Squinted. Two guys in suits. Didn't look familiar. He cracked the door.

Ralphie said, "Sup."

"We're from the FBI. Need to talk to you."

"'Bout what?"

"That patient there."

"In the middle of the autopsy."

"Don't matter. Racing against time here."

Silence.

From deeper in the room, Ross: "Who's that Ralphie?"

"Says FBI."

"Fifteen minutes, okay?" Ross didn't take his eyes off Javier. "Almost done."

"We need to talk to the doctor in charge." The guy stared down Ralphie. "You him?"

"I'm the diener"

"The what?"

"Diener. Pathology assistant."

"Great." The guy brushed past, a little elbow jab for Ralphie. "Can't wait."

The door swung shut. The other guy waited outside.

Ross stood beside the body, gloved hands out in front, neck twisted, looking over. Tugged the mask down around his neck. Ralphie stood by the door, hands at his sides, fists balled. The guy stood between them, closer to Ralphie, hands clasping the lapels of his coat, grinning.

Ralphie sensed something wasn't right. "You guys usually wait till we're done. Give us our respect."

"This is a very unusual circumstance."

The guy reached into his coat. Came out with a pistol. Held it up, looking at Ralphie. "9 mm Semiautomatic. 15 round clip. Can put a few in you. A few in your boy there, just like that. Like a little sing song. Even have a few left over."

"*Que coño?*" Ralphie stepped toward the guy.

"Easy, hotshot." The guy leveled the gun at Ralphie's chest. "What are you? The doc's secret service boy?"

Ralphie hesitated.

The guy looked around, made a scrunched up face. "Man this room smells nasty."

Ralphie leaned in. "You just turn around it bothering you so much." Jerking his head to the door.

"Okay wiener man. Whatever you are. You a big hotshot, right? We here for our shit. We need our shit like now. You got our shit?"

"You ain't getting no shit, amigo."

"Ralphie," Ross said, voice different now, softer. "Let the guy talk."

"Smart move. Guess that's why you the doctor. Can make this easy or hard. Actually I wanna make this quick cause the smell is killing me. Don't wanna get no cancer or something breathing this shit. Doc, can I get cancer breathing this shit? Well I guess not or you wouldn't be breathing it, right? How the hell you work like this?"

"Who're you guys anyways?" Ralphie said.

"You don't worry," The guy said. "Wait. You know what?" He looked over at Javier, thought about the heroin, nodded. "You just call me Scag. Okay?"

"I got a better one," Ralphie said. "How 'bout *Pinga?*"

"Funny." Scag relaxed on his heels, spun quickly, cold-cocked Ralphie across the head with a handful of metal. A spray of spit arced. Ralphie crumpled and met the tile floor. Ralphie struggled, a little dazed, got onto an elbow, took a kick to the head with a steel-toed boot. He stayed on the floor, out cold, on his stomach.

"Like I was saying, Doc." Scag massaged his knuckles. "How you work in this shit?"

Ross didn't move. He spoke deliberately, stone-faced. "You. Get. Used. to it."

"Not me. Nope. Never get used to this nasty shit smell. Guess that's why I never went to med school huh, Doc?"

Ross squinted. Evaluated Ralphie. "Whatever."

"You know? I seen dead bodies before. Was okay with it, but never like this with all the shiny lights and guts hanging out. All naked, opened up. Creepy, man."

"Another reason I guess you didn't go to medical school."

"That's it, Doc. You enjoying yourself now. What I like to see. Nice and easy. I bet you can guess why I'm here. Being you all smart and stuff, huh? You get my shit from Javier?"

"I got it, yeah. Who the hell are you anyway?"

"Wow. Man, you gettin' nasty. Don't think I ever hear a doctor talk that way. All street and gangsta. You allowed to do that, Doc? Say *fuck* and *shit?*

"Actually, that would be intercourse and feces. That's what you would learn in med school."

"That's nice with the words and all. You really teaching me nice. All the big science words. Glad I came today. Now you don't worry 'bout who I am. I'm Scag remember? Let's just say the Big Boys sent us."

Ross wondered if he was pushing it. "Fine."

"Fine. I like that. Starting to get into the whole thing now. Things are gonna go just fine. Now Doc, you think you can teach me a little more shit while I'm here? Like a little bonus or something? Maybe teach me some amatomacal shit or something?"

"If you like. Be glad to help out. Better the world some."

"Man, you funny. A funny cool doctor. Street doc. Ain't that a riot?"

"Just take the stuff, okay? It's right here."

"That all of it?"

"Think there's more in the colon. Was just about to retrieve it."

"Retrieve it from the colon? Like the ass? Retrieve? I like that too. Man, I learning all sorts a stuff from you. We'll wait, Doc Fuckface."

Scag approached the table. Had his back to Ralphie. Leaned in to better see in front of Ross. Kept a slight distance.

Ross slowly, mechanically, picked up the blunt-tip scissors from the counter, started to cut the top wall of the sigmoid colon along its length. As if he were cutting a sheet of wrapping paper.

Ralphie stirred on the floor. Rubbed his head. He glanced at Scag. Made a mad crawl, like some rabid animal. Grabbed Scag around the knees, pushed off, hooking his hands, squeezing and pushing.

Scag lost his balance, tipped, reached for air, tumbled over. Cracked his forehead on the table edge, sending the pistol skittering across the floor. Scag's hand caught in Javier's vacant chest cavity, dragged the body half off the steel, so that Javier's head and chest were dangling with stiff arms overhead now.

Scag landed on his back, face to face with Javier. A gush of viscous body fluid poured from Javier's chest cavity, splashed onto Scag's face and neck. He didn't move.

The door burst open. The other guy rushed, gun drawn, looking around. Trying to figure what the hell was all the racket.

"Hold it!"

He saw Scag, supine and unconscious. Forehead gash. Ralphie climbing to his feet, turning. The guy reacted, from the gut, pumped off a round. Sent Ralphie to the floor, against the wall. He sat still, his shoulder looking like fresh ground beef.

Nervous, the guy looked around, agitated, said to Ross, "Come on man. Just gimme the shit. Give it to me. Let's move it. MOVE IT!"

"Okay okay." Ross tried to calm things down. *Don't get shot.* "It's not all out yet. There's a bunch in the colon. Was just going to cut it out."

"Come on come on, then. Cut it out. Get it to me." He leaned. Beckoned Scag. "Yo. Get up, man. GET. UP."

Scag stirred.

Ross watched.

Ross knew this was it. His only chance. He cupped a load of small intestine. Both hands. Webby mesentery. Unraveled, floppy loops of wet sweet Italian sausage. Lifted it. Sent it flying. Slammed the guy's face. Encased his head. He let out a muffled yell. Reflexively dropped the gun, hands grappling. He danced back, arms flailing, as if fighting some alien octopus.

Ross turned swiftly, like a dance move. Lifted the long steel knife from the counter, an automatic reaction. An uncharacteristic throaty savage yell. Jabbed forward as if holding a dueling sword, buried the blade in the guy's neck, right through a mushy sausage segment. Ross stood frozen, arm still extended. Watched the guy stumble around drunkenly.

Gurgling. Oozing. Ross couldn't help but think which structures his weapon had traversed. Probably just below the level of the vocal cords. Maybe through thyroid cartilage. Esophagus? Thyroid isthmus? Pretty damn good placement.

Scag was coming around. Rubbing his eyes. Moaning. Face and shirt slick with wetness. Mumbling fast. Something along the lines of getting Javier's shit. Scag's partner pedaled in reverse, crashed back-first into a cabinet. Ross slipped into the cooler, thudded the heavy reinforced door closed.

Scag glimpsed through burning eyes. Grabbed at the basin full of heroin capsules. Frantically stuffing his coat pockets, moving quickly, starting to hear some commotion in the hallway. Trying to get all his shit. Scag spotted the gun. On the floor. Swept it up, took a step to the cooler, grabbed the handle. Tugged. It was stiff. "Get you next time, street doc!" He started for the door. Freedom. He skidded on the wet tile, almost lost his footing.

Hand gripped door handle. That's when he heard it.

It was Ralphie, from across the room. Weak. "Yo, amigo."

Scag looked round, turning his head first, slow motion-like. Knew he was in a bad position. His back to the main action. Swung his body. Then the gun-arm. Knew it wasn't going to be fast enough.

He glimpsed Ralphie. Just a flash, a fleeting image like a fuzzy bad dream. Sitting against the wall, shit-eating grin. One arm limp, the other outstretched, reaching for its life. His fist tight, crushing the pistol. The black metal glowed in the harsh light.

Ralphie ticked his head at the gun. "Think you forgot something."

Cannulation

Amazonia

July 1, 1989

"Doc-tuurrr!"

I knew as soon as I heard it that things were going to hell. I mean, all I had to do was stay out of trouble for two days in the jungle. Two days. Just two days before I would catch up with the rest of the group. I had arrived not three hours ago. I was in the hut getting acclimated, organizing my belongings (which weren't much), trying to get used to the godforsaken heat and humidity.

I missed my two-stop flight to Manaus and had to sleep on the tiled airport floor given there was only one flight a day to this Brazilian city. I felt like I was getting a cold and I hadn't slept well for three days, trying to finalize everything for this once-in-a-lifetime trip.

Then the layover in Peru. It was pouring rain there too, with severe winds and lightening, which delayed departures for hours. Then there was some electrical problem on the plane and we had to sit on the tarmac for five more hours.

"Doc-toooorr! Doc-toooorr!"

The sounds were louder, getting closer. I could hear a commotion building, many many voices now. The torrential rain started again, hammering away on the grass-thatched roof, pouring off the sides to the dirt like a waterfall, splashing and swishing. My body was dripping as well, drenched in sweat.

And the boat ride up river. Just outside Manaus I got on a river-boat, which was relatively comfortable compared to what I had been through up to that point. It had three levels. I was able to sit on the high deck, recline and watch the river's winding, bending course. The river seemed swollen and full, spilling over the banks, extending inland. The rainy season had just ended but that didn't mean much in a tropical rain forest.

The boat was loaded mostly with tourists, wannabe explorers. As we continued along, I watched the city dwindle away into smaller buildings then single floor shacks and then dense green forest, its canopy extending for miles and miles in every direction.

I switched over to a single canoe at Puyo that the mission had arranged, had it there waiting for me. There, I met my guide, Kiko, a more or less civilized Indian, a descendant of the Mayorunas. Spoke decent English and could speak many native dialects. He was to accompany me until I met up with the rest of the mission.

The canoe had a small outboard motor and was manned by another less civilized native, related to the Yanomamo tribes. Spoke no English. We started our trek farther up river, deeper into the rain-forest through towering thick walls of green. Sporadic villages dotted the shore.

We floated past a naked boy standing at the river bank, bow and arrow in hand. It seemed like he was aiming at us. "What's he doing?" I asked Kiko, lowering myself in the canoe.

"Fishing."

The boy released the arrow into the water and we could see some-thing thrashing and flopping about. For a moment, I felt as if I could see into the past and I thought about Percy Fawcett, an early twen-tieth-century British explorer I had recently read about who spent his life in search of El Dorado, supposedly an ancient city filled with trea-sure deep in the Amazon. He had befriended many native tribes in his travels, but he ultimately disappeared in the jungle, thought to be at the hands of hostile Indians. Many people also disappeared looking for him.

A short time later, the outboard engine died and the native stared at it for a while and then banged it with bare fists before he picked up a paddle and finished the trip by hand.

Along the way, we watched a frenzied slush of piranhas devour some unknown carcass bobbing beside us. Later, Kiko pointed at something floating in the water that I thought was a tree trunk. I shrugged and Kiko said flatly, "Anaconda."

"Ya ya ya. AAAyoooo. Doc-tooorrrrr!"

They were real close now, a wild hoard approaching my hut. Lots of chattering, some moaning, deep breathing and stomping of bare feet in mud and puddles. Rain drumming.

Earlier, I was greeted warmly in the village. In fact, I was made to feel kind of like a God. Natives bowing at my feet, wide wild hand gestures and glaring, smiling faces. Kiko told me that this evening there was going to be a special ceremony in my honor, the poison frog ceremony, by way of greeting, and I said, "Cool."

The natives were happy of course, grateful actually, given my mission had just passed through and treated some of their sick. My colleagues two days ago had fitted many of the natives with crude eyeglasses and given out some anti-malarial medications and mosquito nets.

The mission was on its way to a village far upriver that was considered home base, with a dedicated medical facility, so the team could do some minor eye as well as head and neck surgeries: cataracts, branchial cleft cyst drainages, thyroglossal duct cyst repair, cleft palate and the like.

As a fresh out of residency orthopod, my job was going to be minor musculoskeletal procedures; clubfoot repair, congenital as well as post-traumatic hand deformities, resetting some old fractures that had resulted in unnecessary motion limiting deformities. Stuff like that.

"Doc Doc Doc-tooorr!! Ayayayhaaaa!"

This had been my dream since med school. To come to an underserved area, volunteer my newly acquired skills. Give back. When I heard about this medical mission I was overjoyed. A month in the Amazon jungle, living with native Indian tribes, some of which had had only minimal contact with the outside world, learning about their culture. I was fascinated.

But things weren't going as I had imagined. Two days. Two days and I was going to meet the rest of the mission up river, continue on together. Like it was supposed to be. As a group. Safety in numbers. The hoard was right outside the hut. Ready to enter.

I surveyed the space. The hut was round, fifteen feet in diameter. Single pole in the center. A small bed of woven material on the floor and a hammock hanging along the wall on one side. A small table constructed of contorted tree limbs and bark.

My bags. A small opened suitcase with the standard shorts, t-shirts, underwear, toiletries, flip-flops, a pair of sneakers. Not much else. The other smaller bag was my medical stuff. A kit that included a scalpel, a #11 curved blade, a pack of absorbable catgut suture and a pack of nonabsorbable proline suture, a hemostat and a Penrose drain. Basic surgical stuff.

Another compartment housed two 1 cc vials of morphine, a 20 cc bottle of lidocaine, an IV catheter with extension tubing, a bag of normal saline, some sterile gauze, one set of sterile gloves and a container of betadine. The mission had complete supplies for the more involved, complicated procedures. This was just my personal stash.

I also had several books, two of the four volumes of Campbell's Operative Orthopedics, Farquharson's General Surgery text and Manson's classic Tropical Diseases text. I braced myself.

Bam. A group of natives spilled into the hut through its small door, hunching over, dripping wet, sweat mixed with rainwater. They carried a naked man. Two natives above, one hooked into each armpit, another two men below, gripping his feet and lower legs.

They were having an awkward time of it, given the man was writhing in pain and was crunching into the fetal position. Both of his hands were between his legs. Kiko was waving them in, "Over here, over here," pushing them toward the cot where they plopped him down. The man continued to writhe and moan.

"What happened?" I was talking to Kiko, but had a good look at the group around me. About seven men and two women. Brown skin glistening, heavy breathing and gasping. They were all mostly naked, save for some penile sheaths on the men and a thatched bottom on the women. The men's torsos were painted with red stripes. The women's breasts swung low and flat, having never been in contact with a bra.

Several men had large plate-like discs stretching their earlobes, others with painted faces, straight objects protruding from their cheeks and noses, resembling whiskers. Bowl haircuts. The men chattered back, and then they all started chanting the same thing: "Kan-deer-oo, kan-deer-oo, kan-deer-oo."

"What are they saying?"

Kiko's face was grim. "Candirú," he said. "They're saying Candirú."

I thought: candirú candirú candirú. Sounded familiar, but wasn't sure.

"What's that?"

"Vampire fish," Kiko said quickly. "Very bad. Very evil."

Vampire fish. Yes. Coming back now. "Ask them what happened exactly."

Kiko turned, chattered again. Several Indians spoke at once. "They say he was bathing in the river. Then he screamed. He fell back. They dragged him out of the water. Then they saw it."

"Saw it?"

Kiko nodded slowly, ticked his chin at the man. "Look."

I stepped closer to the man. His body was contorted and flexed. His torso was also painted. "Hold his arms and legs down."

Kiko barked orders and several natives responded. They pulled the man's legs and arms out and away. He fought. They pulled.

I bent and looked at his genital area. "Goddam."

A man yelled, "Kan-deer-oo!" and scurried from the hut.

I bent even closer. There was a two inch silver, almost transparent fish-tail protruding from the man's penis. It was wiggling its way inside, even creeping in a couple millimeters as I watched. The man's penis moved in rhythm with the fish.

It was coming back to me. This kind of fish. Entering the urethra. I vaguely remembered it from med school. One of those horrifying things you learn about that never leaves your mind. With thumb and index finger I went to pinch the tail, see if I could pull it out and the natives started to yammer and yell. I looked at Kiko.

"Legend is if you pull it out there is instant death from bleeding," Kiko said. "And the tribe's men are cursed forever."

I put my hand up in a calming gesture and moved slowly. I had to at least try, get a feel. I pinched the slippery mucous-covered tail, couldn't get a grip right away, then managed to get hold. I held the penile shaft in one hand for counter traction and tugged gently. Nothing. In fact, I think the thing scurried in another few millimeters. I tugged a little more forcefully and then there was the slightest hint of blood. Crap.

The man was screeching now, trying to pull and twist his limbs free. One foot came free, kicked high in the air, just missing my head. The yelling and yammering started again. More blood oozed around the fish.

I backed off. "Okay. Okay."

I figured I'd get the guy stabilized. I had my surgical text and the Amazon text. I had to look this thing up. I moved quickly now, getting a little nervous. The natives let go of the man and he resumed the fetal position, screaming louder. I pulled the small table closer to me, put the medical kit on top, opened it. I grabbed the textbooks from my bag and stacked them on the table next to the kit. "I gotta get an IV in," I told Kiko. "I have one bag of saline and some morphine."

I grabbed the rubber Penrose drain and motioned for the men to hold the native's arm out. I wrapped the tourniquet and quickly placed the IV. I connected a section of tubing and then the saline and gave it to Kiko. "Hang this on the wall." I drew up one vial of morphine into a syringe, pushed it into the port on the IV.

The man's muscles immediately started to loosen and the other men could let him go and he lay there lax, breathing deeply, the fish wiggling gently between his legs. Expanding smears of blood on his thighs. Okay, I had a moment now. Figure out what to do.

I flipped open the text on tropical diseases. I smirked to myself, thinking I was never actually going to need this book. Thought it would be interesting. I went straight to the index, C-C-Ca, *candirú candirú*. There it was. I flipped to the page and read:

Candirú (Vandellia cirrhosa) also known as the Vampire fish or Terrifying Toothpick fish. A freshwater fish belonging to the catfish family. Shaped like an eel, is a fast, powerful swimmer and is virtually transparent, making it almost impossible to see in the water. It is found primarily in the Amazon and Oranoco Rivers and has a reputation amongst natives as the most feared fish in the water.

Candirú is a parasite. It has sharp teeth and backward pointing spines on its gills. It is urinophilic, attracted to urea and ammonia, which are by-products excreted through the gills of fish. The Candirú follows this scent underwater, and then rapidly inserts itself inside the gill flap.

The backward spines open like an umbrella and hook into the fish's flesh, then uses its sharp teeth and slurping apparatus to tap into an arteriole and feast on the host's blood

First described in The American Journal of Surgery in 1930 by Eugene W. Gudger, PhD et al....

Okay. Can't pull it out then. Those backward spines would rip the urethra to shreds. Explains the bleeding. I went on to read about the rare reports of the fish entering the human urethra, anus and vagina while urinating in the Amazon. Only several reports and even those were not well-documented.

I look up and it is eerily quiet. All the natives are staring at me. I can't tell if it's with respect or hatred. "What are they doing?" I asked Kiko.

"They're waiting."

"For what?"

"For you to fix him."

"Well tell them it's not that easy." I looked down and saw that there was more bleeding. Pooling between his legs.

"They tell me this man is a key tribal leader, a Chief," Kiko said through tight lips and a face of stone. "He has fathered many of the children in the village and is expected to father many more."

"Well," I said, rubbing my chin. "I don't know about that."

"They say his "instrument" is sacred and they're having a very difficult time with a white man even just touching it."

"Great." I could see the Candirú had gone farther into the urethra. The bleeding was steady now. We were at least two days away from any decent medical facility. Seemed it was all up to me. And I was an Orthopedist. "Tell them I'm doing the best I can." I then found several paragraphs on therapy. There wasn't much. There just wasn't that much experience. All it said was that surgical removal is recommended and at times total penectomy is indicated, actually preferred by the patient due to the intractable pain and bleeding.

Removal of the penis. The patient pleads for it.

I had one bottle of morphine left, a good amount of lidocaine for local anesthesia, some betadine, the scalpel, and two packets of suture material. I was going to have to attempt to excise it from the urethra. My only chance. I could see that the bleeding was worse now. "I'm going to try to remove it surgically. Tell them."

Kiko exchanges with the tribesmen. They looked very angry, raising their voices. Two of them left the hut. There was yelling outside.

"What'd they say?"

"That they don't want you to do anything. They want to pray, have a kind of ceremony to release the fish. The also have special juices they can make. Takes time though."

"What? Chief is bleeding here. There's no time for praying or juice or anything if they want him to live. Look at the blood!" I heard some drums in the distance. Chanting. Rattles.

"Tell them I'm just going to make a tiny incision. To help release it."

The Chief started to rouse again, moaning. I gave him the other half of the morphine. The last of it. He slumped, heavily sedated.

"Tell them if I can get it out, stop the bleeding, we can take him up river in the morning, get better attention. He should do fine then."

"They'll not let you take him."

"I have to do something."

"Wait."

"For what?"

"Instruction."

"Just tell them I'm gonna try!"

"Doctor..."

I fingered the scalpel, clipped the blade on. I wiped the penis with betadine, drew up some lidocaine. I turned his penis up, injected lidocaine along its undersurface in the midline so that I could make the incision along the corpus spongiosum, which housed the urethra.

The activity in the crowd increased and there was loud mumbling. Kiko said, "Doctor please..."

"Hold on, dammit."

I could see the fish had continued farther in, now with about an inch of it sticking out, its body swollen with blood, engorged, causing the penis to become taut with the increased pressure.

The crowd of natives was grumbling and as I moved the blade toward the skin I heard a loud crack and it was momentarily black and the next thing I knew I was sailing over the small table, knocking it on its side, pain ripping through my skull, slamming over my medical kit and books. My face was in the mud.

When I opened my eyes, I could see the books and contents of my medical kit scattered in the mud near my head. So much for sterility.

Kiko yelled and there was some scrambling and more yelling as I got to one knee, feeling groggy, and looked back at the crowd. Several men had clubs raised overhead. One took a swing and missed this time. "Wait!" I said. I thought I could feel a loose tooth. "Just wait!"

Kiko got between me and the men. He talked to them, yelling, gesturing, calming them down. Reassuring them.

"Tell them he's going to die!" I said. "Soon! Look at the bleeding! Tell them, dammit!"

For the first time Kiko screamed loudly, getting in their faces. I could also see he had a small black revolver in the palm of his right hand. The yelling continued and there was some shoving and then things seemed to slowly simmer down.

"Tell them they have to wait outside. I'm not doing this with them here. No way. Tell them to pray. Go!" Kiko convinced them to walk outside. I had no idea what he told them but I'm sure the exposed gun didn't hurt.

I got up, brushed off my muddy wet hands, streaked with blood. I picked the medical items off the floor. "Crap," I said. "Kiko, I need a small fire in here. Fast!" Kiko went out and brought back a flaming torch and sticks. He started a fire on the ground off to the side in what looked like a fire pit, probably for cooking. "We gotta move quickly." I swiped the mud off the scalpel and clamp and held the tips over the fire.

The bleeding was gushing now. I donned the sterile gloves from a paper packet. I held the Chief's penis and started to make the incision. The glowing hot clamp helped to cauterize some of the small bleeders as the skin splayed open. I could see the belly of the fish. I was careful not to cut into it because there'd be massive hemorrhage for sure.

I continued the incision and could see that the fish continued most of the length of the penis. If it had gotten deeper into the prostatic urethra, I was screwed. There'd be no way to get it out without significant damage. It suddenly occurred to me that I was in way over my head. In this hut in the middle of nowhere. Heat. Rain. Mad natives.

I looked at the Chief, urethra splayed open, body twisted. Blood steadily oozing into the surgical field. I opened the pack of gauze and covered the surgical site. I took a deep breath. There was no way I was going to be able to pry this fish out. I poked at it and prodded. Nothing. Its barbs were dug deep and because of its communication with the Chief's circulation, it was akin to a blood-filled artery now.

I looked up at Kiko. Even with his dark brown skin, he looked pale. The firelight flickered off his face. He could tell I was lost. My eye and cheek were swollen. My head hurt. I wanted out of there. Kiko said, "We should go."

"He'll die. I can't."

I could hear the drums in the distance, the rain hammering again, some more rattles.

"The drums are not good."

"I have to save him."

Kiko went to the door and peeked out.

I picked the surgical text off the floor, righted the table and set it down. I wiped off a glop of mud and went to the index. P-P-P Pe-Penectomy, total, partial.

"What're you going to do, Sir?"

I exhaled deeply and hoarsely. "I'm gonna have to take the penis."

"No Sir." Kiko almost yelled it. Desperation in his voice. He came close. "No Doctor. Please. Don't do it. We'll never leave."

"The Chief is gonna die. Soon. Get it? Look at the bleeding. Not to mention this goddam fish is obstructing his urethra. He can't piss. And then there's infection. This is a disaster! They're your people. Talk to them!"

"They're not my people!"

"Close enough!"

I dragged the table close to the bed, pages wide open so I could see the diagrams, as if I were baking a cake, studying the recipe.

Kiko mumbled. "Oh please, sir. Please, please."

"You have a better idea?"

Quiet then, resigned. "No."

"Then get this fire burning!" Something had changed deep in my chest. Maybe delirium. Fear? Futility? I felt raw and almost crazed. Strong. My eyes widened, heart drilling. I could tell the way Kiko looked at me now that he was scared. Scared of me.

I cooked the scalpel blade over the flames, grinning. Kiko darted around, tossing more material on the fire. I drew up the rest of the lidocaine, injected it around the base of the penis, around the pubic bone. The numbing would last several hours and I had a little more after that. I splattered on betadine in wide arcs. I burned the clamp, again to use as cautery. It was red hot, like a branding iron. I glanced at the textbook then went to work.

It had been a long time since a urology rotation early in my residency, but it started to come back. My mind was racing. I got in the zone. I made a wide skin flap at the base of the penis, including some scrotal tissue. I then made the circumferential incision at the base, quickly burning the bleeders as I went. I'd burn, then put the tip back in the fire. Burn again.

I continued the longitudinal incision along the urethra to meet the base and I could see the fish's head, trying to burrow its way toward the bladder, its own El Dorado. Great. It wasn't too far in. This just might work. I cut and burned, cut and burned. I could hear the sizzle of flesh with each burn, like after a burger is thrown on a hot grill. It had that distinctive fleshy smell too—a char-broiled breeze. I inhaled and felt a wild euphoria set in.

Before I knew it, the penis was hanging by a thin strand of tissue. I swiftly sliced it and the flesh fell into my hand, detached. I quickly plopped it on the Chief's stomach. The fish was still alive, bending into a "U" and then straight again. Back and forth.

A gush of urine squirted upward like a geyser from the urethral stump. I let it empty, warmth flowing and cascading to the floor. I then widened the urethral opening and threaded the thin rubber

Penrose drain into the bladder to act as a catheter. I sutured the flap closed using a purse string technique.

I stepped back and I noticed that I was out of breath. My hands were shaking and I felt light-headed. I was actually pretty proud of myself, and in some bizarre way, admired my handiwork. There was no bleeding. I tuned to look at Kiko. His hands rested on his knees, bent over, opalescent strings of vomit hanging from his full lips.

I stood erect, aware again of my surroundings, the drenched shirt stuck to my body, the pain in my own skull. Droplets of sweat dangling from my earlobes, nose. A penisless native Chief in front of me, groin covered in blood, urine, betadine, a rubber drain where the penis should be.

"Done." I nodded and smeared a muddy and bloody hand across my forehead. I heard a plop and saw that the penis-fish had squirmed off the Chief's stomach and onto the dirty wet ground. I picked it up.

It was still moving, the tail just protruding from one end, the bulbous head with small whiskers at the other. I figured I would present this sacred organ to the tribesmen. I would be a hero for saving the Chief's life. It was medically necessary. Maybe they could save the sacred instrument for worship. I limped outside.

One native stood about thirty feet away. I could see a faint fire in the distance and the low sound of drums and voices. The rain was lighter now. A heavy mist cooked up from the ground. The native approached and stopped before me. He wore a feathered headdress, his body painted with slashes of red and black. A large necklace of bone and teeth hung around his neck.

In a slow, deferential manner, I raised the penis-fish high in the palm of my hand and smiled, presenting the gift. "Your Chief is alive."

Kiko came out of the hut, stopped a few feet behind me, palming the revolver.

The native's eyes narrowed and he let out a high-pitched wail.

Kiko said, "Let's go."

"Where? It's dark. I want to talk to them. Tell them I saved the Chief's life."

The native screeched, backing up, hands waving.

"We should go, sir."

"No! The nearest village is two days away. Tell them he's alive! I saved his life! We have to take him in the morning. Get help!"

"They will not let us."

"Tell them..."

It sounded like a tire leaking air, followed by a quick hard thud. I turned and saw Kiko, a ghastly expression on his face, the arrow jutting from the middle of his chest. He fell to his knees in the mud, his eyes following mine, imploring, then flopped to his side. Then the sound again.

This time I felt hotness in my arm and saw that an arrow had completely penetrated my left bicep and was poking out the back of my arm. I heard a yell. First my own and then others. Then the sound again. And again. Arrows rained down around me, another getting Kiko, already dead, in the neck. I reached and reflexively grabbed the revolver from Kiko's hand. I blasted several rounds into the air, more of a scare tactic.

I scrambled around the back of the hut and made a split second decision. My only choice. Run. I darted into the black jungle, toward the river. It was one of those situations when your mind leaves your body, and your body is suddenly capable of adrenaline-charged superhuman feats. I felt nothing.

I heard my own footfalls on soggy earth and mud, branches cracking, humongous leaves slapping me in the face. I saw my body hurdling over fallen tree trunks, twisting between vines, jumping thick snake-like roots. There was no pain. The arrow still in my arm.

After what felt like an hour, which was more accurately about a minute, of full-on zigzagging sprinting, I could make out the river in the darkness. Several canoes rocked by the bank. I heard my legs splashing in water, without sensation of hot or cold, then a thump after I pushed off and landed on my side in the canoe, rocking slightly along the water's smooth surface.

I dropped the revolver in the canoe and grabbed the paddle and dug into the murky blackness. I slid away in complete darkness, not knowing if I was going upriver or downriver. I didn't care.

I stopped paddling after a while and glided along, pain and awareness making their cruel entrance back into my consciousness. I cracked off the long portion of the arrow and threw it into the river, pressed my arm to slow the bleeding.

It was only then that I could hear the low staccato of voices. Faint splashing in the distance, paddles chopping water. I couldn't tell if the noises were coming toward me or away.

But I had a good head start. I straightened my back, inhaled deeply. Winced.

And resumed paddling.

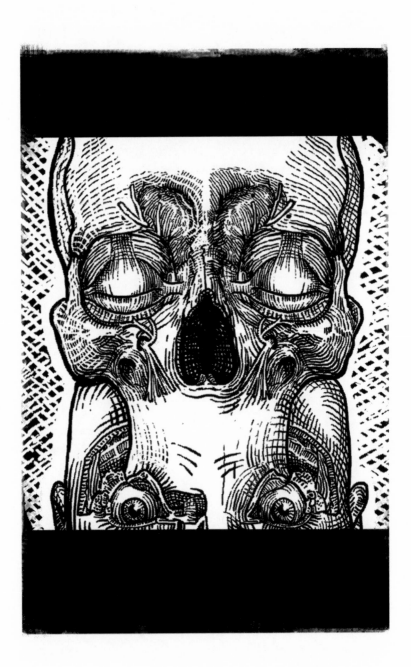

A Blind Eye

"HAVE YOU BEEN USING THE DROPS I PRESCRIBED LAST VISIT?"
I scan her chart. It says Mrs. Jankin brought her infant daughter here
to the clinic about two weeks ago. I vaguely remember her but I definitely remember her cute baby, Molly.

"Of course," Mrs. Jankin says.

Molly had what I thought was bacterial conjunctivitis of both eyes.
I noted subtle corneal abrasions as well, possibly from scratching or
rubbing. I prescribed antibiotic drops last visit. She was supposed to
follow-up a few days later but didn't show. The note in the chart indicated that the clinic staff had tried calling but the listed number was
apparently disconnected.

"Well." I look down at Molly on the exam table—puffy eyes, red
and indurated. I tuck the blanket back up around her chin. "It seems
she's gotten a little worse. Have you noticed any other problems? Like
fever, diarrhea, cough?"

"Nope."

"She eating okay?"

"Seems."

"Sleeping well?"

"Yup. Seems real tired. Sleeps all the time."

"Well, her exam is okay except for the eyes. And her vital signs
and temp are normal. So, I'm going to prescribe something a little
stronger. But you really need to come back in a couple days. We need
to keep on top of this."

"Okay, Doctor."

I wink at Molly, touch her smooth cheek. She kicks, chubby legs pedaling. Her arms flail in jerky circles. I fill out a script, rip it from the pad and hand it over. Mom and baby are on their way.

I take a moment to write my note, and decide to review the chart in its entirety. I have a gut feeling that maybe something is a little off. Missing appointments is always a red flag but people have busy lives, right?

I look at the address. A nearby neighborhood, lower middle class. Not that that means much. Mom is thirty-two years old. No other children. Unemployed. Divorced. The ex-husband's details aren't listed. I feel like I'm being stupid, maybe even a bit paranoid. But I've been down this road and so have several of my colleagues. I've called Child Protection Services before, only to come up empty-handed. Then a family is unfairly flagged.

A case still haunts me from when I was an intern. I saw a baby during a routine well-visit and the mom expressed concern over two small bumps on the baby's chest. The bumps seemed bony and I was not that worried, but I consulted the covering attending physician and we ordered x-rays. There were two healing rib fractures. The chief doctor called Child Protection Services, thinking they were the result of abuse. More x-rays were ordered and several other old fractures were noted.

The parents were questioned and it seemed the answers were not good enough, even though the baby was clean, well-dressed, well-fed, and happy. Even through the baby had painted toenails. The mom told me that bone problems ran in her family and I relayed that information to the senior doctors, but no one listened. The baby was admitted to the hospital for observation. The next day a social worker informed the parents that due to the injuries and the interviews the baby was going to be put in foster care. They were told making a scene would certainly make things worse.

The parents reluctantly handed over their baby and wept. The parents wrote out her schedule and helped buckle their baby in the car seat. The car pulled away. The mother bolted across the parking lot screaming, "They stole my baby!" The father ran too. They both fell to the ground in the rain sobbing, the mother curled into a ball in a puddle.

A series of emergency hearings were held. A judge ruled that there was abuse and the baby was to remain in foster care. The husband was arrested. The parents fought back. They fought with everything they had, which wasn't much, and eventually lost everything. First their jobs, insurance, then all of their savings. But they didn't lose hope.

After a year and a half, I heard, the baby was found to have osteogenesis imperfecta, a genetic disease that affects collagen production and weakens bones, resulting in multiple fractures at the slightest trauma. Funny thing is, this disease was suggested to the social workers and others by the mother after doing her own research but was dismissed as an excuse, a cover-up for the husband.

After finally getting the attention of a lawyer, and a major legal battle, the baby was eventually returned to the family but of course not without significant psychological, financial, and emotional trauma to the family.

I've been overly cautious since. And as far as Mrs. Jankin and little Molly go, I had a baby with an eye infection. As of now, all Mrs. Jankin was guilty of was a missed follow-up appointment. Hardly a crime. And she did come to the clinic today, no?

Mrs. Jankin placed Molly in her crib. Molly had wailed all the way home from the clinic. And it was such a long walk. Mrs. Jankin's feet hurt. Mrs. Jankin didn't stop at the pharmacy for the new prescription. Passed it right by. Heck, she had no insurance. No money. How was she supposed to pay for that stuff?

She had lied to the doctor at the clinic. She did have eye drops left. Just not the ones from the pharmacy. She never filled that first prescription either. She made her own "special" eye drops. Like a home remedy. What did those doctors know anyway? She had plenty of drops left. See? Much cheaper too.

She wrapped Molly tightly in a soft blanket, like a cocoon, to keep her arms and legs from moving around, messing things up. She filled the dropper with a gentle squeeze, then applied firm pressure to Molly's forehead with the palm of her hand, to keep her head still. With thumb and forefinger of the same hand, she separated the lids of Molly's right eye. She positioned the dropper overhead, steady, watched the liquid form into a drop, then elongate and plop, right onto the eyeball.

Molly shrieked as usual, a blood curdling high-pitched sound like babies do, till her face reddened. This annoyed Mrs. Jankin. *What the heck was she screaming at? I'm just trying to help.* Mrs. Jankin made her scrunched-up face. The one that made her feel all put together. She took a breath and let it out through pursed lips.

Molly had a hard time getting her breath for a moment. When she cooled off a little, settling down like a good baby, Mrs. Jankin moved her hand so that her fingers could spread the left eyelids.

From the next room, Mrs. Jankin's new boyfriend Max, who had been trying to take a nap, yelled, "Shut that kid up will ya!"

Under her breath, Mrs. Jankin said, *"Chillax, Max."*

"Whassat?"

"I said okay, Max!" Mrs. Jankin smirked. Shook her head. She steadied the dropper over Molly's left eye, watched the drop form and ever so slowly, stretch and elongate.

Then fall.

"What happened?" Molly lies on the examining table in front of me, somewhat lethargic, both eyes massively swollen, discolored. There's a new bruise over the left side of her head.

"She fell off the changing table."

I don't like the look of this. I motion the nurse over. She comes at once, recognizing the panicked expression on my face. "Yes?"

"Call CT. Now." I hold Molly's tiny hand. "We need to scan this baby's head."

The nurse darts off and I turn back to Mrs. Jankin, who seems oddly calm.

"Have you been giving Molly the drops?"

"Yes."

"You filled the prescription I gave you?"

"Well."

"Well what?"

"I have my own drops."

"Your own?" My head hurts. This isn't making sense. "You have them with you?"

Mrs. Jankin stares blankly into space.

"I need to see them. Please. Molly is critically ill."

She turns slowly, unzips the tattered purse on her shoulder, and roots around. "Here."

I grab the dropper bottle and examine it. Clear, no label.

"What are these?" I start to unscrew the cap. "Where'd you get them?"

"I made them."

With that, I pass the open bottle under my nose and immediately whip my head back and swing my hand to face. My nostrils burn, eyes water. I let out a muffled gasp.

"What *is* this?"

Mrs. Jankin stares at me, shrugs.

Transport appears, angling a stretcher alongside the table for Molly.

I step back while they transfer Molly to the stretcher.

"Non-contrast Head CT," I tell them, capping the bottle. I turn to Mrs. Jankin, my fury starting to take shape and build. "What the hell is this, lady!?" I blurt, losing control, holding myself back, wanting to shake some sense into this woman.

Mrs. Jankin looks dazed. All she says is, "Drops."

I call Security.

Two hours later I'm in the pediatric ICU. Molly is sedated and intubated. The head CT revealed a small subdural hematoma. The bruise on her scalp was felt to be made from an open hand.

She's going to be okay. At least as far as the bleed goes.

I sent the homemade drops to the hospital lab for stat analysis. The head tech called me frantically a short time later.

"You wrote that these are *eye drops?*" The tech says over the phone.

"Yeah." I can't see his face but I can pretty much guess the expression by the sound of his voice. "What's in it?"

"Oh boy," he says, probably shaking his head. "You ready?"

"Yeah."

"Bleach."

"Bleach?"

"Yes," he says. "Pure...household...bleach."

Silence.

"You okay, Doc?"

"I guess."

After I hang up, I can hardly talk. I take a few minutes, then call the security office and break the news. Social Services is already there. Mrs. Jankin is taken into police custody.

I rush up to the ICU.

I look at Molly in the bed, intubated, swollen slit-like eyes, bruised head. My heart sank.

Pure bleach?

I'm not sure how much vision Molly lost at this point, but there's a good chance she'll be totally blind.

I fight back tears and wonder if I could have done more.

I run a finger along Molly's cheek. The monitors buzz and hum. Molly's limbs lack the usual excited baby kicks, swings and jabs. Her arms slump at her sides, due to sedation, the small endotracheal tube juts from her lips, taped to her cheek. Her bulbous eyes are crusted and glistening from ointment. I curse under my breath, my fists balled.

I decide never to let gut feelings go unchecked. I wouldn't let someone I had a strange feeling about just walk away without at least discussing it with a colleague or some other third party. Without probing deeper. From this moment on, I am going to err on the side of ultra-protector. Molly and the many more like her need to see the world for what it is, a place of right and wrong, damage and repair—inseparable as two crossed fingers, two serpents intertwined.

Glenn Gray is renowned among noir writers and readers for his powerful, visceral stories, which have appeared in a wide range of print and online publications and anthologies. He is at work on his first novel. Beyond his writing career, Glenn is a practicing physician specializing in Radiology. He lives in New York with his wife and three daughters.

Stephen Fredette (illustrator) is an artist and musician who lives in Hull, Massachusetts.

The author would like to thank the magazines, ezines, anthologies, and ebooks where some of the stories in *The Little Boy Inside and Other Stories* originally appeared, often in very different form.

"The Little Boy Inside"—*Beat to a Pulp, Beat to a Pulp Round 2 (anthology)*

"Bigorexia"—*Beat to a Pulp*

"Disintegration"—*Pulp Modern, Volume 1 (anthology)*

"Mr. Universe"—*Thuglit, Cherry Bleeds,* and *Thuglit Presents, Blood, Guts and Whiskey* (anthology)

"Headless in New York"—*Underground Voices*

"Diary of a Scutmonkey"

   "Disimpaction"—*Beat to a Pulp*

   "Insertion"—*Dogzplot* and *Flash Fiction Offensive*

   "Penetration"—*Muzzle Flash* and *Flash Fiction Offensive*

   "Inflation"—*Muzzle Flash* and *A Twist of Noir*

   "Rupture"—*Powder Burn Flash*

   "Retraction"—*Muzzle Flash, Out of the Gutter 3 (anthology)* and *Out of the Gutter, Baddest of the Bad (anthology).*

"Venice Beach Birthday Boogie"—*Needle: a magazine of Noir* and *Noir at the Bar, Volume 2 (anthology)*

"Jacked"—*Thuglit*

"The Wood"—*Out of the Gutter 5 (anthology)*

"Balls to the Wall"—*Pulp Pusher*

"Obstruction"—*Grim Graffiti* and *Beat to a Pulp, Hardboiled (ebook)*

"Cannulation"—*Beat to a Pulp, Round 1 (anthology)*

"A Blind Eye"—*Protectors: Stories to benefit PROTECT (anthology)*

CONCORD
ePRESS

Where eBooks Support Free Books

The **Concord Free Press** is a labor of love supported by the generosity of hundreds of individuals. Via the Concord ePress, we publish great books (ebooks and limited-edition paperbacks) in collaboration with a wide range of authors—who believe in what we're doing and want to be part of it. When you buy one of our books, half of the proceeds go directly to the author and the other half goes to support the **Concord Free Press**.

So check out our latest books today—and support the Concord Free Press.

www.concordepress.com

CONCORD
ePRESS